I0876619

A Plain Confession

Books by Suzanne Woods Fisher

LANCASTER COUNTY SECRETS

The Choice

The Waiting

The Search

STONEY RIDGE SEASONS

The Keeper

The Haven

The Lesson

THE INN AT EAGLE HILL

The Letters

The Calling

The Revealing

AMISH BEGINNINGS

Anna's Crossing

The Newcomer

The Return

THE BISHOP'S FAMILY

The Imposter

The Quieting

The Devoted

NANTUCKET LEGACY

Phoebe's Light

Minding the Light

The Light Before Day

THE DEACON'S FAMILY

Mending Fences

Stitches in Time

Two Steps Forward

THREE SISTERS ISLAND

On a Summer Tide

On a Coastal Breeze

At Lighthouse Point

CAPE COD CREAMERY

The Sweet Life

The Secret to Happiness

Love on a Whim

NATIONAL PARKS SUMMERS

Capture the Moment

Chase the Light

DOCTOR TO THE AMISH

A Healing Touch

A Hidden Hope

The Moonlight School

A Season on the Wind

Anything but Plain

Lost and Found

A Year of Flowers

A Plain Confession

SUZANNE WOODS FISHER

Revell
a division of Baker Publishing Group
Grand Rapids, Michigan

© 2026 by Suzanne Woods Fisher

Published by Revell
a division of Baker Publishing Group
Grand Rapids, Michigan
RevellBooks.com

Printed in the United States of America

All rights reserved. No part of this publication may be reproduced, stored in a retrieval system, or transmitted in any form or by any means—for example, electronic, photocopy, recording—without the prior written permission of the publisher. The only exception is brief quotations in printed reviews.

Library of Congress Cataloging-in-Publication Data
Names: Fisher, Suzanne Woods author
Title: A plain confession / Suzanne Woods Fisher.
Description: Grand Rapids, Michigan : Revell, a division of Baker Publishing Group, 2026.
Identifiers: LCCN 2025048694 | ISBN 9780800745301 paperback | ISBN 9781493455546 ebook
Subjects: LCGFT: Fiction | Christian fiction | Romance fiction | Novels
Classification: LCC PS3606.I78 P57 2026
LC record available at https://lccn.loc.gov/2025048694

Most Scripture used in this book, whether quoted or paraphrased by the characters, is taken from the King James Version of the Bible.

Scriptures marked NIV are taken from the Holy Bible, New International Version®, NIV®. Copyright © 1973, 1978, 1984, 2011 by Biblica, Inc.® Used by permission of Zondervan. All rights reserved worldwide. www.zondervan.com. The "NIV" and "New International Version" are trademarks registered in the United States Patent and Trademark Office by Biblica, Inc.®

This book is a work of fiction. Names, characters, places, and incidents are the product of the author's imagination or are used fictitiously. Any resemblance to actual events, locales, or persons, living or dead, is coincidental.

Cover image of Amish woman and cover design by Laura Klynstra.

Baker Publishing Group publications use paper produced from sustainable forestry practices and postconsumer waste whenever possible.

26 27 28 29 30 31 32 7 6 5 4 3 2 1

The stronger the telescope,
the more stars there are to count.
—Matshona Dhliwayo, philosopher

Cast of Characters

Ruth "Dok" Stoltzfus (age 60), raised Amish and left as a teen to pursue a career in medicine. Now a beloved doctor to the Amish, known for making house calls. Sister to Bishop David Stoltzfus. First introduced in *The Devoted*.

Darcy Delaney (age 32), traveling nurse, temporarily filling in at Dok's office for her best friend Evie Miller King. New to Stoney Ridge.

Annie Fisher (age 21), Amish, works as a dispatcher for emergency calls after completing her EMT certification. First introduced in *A Healing Touch*.

Gus Troyer (age 25), Amish, works as an EMT. Quite fond of Annie Fisher. First introduced in *A Healing Touch*.

Bishop David Stoltzfus (age 58), Amish, husband to Birdy, father to many, a true shepherd to his flock. First introduced in The Inn at Eagle Hill series.

Sam Mustang (age 41), NASA analyst, has come to Stoney Ridge to find someone from his past and make amends.

Birdy Stoltzfus (age forty-something), wife to the bishop, mother of two spirited boys, stepmother to David's brood from his first wife, Anna. First introduced in The Bishop's Family series.

Charlie King (age 30), newly minted doctor who is working for Dok Stoltzfus, with hopes to become her partner in the practice. Recently married Evie Miller. First introduced in *A Hidden Hope*.

Evie Miller King (age 29), married to Charlie, works as a nurse at Dok's office. Broke her leg during her honeymoon so best friend Darcy is covering for her during her recovery. First introduced in *A Hidden Hope*.

Matt Lehman (late fifties), Dok's husband, police officer. First introduced in *The Devoted*.

Hank Lapp (ageless), Amish, husband to Edith, likes to get involved in everyone's business. First introduced in *The Keeper*.

Edith Lapp or Eddy (won't admit her age), Amish, long-suffering wife to Hank. First introduced in *The Keeper*.

Sally Fisher (mid-fifties), Amish, mother to Annie, and a raging hypochondriac. First introduced in *A Healing Touch*.

Sarah Blank (mid-twenties), Amish, works as a clerk at the Bent N' Dent. Known for being on the nosy side of nosy. First introduced in *A Healing Touch*.

Gabe (around eighteen-to-twenty months old), foster child for Dok and Matt. First introduced in *A Healing Touch*.

Glossary

Penn Dutch Terms

Ausbund—The traditional Amish hymnal used during church services.

Attnung or Ordnung (high German)—The specific practices as lived by that church district. Each Amish church is a stand-alone, so rules and customs vary. However, most Amish churches share cardinal values, like Plain living and pacifism.

Attnungsgemee or Ordnungsgemee—Council Meeting (Preparatory Service)

This special service takes place two weeks before communion, which is usually held in spring and fall. It's a time for every church member to reflect: Are they in agreement with the Ordnung—the church's rules? Are they at peace with others? Is there anything "standing in the way" of sharing communion? If there are faults or conflicts or sins, they're to be confessed and made right. Council Meeting is, at its heart, a time of cleansing and renewal. The Amish believe no one should come to the Lord's table carrying anger or bitterness in their heart (1 Cor. 11:28–29).

Bann—Excommunication or shunning, when a baptized member is disciplined by the church.

Gelassenheit—A central Amish value, meaning humility, submission, and yielding to God's will.

Hochmut—Pride, considered the opposite of Gelassenheit.

Astronomical Terms

binary star—Two stars that are linked by gravity and orbit around each other, like dance partners circling a shared center. Sometimes both stars are visible through a telescope; other times, one is hidden.

exoplanet—A planet that orbits a star outside our solar system. Thousands have been discovered, ranging from rocky Earth-like worlds to gas giants larger than Jupiter.

meteor—A tiny bit of space rock or dust that burns up in Earth's atmosphere, creating a quick streak of light. It's often called a "shooting star" even though it's not a star at all.

nebula—A vast cloud of dust and space where stars are born and die.

One

Dok Stoltzfus was juggling a box of bandages under one arm and a package of antiseptic wipes when she heard the front door to the office open and Charlie, her apprentice doctor, call her name. “Be there in a minute.” She tossed the box of bandages toward Darcy, who caught it one-handed, still balancing on the stepladder.

With her hand on the door, Dok hesitated, watching as Darcy set the bandages on the shelf and brushed a loose strand of hair behind her ear—hair that refused to stay in its ponytail. Perched on tiptoe, light-blue scrubs mirroring the color of her eyes, she worked with quiet precision: bandages stacked by size, antiseptic wipes lined up in perfect rows. For a small-town clinic, it was probably more order than necessary, but Dok kept that thought to herself.

She needed Darcy too much. Liked her too much.

The cheerful, chatty traveling nurse had blown into Stoney Ridge for Evie and Charlie’s late December wedding, covered for Evie at work during their honeymoon, then stayed on when Evie’s ski accident sidelined her indefinitely with a broken femur. That was weeks ago. Dok kept waiting for Darcy to mention her next contract, kept bracing herself for the inevitable goodbye. Preparing for the scramble to keep the office running smoothly. She was still grieving the loss of Annie Fisher to the dispatcher's job—the right move for Annie, but it had left a gaping hole for Dok to fill.

She stood at the doorway of the waiting room, listening to Charlie as he interacted with a male patient she didn't recognize. He was chatting away about planetary alignments—not a topic she would have expected from him. Then again, she never talked to her staff about anything beyond patient care. "I didn't know you were an astronomy buff."

Charlie whirled around. "Not hardly. But it's all Darcy talks about."

Dok blinked. She had no idea. Matt's voice echoed in her head: *"Ruth, these people spend more time with you than I do. How could you not know what they're interested in?"* Her husband was always after her to slow down, to make the effort to get to know Charlie and Evie and Darcy instead of just work alongside them. So . . . perhaps he had a point.

"Dok, this fellow would like to talk to you."

Dok's attention turned to the man. He seemed completely out of place in a rural Pennsylvania town that was more than half made up of Old Order Amish farming families. He looked like a cowboy from the Wild West—weathered, rugged, with a quiet intensity. "Actually, office hours are over for the day. Perhaps there's an opening in tomorrow's schedule. Unless"—there was something in this man's eyes that struck Dok as just a little bit desperate—"you've got an emergency?" Hopefully not.

The man lifted his hand. "I'm not here as a patient. I was just hoping I could have a moment of your time. It won't take long. I'm willing to pay for it."

A second opinion. Okay, then. Second opinions were vitally important. It was hard to say no to the cowboy when he was standing right in front of her. "I can spare a few minutes. Follow me to my office."

She went down the hall and sat at her desk, gesturing a hand to the chair across from her. "So, I'm Dr. Stoltzfus. And you are . . ."

"Name's Sam Mustang."

"Like the horse?"

"Like the car."

Too bad. Dok would've preferred the horse. "Hello, Sam," she said, reaching over the desk to offer a handshake, feeling a slight tremor in his grip. "So what can I do for you?"

Sam eased into the chair across from her. "I saw a television feature about you."

Dok tensed. *That*. A year or so ago, she had been talked into appearing in a short segment on a local news station and wished she'd never agreed to it. A journalist and a television crew followed her around for a few days and what resulted was a long—*not* short—feature dubbed "The Doctor Who Still Makes House Calls." To Dok's shock and dismay, the piece was picked up across the state of Pennsylvania, and suddenly her rural practice was in high demand, out of control, with an endless waiting list. "How can I help you?" she said, glancing at her wristwatch pointedly.

"So you grew up Amish. And your brother is the bishop."

"That's true."

"You know the Plain People well."

"I do. And then they still surprise me."

Sam met her gaze, his expression thoughtful. "I grew up not far from here in an unincorporated area between Stoney Ridge and Gap. Raised Amish. Left when I was sixteen. Didn't think I'd be back. But here I am."

Dok softened. It was a story she was very familiar with. She had left at about the same age and didn't think she'd ever return. But here she was. "So what brings you back?"

"There's something I need to clean up before . . . well . . ." Sam cleared his throat, as if he was trying to get words out that didn't want to be said aloud. "I've been diagnosed with limb-onset ALS."

Ah. So that explained the tremor in his handshake, the way he had eased himself into his chair—a little too slowly for a man his age. Dok kept her gaze steady, her expression calm, even as the weight of his words settled into the space between them. She knew what lay ahead for this man. She could tell that he knew it too. She didn't break eye contact, and when she spoke again, it was with a tone that was both neutral and professional. "When did you first notice the symptoms?"

"Last summer. Weakness in my legs and arms. At first I thought maybe I'd just overdone it after a hiking trip, but . . ." Sam shrugged, a small grimace tugging at his mouth. Or maybe a twitch? "Turns out, it wasn't that."

Dok nodded. "And now?"

"More weakness. Muscle loss. Coordination trouble."

"What are you taking for it?"

"Riluzole. Baclofen for muscle spasms."

"Do you have much pain?" She noticed he kept rubbing his knees like they hurt.

"A little. Here and there. Some headaches."

"How old are you?"

"Just turned forty-one."

Dok stilled. She would've guessed he was closer to fifty, but that might be the effect of the disease. "We can run some tests—" she said, reaching over to grab an order form.

Sam lifted a hand in the air. "Hold on. I'm not here for a second opinion." He shifted in his seat, his fingers shaking nervously against his knee. "I'm here to make amends."

Dok put the order down. "Go on."

He dropped his chin. After a long moment, he raised it. "I need help finding my child."

Dok's brow furrowed. "Your child?"

Sam nodded, his hands clasped together, tight. "I don't know much. Don't even know if it's a son or daughter. Like I said, I left Stoney Ridge when I was sixteen. Had a girlfriend here—she got pregnant. We were both too young. And I . . . I didn't handle things well."

Dok said nothing. She waited, allowing him to continue when he was ready.

"I faked my own death," Sam said, his voice cracking slightly as the words left him. "A drowning in Blue Lake Pond."

Dok raised an eyebrow, surprised, but her expression remained calm. "Well . . . I didn't expect that."

"No, no one did." Sam let out a long sigh, rubbing his hand over his face. "Not my finest moment."

Dok rested her forearms on the desk, her gaze unwavering as she studied him. "How long ago?" She wondered if her brother David knew of the incident.

"Twenty-five years ago."

No. David would've still been living in Ohio. "And now?"

"Now, I want to make it right. I don't have much time, and I don't even know where to start. The church is gone. That was the first thing I checked on. The farm where my girlfriend's parents lived is now a senior living facility. I thought things would've stayed the same in an Amish farming area in twenty-five years, but I don't even recognize it anymore. Only a few natural landmarks."

"Twenty-five years is a long time. Even here."

"So it seems," he said, nodding. "All I have to go on is her name. Mary Zook."

Dok tilted her head slightly, still trying to piece it all together. "That narrows it down to a few dozen."

Sam gave a small, weary laugh. "Yeah, I know. Plus I'm sure she's married with a different last name."

Dok pulled out a Post-it Note to write on. "What about her parents' first names?"

"Her dad had passed. I never knew his name. But her mother was Katie Zook."

Dok knew of at least fifteen women in her practice named Katie Zook, all different ages. She leaned back in her chair, taking a moment to consider his request. "Seems as if a private investigator is your best bet."

"You'd think so," he said. "But two separate PIs came up empty-handed. The Amish are spectacularly skilled at living under the radar."

Dok smiled. So true. Just trying to keep up-to-date medical records on her Amish patients was met with grave suspicion. "Let's rule out the obvious. I assume those PIs checked county birth records."

"They did. Nothing. Nothing in hospital records. And no midwife to the Amish would talk to them."

"What if she'd had a miscarriage?"

"It's possible, but . . ."

Doubtful. Teenagers' fertility success was remarkable. "Any chance the pregnancy didn't go full term?"

He seemed startled by the thought. "Mary would've had the child."

Dok could see he seemed certain about that. "Maybe she had the child elsewhere. She might have been sent off to a relative if her family wanted to keep things quiet."

"Right. I've thought of that."

"Any chance she left the Amish?"

"Not likely. One of the PIs tried to network with those ex-Amish support groups, but nothing came from it." He let out a huff. "Dr. Stoltzfus, I've had a lot of regret about what I did. I want to make things right, but I'm not looking to disrupt Mary's life, or the child's."

"A twenty-five-year-old is hardly a child." Though Dok wasn't interested in disrupting someone's life either. At any age.

"All the more reason to approach this situation carefully. I'm hoping you might be able to steer me in the right direction."

Dok studied him a minute longer. Regret was easy to fake,

but Sam Mustang seemed sincere in this quest. He hadn't once tried to justify himself. And she was all for making amends. She'd seen enough lives torn apart by silence to know the healing power of a well-timed truth. "Finding the right Mary Zook might take time."

"Yeah, I figured as much. For now, I'm on medical leave from work. Starting the process for disability."

"So you'll be in the area for the foreseeable future?"

"Yes."

Sam Mustang was a man who used an economy of words. "No promises," she said, "but I'll do a little digging. See what I can find out."

The relief was instant. Sam's shoulders dropped an inch, the tight line around his mouth eased. "Thank you."

Before anything more was said, her phone rang and Sam rose, lifting his hand in a quiet farewell. "I'll let you get back to work."

The phone trilled again.

"I'll be in touch," she said, one hand reaching for the receiver. By the time she looked up again, he was already gone. It took her a second to realize she hadn't asked for a number. No address. No way to find him again. All she had to go on was his name and a twenty-five-year-old memory of an Amish girl named Mary Zook.

Darcy tidied up the waiting room, sorting the magazines as Charlie sat at the little receptionist's desk to finish up some end-of-the-day paperwork. After working side by side with him these last few weeks, she was starting to see why Evie had always been such a Charlie fan. He was a genuinely nice guy, with a dry, brotherly sort of humor—and smarter than Darcy had ever given him credit for. A flicker of guilt tugged at her when she thought of how often she'd tried to talk Evie out of that epic crush on him. Usually, Darcy's man-radar was dead-on. But Evie had spotted something in Charlie she'd missed. And now, Darcy had to admit, Evie had been right all along. He was a good guy. A good doctor.

She held up today's newspaper that a patient had left behind. "Look at this, Charlie. Just like I was telling you—it's all over the news. A great planetary alignment. Seven planets! All in a row." She seesawed a hand in the air. "Sort of in a row. It's supposed to be spectacular. All the planets on the same side of the sun and all visible at once."

Charlie glanced up from his paperwork. "Didn't that just happen?"

"You're thinking of Jupiter and Saturn. That was the Great Conjunction of 2020. This is soooo different—"

"Is it?" Charlie shrugged. "Is it really? Planets and stars all look pretty much alike."

Darcy gasped at such an ignorant remark but, for now, decided to overlook it. "I need a good spot to see this tonight. Where's the best vantage point around Stoney Ridge?"

Before Charlie could answer, a deep voice spoke from behind her.

"Wonder Pond."

She turned to find an extremely handsome man standing at the doorjamb to the waiting room. Like, drop-dead gorgeous. He had the kind of face that belonged in old Hollywood films—sharp cheekbones, square jaw, hooded eyes lined by thick eyebrows. And if a cleft in his chin wasn't enough, he had a NASA emblem on his jacket. She tried very hard not to stare, slack jawed.

"Sam Mustang, meet Darcy. She's filling in for my wife Evie as Dok's nurse."

Thank you, Charlie! He'd given Darcy a moment to reset. To pull herself together. *Sam Mustang.* With a name like that, and looks like his, maybe he was a movie star. "Wonder Pond?"

She cleared her throat, trying to act super cool. "I haven't heard of it."

"Highest elevation around. No artificial light." Sam Mustang paused. "Best viewing for stargazing in all of Lancaster County, in my humble opinion."

Charlie let out a low whistle. "Well, there it is. Darcy, I think you've just lost your title as Stoney Ridge's top celestial amateur."

"Hey." She shot Charlie a look. "I know stuff."

The man gave her a considering glance, as if he wasn't sure if he believed her.

"So how do I get to this Wonder Pond? Is there a trail?"

Sam started to explain, then stopped. "Look—I'm going up there tonight. You can tag along if you want."

Tag along? Like he was doing her a favor. Darcy folded her arms. She felt a tiny bit miffed.

"But one condition. You can't talk while up there." His expression didn't change.

Charlie snorted. "Yeah, well, that's not happening."

Her mouth opened. Then closed. Now she felt very miffed—with both of them.

"I'll be working," Sam said, "so I'll need quiet."

"Really?" Charlie said. "Like you're paid to stargaze?"

"Something like that."

Something like . . . what? Darcy's curiosity ratcheted up a few more levels. Just what did this guy do for a living? How much did he know about astronomy? "I'll think about it," she said.

He nodded once. "I'll be at the trailhead to Wonder Pond on the corner of Gap Road and Stoney Ridge Road at nine p.m. If you're there, fine. If not, fine. I'm not waiting." Then he turned and walked off.

She glanced once more in the direction Sam had gone.

Oh yeah. She would definitely be there.

Dok's hand tightened on the phone. "I'm sorry. Would you repeat what you just told me? Slower, this time?"

A pause. "It's Sandra. From the county's social welfare department."

Sandra? She hadn't heard from the social worker since the court had ruled to give full parental rights of their foster baby Gabe to his teenaged father. A raw, painful decision for Dok and her husband Matt, one in which their only choice was to accept it. "What's happened to Gabe?"

"The child's father has requested that the boy be returned to you and your husband for emergency foster care."

Dok gripped the edge of her desk. Sandra's words made no sense at first, like puzzle pieces that didn't fit together. "What? Why?"

"Why does he want you to care for the boy? I suppose he thinks you'd want to foster him again. Now, normally, this isn't how the system works. A parent doesn't just tell *us* where to place the child. But in this case, knowing how you felt about the boy, the system can bend a little. The court isn't heartless, after all."

Really? It had felt pretty heartless when Dok and Matt were told they had to hand Gabe over. "What I meant was, why is the father returning the baby to foster care? He worked hard to keep Gabe—to get him *out* of foster care."

"He said the child has some concerns beyond his ability to provide for him."

Dok sat up straighter. "What kind of concerns?"

"Well, that part's a little vague," Sandra said. "But you're a doctor. You'll be able to figure it all out."

The pieces clicked together with a sickening clarity. "I'd like a little more information. What kind of concerns? Cognitive? Physical? What tests have been run?"

"Hmm, not sure if any tests have actually occurred. But you'll know what he'll need."

"Hold it," Dok said sharply. "I didn't say we'd take him."

"But you'll consider it."

Dok exhaled. "I need to talk to my husband." Though she knew what Matt would say. He had a heart the size of Pennsylvania. He'd say yes before she even finished the sentence. And that meant the real decision would rest on her.

"So this would be emergency foster care?" Dok said. "Until the father wants him back again?"

Sandra's silence stretched just long enough to make Dok uneasy. "The father has started the process to rescind all parental rights."

What could be wrong with Gabe? He'd been growing normally when he lived with them. Yes, he'd been a mellow baby, maybe more than most, but he had hit all the right milestones, had formed a strong attachment to them. "Sandra," Dok said carefully, "if the father is rescinding his parental rights, that means you're looking for a permanent family to adopt him. Am I right?"

Another hesitation. "The child's welfare is always our top concern."

Dok swallowed. *This didn't sound very temporary.* "I need to talk to my husband." To think this over. To pray.

"Of course, of course. But I'll need an answer by tomorrow."

Dok hung up and stared at the phone.

She pressed her fingers to her forehead and shut her eyes. If she let herself, she could still picture Gabe's tiny fingers curled around hers, his sleepy little sighs in the crook of her arm. Gabe wasn't a baby anymore. He was a toddler now—walking, talking, forming memories that didn't include her and Matt.

By this time tomorrow, she and Matt would need to tell Sandra their answer.

She could say no. A simple, reasonable response.

Matt had bought a used RV with big plans to travel the country. Dok finally had someone to help her with her practice—not really a partner-someone, but Charlie was coming along, making progress as he gained experience. And Evie was a big plus.

Dok could say no. She could call Sandra back right now and say no. Matt might be upset with her, but he'd understand. Eventually.

Or she could say yes. Their hearts would open, only to be broken again when the boy-father changed his mind, which he probably would. He'd done it before.

She had an odd sense of coming change, like standing in a field when the air goes still and electric just before lightning splits the sky. Dok lowered her chin. Penn Dutch, her first language, rarely slipped past her lips in prayer except in moments like this, when English felt too small to hold what needed saying.

"Liewer Gott," she whispered, "Ich weiss net, was Ich soll duh." *Dear God, I don't know what to do.*

Two

Annie Fisher gripped the handlebars of her scooter, pushing off with one foot as she made her way home. The late afternoon air held February's particular kind of cold—the sort that found its way through every layer of clothing. The fields stretched bare and colorless, dotted with stubborn patches of dirty snow that refused to melt, the ground beneath iron-hard with frost. Waiting, waiting for spring to come.

Much like her heart was waiting.

She exhaled, watching her breath drift in a small cloud. Her thoughts kept circling back to her new job, and to her very special friend, Gus Troyer, in his EMT job.

Annie and Gus had hoped to work together. Back when she'd been taking classes to become an EMT, she and Gus had dreamed about being a team, riding together in the ambulance, responding to emergencies side by side. Gus had been made for this kind of work, for the quick decisions, the life-saving action. And Annie thought she had too. She thought she'd gotten an unmistakably clear signal from God to pursue this work. Dok advocated for her, the bishop agreed, her parents might not have been jumping for joy but they acquiesced. After all, you don't say no to a bishop. Everything was looking good.

Until Annie's motion sickness put a stop to it.

No amount of stubbornness or wishful thinking could change the fact that riding in a moving ambulance made Annie sick as a dog. Worse than a dog. It hadn't mattered that she could handle the pressure, that she knew how to stay calm, that she wanted to be out there in the field with Gus with all her heart. Her body had absolutely refused to cooperate.

She might have been lost after that, floundering, if not for Dok Stoltzfus.

"Emergency call responding is only half the job," Dok had told her. "Somebody starts the process to get help to a situation. Somebody is keeping things calm before help arrives."

And just like that, with a little nudge from Dok, Annie had found her place.

She had been hired as a dispatcher. Just an entry-level position—an administrative dispatcher at a local fire station, handling nonemergency calls and coordinating routine operations. Somehow, she had been assigned to Gus's fire station in Gap. She had no idea how that happened, but she suspected Gus had something to do with it. In the end, it was probably best not to ask. She still needed to prove herself on her own merits.

When their schedules lined up, which was often, Gus would pick up her and her scooter in his buggy and take her to work. If he was still out on a call by the time her shift ended—which was also often—she'd scooter home or, if the weather was bad, her dad would come get her. Eventually, she hoped to be transferred to Manheim, where the Lancaster County-Wide Communications Center handled all 911 calls for police, fire, and emergency services. Manheim was more than twenty miles away, and she wasn't sure how she'd manage the commute—not with her motion sickness. But as Dok often reminded her, one step at a time. Lehne nicht der Druwwel von dem Mariye. *Don't borrow tomorrow's troubles.*

For now, Annie was grateful to gain experience in a familiar setting. And, as Gus liked to say, they *were* working together. Maybe not as EMTs, but pretty close. From her window, she could see when he headed out on a call. She always took a moment to say a quiet prayer—for whoever needed help and for Gus who provided that help.

As she scooted past a stretch of fenced-in pasture, the scent of cold earth and woodsmoke in the air, she let her thoughts drift further. Gus had hinted, more than once, about getting engaged this spring. She knew he was eager. He'd made it clear that he was ready.

She was the one who hadn't been ready. Something had held her back, something unspoken and uncertain, like a road stretching ahead that she wasn't quite ready to travel.

Until today.

It was the first time she had heard his voice, not the paramedic's, on the call—so calm, focused, full of quiet authority. She had listened to the way he took control of the situation, his words measured and sure, his knowledge and skill on full display.

Annie remembered the day Gus had arrived to transport the abandoned infant from Dok's office to the hospital. It was her first glimpse of him. She'd never known an Amish EMT existed, had never imagined it was possible. Yet there Gus was, in his EMT uniform, competent and calm, living proof that two worlds could intersect. From that day forward, becoming an EMT became Annie's dream.

Annie and Gus's friendship blossomed steadily as she pursued EMT classes. She was painfully shy, easily flustered, and preferred to fade into the background whenever possible. But Gus seemed to understand her in a way few did. He knew that silence didn't mean emptiness—that Annie's quiet held depth.

He had a gift for drawing her out, helping her find the words she didn't know she had. In that way, he reminded her of Dok.

And today, hearing Gus's voice steady and sure in the middle of a crisis, Annie felt something shift. She knew, with a clarity that surprised her, that she loved him. Not only that, but she knew she could trust him—with her heart, with her future.

She knew she was ready.

Annie smiled to herself, the cold air stinging her cheeks as she pushed forward, the quiet countryside stretching out before her.

The next time Gus brought up their future—and she knew there would be a next time—her answer would be yes.

Dok stepped into the house, rolling her shoulders to shake off the weight of the day. The scent of cinnamon and cumin filled the kitchen, and she spotted Matt at the stove, stirring a pan with practiced ease.

"Smells amazing," she said, setting her medical bag on the counter.

Matt glanced over his shoulder, grinning. "Moroccan chicken."

She sniffed the air. "Making sure I don't starve?"

"Making sure you don't get cranky." He turned off the burner. "Long day?"

She pulled a glass from the cupboard, filling it with water before leaning against the counter. "Good day with a long ending."

Matt raised an eyebrow. "Interesting patients?"

"That's one way to put it." She took a sip of water, then shook her head. "After the office closed, a man came in today with an interesting reason for returning to Stoney Ridge. Formerly Amish. Left the area when he was sixteen years old. And when I say left, I mean"—she set her glass down and leveled him with a look—"he faked his own death."

Matt dropped the spoon onto the stovetop with a clatter. "He what?"

"Mm-hmm." She crossed her arms. "Got his girlfriend pregnant, panicked, and decided the best solution was to disappear."

Matt let out a low whistle. "That's a new one."

"Right? And now, decades later, he's back to make amends."

Matt folded his arms, leaning against the counter. "How exactly does one make amends for something like that?"

Dok sighed. "That's what he's trying to figure out. He doesn't know anything about the child. Not even if it's a son or daughter. The only thing he knows is the mother's name—Mary Zook."

Matt gave her a knowing look. "Well, that narrows it down."

"That's what I told him." She shook her head. "I said I'd see what I could do to help track down which Mary Zook it might have been."

Matt's brow furrowed. "Ruth, if you do happen to find the right Mary Zook out of dozens of Mary Zooks, it sounds like something that could open a can of worms."

"I had the same thought." She exhaled. "But he's dying, Matt. ALS."

Matt's expression shifted, the weight of that landing hard. "That's rough."

"Yeah." She pressed her lips together. "He said he wants to clean up his mess before he goes."

"Well, good for him." Matt turned back to the stove, giving the pan one last absent-minded stir.

Dok hesitated before speaking again, knowing the next topic would hit much closer to home. "Just as I finished up with him, the phone rang. It was Sandra."

He had crouched down to look through a cupboard and pulled out a platter for the chicken. "Sandra who?"

"Sandra—Gabe's social worker."

Matt glanced at her, more alert now. Slowly, he rose and set the bowl on the counter. "And . . . ?"

"She had an update on Gabe." Dok took a breath. "Apparently, his father is officially rescinding his parental rights. He told Sandra he was unable to provide care for him."

Matt's whole body stilled. "So what happens now?"

"She's looking for an emergency foster home. And she wanted to know if we'd be interested."

"Of course you told her yes."

Dok let out a slow breath. "I told her I'd think about it."

His forehead creased. "Think about it?"

"Yes, Matt. Think about it. Talk about it. This is a big deal." She crossed her arms. "There's a reason his father had given up his rights. It sounds as if Gabe might have some developmental delays. Serious ones."

Matt ran a hand through his hair. "But he was fine when he was with us." He frowned. "What exactly did she say?"

"She said he has some . . . issues. She didn't say what, just that there were concerns."

Matt absorbed that, his jaw tightening slightly. "And the father *gave* him up?"

"That's what Sandra said." Dok rubbed her temples. "I don't know, Matt. Foster care isn't easy, and Sandra admitted she wants to find a permanent home for him. We need more information before we make a decision."

Matt blew out a breath and nodded, but she could see the wheels already turning in his head. Despite a career as a police officer, and a stint in the military before that, he was always led by his big heart. He wasn't the kind of man who could hear about a child in need and not want to jump in. Especially if that child was Gabe. He had adored that baby.

She stepped closer, resting a hand on his arm. "I know you want to say yes right away. But we need to be smart about this. You remember how much we had to change in our lives to provide foster care for Gabe. Everything now will be . . . magnified.

If he does have developmental delays, it'll require a great deal of intervention."

He looked down at her, his expression softer now. "I get it. But there's something about that little boy. There's always been something special about him. I can't help but think God has a plan going on behind the scenes. Something he wants from us."

Dok had the same feeling, and it was a little bit terrifying.

"When do you need to give Sandra an answer?"

She scrunched her face. "Tomorrow."

Matt sighed, then shook his head. He turned back to the stove, picking up the tongs to move the chicken pieces onto the platter. "Well, in the meantime, we're eating my magnificent Moroccan chicken. And while we eat, we'll talk it through."

"That sounds like a plan." Dok smiled, some of the tension easing from her shoulders. Some, but not most of it. She already knew what their answer would be.

Darcy Delaney checked the time on her phone and frowned. Had Sam Mustang blown her off? She pulled her coat tighter around herself, shivering a little in the chilly night air. The binoculars hanging around her neck felt like an ice cube. She should've brought a warm beanie, at least. She thought about it, but she'd been having a rare good-hair day. At work, she tried to keep her uncontainable hair in a ponytail; tonight, it spilled loose over her shoulders. A hat would only flatten it, leaving the dreaded hat hair. Not a good look. She gave a small shiver and silently chided herself—vanity was a poor trade for warmth.

Why was she even here? Why had she come?

This was a bad idea. A terrible idea. Sam Mustang might be a serial killer, for all she knew.

Probably not, since Dok seemed fine with him being alive and breathing in her office just a few hours ago, but still. For some reason, Dok hadn't created a patient file for him. No reason for the visit. Darcy knew, because she had checked. So maybe even Dok had some suspicions about this guy.

She should go. Leave now. Even if it meant missing a great planetary alignment. From where she was standing, with a naked eye, she'd seen Venus, Jupiter, and Mars. Through her freezing-cold binoculars, she thought she might have spotted Saturn and Mercury. So Uranus and Neptune might have to wait for another day. She sighed, disappointed. A great planetary alignment might not happen again for years and years. But better to be safe—and warm—than risk her life with a sketchy stargazer.

Just as she pivoted on her boot heels to head back to her car, a truck rumbled up the road and pulled over. Hand on her car door, Darcy stilled as Sam Mustang climbed out of his truck, walked around to the passenger side and rummaged around, then pulled out a long, narrow case.

Her heart skipped a beat. She recognized *that* telescope case. She'd seen it once before, in Alaska. Looked through it to see stars that she didn't even know existed. If that telescope was the same make, she was in for a celestial treat.

Sam walked up to her, holding the case against him like it was full of gold . . . and in a way, it was. "Ready?"

That was it. No apologies for being late, no pleasantries. Just "Ready?"—like she was the one who'd kept him waiting.

She should leave on principle. Get into her car and drive away. But . . . that telescope. She couldn't walk away from *that*. Not tonight. Not on the night that seven planets aligned.

So, instead, she followed after him, slipping through the gate he held open for her. He set a fast pace up the trail toward Wonder Pond and she walked behind. He didn't say a word, and she was determined to prove she could be quiet. But the higher they climbed, the steeper the trail became, Sam's pace slowed and his breathing grew heavier. Enough so that she broke her promise of silence. "Want to stop and catch your breath?"

"No time for that," he said.

She scoffed a laugh. "Well, it's not like the stars are going anywhere."

Ignoring Darcy, Sam kept walking. *A real chatterbox, this guy.* Conversational skills, she had already noticed at Dok's office, were not this man's strong suit. She asked herself once again why she had agreed to tag along with him tonight. It was cold, really cold. This was February . . . in Pennsylvania!

And normally, Darcy could get anyone to loosen up and start talking. Not Sam Mustang. He was difficult to talk to. She let out a sigh and didn't even care if he noticed, which he didn't. This could be a long night.

When they finally reached the top, Darcy looked out at Wonder Pond and . . . had to wonder. There really wasn't much to feel in awe about. Just a dark stretch of still water, framed by trees, nothing particularly magical. She put her hands on her hips. "How in the world did it get the name 'Wonder Pond'? Isn't it just a cow pond?"

"Look up."

So she looked up.

And there they were. The stars. So many of them that she nearly gasped. So close she could practically touch them. "An Amish patient told me that tonight would be . . . oh, what was the word? It was so funny sounding. Sheedunk?"

"Schtichdunkel. Dark as pitch."

"That's it! No moon tonight." And the patient was spot on. It was dark, which meant the stars stood out like someone had punched holes in the blackness. If Sam Mustang weren't so opposed to chatting, she'd ask him how he knew such a peculiar Amish word. Evie knew a lot of quirky Amish words too. She'd picked them up from living with her Mennonite grandparents. Darcy wondered where Sam Mustang had picked it up.

Sam set down his case and unlatched it with the reverence of someone handling precious cargo. Inside, nestled deep in custom foam, was cushioned a state-of-the-art Celestron CGX-L 1400 HD telescope. It wasn't just a high-grade scope, it was serious equipment. The kind that cost more than most people's cars—Darcy's Subaru, for sure. She watched as Sam assembled it with practiced efficiency, his movements precise and unhurried, adjusting dials and calibrating settings like he'd done this a thousand times before.

What exactly did this guy do for a living?

He seemed to have forgotten she existed, absorbed completely in his setup. Finally, he stepped back and gestured toward the eyepiece. "Go ahead."

Darcy approached the telescope like it was as breakable as a soap bubble. Almost reverently. As she peered through the scope, her breath caught. The magnification was extraordinary—she could see Jupiter's Great Red Spot with startling clarity, its swirling storms. Saturn's icy rings sharp enough to count. She spotted Neptune, then Uranus. All seven planets lined up in a sort-of row. Her pulse quickened. She'd looked through plenty of telescopes over the years, but nothing with this kind of power. This telescope was even better than the one in Alaska. What she saw through Sam Mustang's scope was absolutely breathtaking.

She was trying very hard to keep her thoughts to herself, but the sight was overwhelming. "It's so beautiful that it almost hurts." She glanced over at Sam, who was staring up at the sky with a quiet intensity. "I've never seen Jupiter's bands look so clear."

"Yeah. Good scope."

Best scope. "And look at its moons. The four Galilean ones are so clear." She stepped back to let him take a turn. "I think the latest count of Jupiter's moons is ninety-seven."

Sam paused to look at her. Just for a second.

She caught the glance and smirked. "See? I know stuff."

He grunted, turning back to the telescope.

Darcy grinned. "And it just goes on and on and on, doesn't it? So much more up there than we can imagine."

"There's a saying," he said, peering through the eyepiece. "The stronger the telescope, the more stars there are to count."

Now it was Darcy's turn to be surprised. She wouldn't have expected eloquence from this taciturn man. Sam was scribbling something down in a notebook. "What are you doing?"

He adjusted another setting on the telescope. "I'm taking calculations."

"For what?"

"Uh . . . it's complicated. Hard to explain."

She raised an eyebrow. "So, do you actually work for NASA? You weren't just wearing a jacket you'd bought in a gift shop? How long have you worked there? What exactly do you do?"

He cast a side-glance at her. "I thought the deal was that if you came along, you weren't going to talk."

Right. He had made that clear. "Just answer that one question and then I'll be quiet."

"I'm a data analyst for telescope missions. And yes, at NASA."

Oh my goodness. Darcy was gobsmacked. There was no other word for it. "But what does that mean? To be a data analyst."

"I study pattern recognition and discovery. Anomalies of stars and exoplanets."

"Exoplanets?" She braced herself for a flicker of condescension, but it never came. If anything, he seemed almost pleased she'd asked—at least, she thought so. Hard to tell with him.

"A planet that orbits a star outside our solar system." He glanced at her. "Basically, I look at beautiful images all day that the Hubble or Webb or Hess have taken."

She nodded, tried to play it cool, but inside she was reeling. A job like that? A telescope like his? And, well . . . a face like that behind it? No wonder she was a little dazzled. "When did you first get hooked on astronomy?"

He tipped his head thoughtfully. "I was just a boy. My grandfather had a backyard telescope and taught me to identify the planets. One night, I saw my first binary stars. Two stars orbiting around a shared center of gravity. Later, I learned they were Mizar and Alcar in the Big Dipper. Binary stars are actually pretty common, visible even with binoculars. In fact, most stars have companions. Not our sun. That's a loner star." He paused. "But binary stars . . . they're like . . ."

"Like . . . cosmic dance partners."

Surprised, a laugh burst out of him.

Darcy smiled, pleased. "Guessing you have some graduate work in astrophysics?"

He murmured something that sounded like a yes.

"So how'd you end up working for NASA? And have you worked on any of the space missions?" She scrunched up her shoulders. "That would be *amazing*."

He straightened to look at her. "I thought you said one question."

Oh. Right. She had said that.

As Sam adjusted the telescope, he muttered something under his breath about atmospheric distortion. Darcy watched as he methodically fine-tuned the focus, then shifted the angle slightly. "What are you looking for now?"

"Messier 31," he said, not looking up. "Andromeda Galaxy. Closest spiral galaxy to us. About 2.5 million light-years away." He stepped back, nodding toward the eyepiece. "Take a look."

Darcy leaned in, peering through the lens, and let out a slow breath. "It looks so hazy, like a smudge in the sky. Hard to believe it's full of billions of stars."

Sam side-eyed her, the faintest flicker of approval in his expression.

She straightened and grinned. "I told you. I know stuff."

"So you do," he said gruffly. But something about the way he said it made Darcy feel like she'd passed some kind of test.

He finished what he was writing down and then dismantled the telescope, taking care to pack it back in the case. It was a slow process. Every piece had a place in its foam cushion.

Before he closed the case, Darcy heard voices and looked up, squinting to see a young Amish couple coming toward them—Annie Fisher and Gus Troyer. Over the last few weeks, she'd crossed paths with them at either Dok's office or the Bent N' Dent, but she didn't realize they were a couple. *Sweet.*

Gus had a small telescope tucked under his arm. The kind that Darcy had. Garden variety.

She waved. "Hi, you two! Sam, this is Annie and Gus." She lifted her palm in Sam's direction. "Annie and Gus, this is Sam Mustang. He's new to Stoney Ridge." Adding in a stage whisper, "And he's an astrophysicist."

Gus's eyes were on Sam's telescope. "That explains why you have such a serious scope." Curiosity was clear in his voice.

Sam didn't hesitate. "Want me to set it up for you? You can take a look."

"No, I don't want to trouble you," Gus said, though he had a look on his face like he would've loved to accept Sam's offer. He lifted his telescope, which had a very bought-at-Walmart look. "This will do us fine."

It will do you fine until you get a look at the sky through Sam Mustang's telescope. *Take him up on his offer!* Darcy wanted to say. When will you ever get the chance again to look through a NASA-grade telescope?

She nearly voiced her thoughts aloud, but Sam had hoisted the strap over his shoulder, holding the case against his chest, preparing to go. It was quite a process to get it unpacked and packed up again. She bit her lip. Maybe it was better not to get a peek through Sam's scope. Better not to know what you're missing.

But then Sam Mustang surprised her.

"If the sky is clear, I'll be here again tomorrow night," he said. "Nine o'clock. Come if you like, and you can look through the scope."

Gus exchanged a glance with Annie, clearly pleased. "We'll be here," he said with an ear-to-ear grin.

On the way down the trail, following Sam who moved rather cautiously and slowly on the descent—giving her plenty of time to mull—Darcy gathered all she'd gleaned tonight about this intriguing, brooding man. He wasn't fazed that Annie and Gus were Amish, acting awkward and self-conscious the way so many non-Amish did. Like Darcy acted around Amish patients in Dok's office, though she was trying very hard to get over that.

Sam didn't mind answering questions—as long as they weren't too personal. Only then did he clam up. And despite his gruff exterior, he was surprisingly generous. He clearly loved sharing the night sky with others. Sharing what he knew about it.

But his social skills, they were appalling. With her, anyway.

Back at his truck, he buckled his telescope case into the passenger seatbelt with the tenderness of a father tucking in a small child, then climbed in and drove away without acknowledging Darcy existed.

Darcy stood in the empty road, watching the taillights of his truck disappear, wondering why a man who could show Jupiter's moons to a perfect stranger couldn't manage a simple goodbye. And why that bothered her so much.

Three

David locked up the Bent N' Dent and headed down the steps to where his mare stood waiting at the hitching post. He reached out to pat her nose, whispering a promise that a good dinner of hay was waiting in the barn—maybe even a handful of oats with a drizzle of molasses for sweetness. She'd earned it. Usually, he unhitched her to graze under a tree, but today, he'd had several errands to run, so the mare had stood idle at the hitching post at various points of the day, remarkably patient. He gave her one more rub, grateful for her steady nature, before turning toward his sister's office.

Ruth had sent word that she wanted him to stop by before heading home. He hoped this visit would be quick, just a word or two, and then he could be on his way.

He gave his customary knock on the doorframe before stepping inside his sister's office.

"Brother or bishop?" Ruth asked without looking up from her desk.

"You tell me." He settled into the chair across from her. "Sarah said you wanted to see me."

"That's right. I did tell her that. Then . . . I asked you here as a bishop."

David's eyebrows lifted. Normally, his sister didn't appreciate his interference as bishop. She was perfectly capable of handling her own problems, thank you very much. "I keep meaning to ask. How's Evie mending?"

"Little by little." She set her pen down and leaned back slightly. "In fact, Charlie had to leave early this afternoon to get back to Windmill Farm. Fern had to head out for a comfort quilt or something like that, and Evie, according to Fern, shouldn't be left home alone. She's still confined to a wheelchair."

Poor Evie. David hadn't seen her, but Birdy had visited and said she had a cast from hip to toes. "Are things going well with Evie's replacement?"

"Darcy? Very well. She stepped right in on day one and hasn't missed a beat." Dok crossed her arms against her chest. "David, I need your help to find an Amish woman named Mary Zook who had a baby twenty-five years ago. She was in a church that used to be between Stoney Ridge and Gap. Gone, now. The church, I mean. Not Mary Zook." She frowned. "At least, I hope not."

"Ruth, I wasn't here twenty-five years ago."

"I realize that. But you know a lot of people who were here and who might be willing to talk to you."

"What's this about?"

She glanced at him. "Still a bishop, right?"

"Still a bishop." In other words, this was confidential information.

"A formerly Amish man came into my office and asked for my help to find Mary Zook. Apparently, he knew her when they were teenagers and he . . . well, let's just say that he had a terrible lapse in judgment."

David smiled. "A description that fits most teenaged boys."

Dok rocked her hand back and forth in the air. "This might've been worse than most."

David leaned back in the chair. He could tell that she intended to give him only the barest of details. He respected that. "So after all this time, he wants to find her? Why now?"

"He's come here to apologize to her. To make amends."

David exhaled. He was all for making amends. It never failed to astonish him to see the healing power of a sincere apology. And yet it also astonished him how seldom they occurred. "I'll see what I can find out."

"Great. But do it very, very carefully. Please don't share this information with anyone, even Birdy. This is a sensitive issue."

As if he didn't realize that! As if he hadn't spent years as a bishop carefully guarding every confidence, every burden that his church brought to him. "Now you sound like a sister." He lifted himself from the chair to leave.

"Hold it. That was only one of the reasons I wanted you to stop by."

David sat back in the chair. "Brother or bishop for this one?"

"Brother." Dok steepled her hands together, which was a sure sign to him that she was about to reveal something personal. "Do you remember the baby we fostered?"

David met her gaze. "Of course. Gabe. How could I forget?"

She hesitated just a fraction of a second. "He's back in the foster care system. His father has relinquished parental rights. Yesterday, I received a call from the social worker, asking if we would provide care for him. Matt said yes, of course. The baby is his niece's, after all, and he feels a familial obligation to step up to the plate. Though no one has seen this niece in a few years. Not even her parents. They have no idea where she is. Matt called them last night."

David studied his sister's face. He could see the tension in her jaw, the way she was keeping her expression carefully neutral. But he knew better. He had watched her struggle with the demands of fostering before—first with hesitation, then with reluctant acceptance, then with a fierce, protective love. And then, heartbreak.

He had seen the toll it had taken on Ruth as the boy's father had come forward and claimed him, watched the way she and Matt had quietly folded up the nursery afterward, one piece at a time, like they were dismantling their own hearts.

And now here they were again, staring at a door they had once walked through, uncertain if they could bear to do it again. "If the father is relinquishing his rights, does that mean the child will be up for adoption?"

Slowly, Ruth nodded.

"What about the grandparents? Are they willing?"

"They live in Florida and have some serious health issues. They're not uncaring, but they just don't have the capacity for a young child. Especially a child with developmental delays."

"Developmental delays? I don't remember that."

"Well, Gabe was still an infant when the court returned him to his father. It's possible that something cognitively or physically has presented itself over the last year. Whatever it is, the father doesn't feel qualified to care for him." She paused, folding her hands together. "David, what if we can't handle Gabe's issues either? What if there's something seriously wrong and we're walking into a situation that's way over our heads? Our capacity?"

Her voice was steady, but David caught the slight tremor underneath. He could practically feel the weight that his sister was carrying, the fear beneath her customary composure. "You don't have to have it all figured out right now," he said gently.

"Don't you think we should have our minds made up to adopt before we bring Gabe into our home? Isn't that the right thing to do, for his sake? Isn't it the responsible thing to do?"

"In my experience, I have found that God seldom reveals the big picture, but he does light the path ahead, step by step."

"Step by step." She repeated it like she was testing the words.

"That's the way God seems to work. He knows we probably couldn't handle it all at once."

Ruth let out a sigh that sounded like one of relief, then gave him a slight smile. It was the first genuine expression he'd seen from her all evening. Before either of them could say more, a knock sounded at the front door of the office. She stiffened. "That's them."

"Who?"

"The social worker and Gabe."

David's eyes went wide. "Now? Right now?"

"Right now. I told her to come at day's end."

David followed his sister to the front of the office as she opened the door. The social worker stepped inside, a thick folder in one arm, and on her hip, she carried Gabe. From the doorjamb of the waiting room, David watched as his sister's expression faltered. The baby—now a toddler—*looked* like Gabe, but he didn't reach for Ruth. He was just a small baby when she relinquished him. Of course he wouldn't have a memory of her. She would be a stranger to him. But he didn't squirm or hide his face in the social worker's shoulder like a typical toddler. He just stared, unblinking, as if the room around him didn't quite register. Something was definitely off.

For a split second, Ruth looked heartbroken. Then, just as quickly, David saw her shift into doctor mode. She stepped forward, gently placing a hand on Gabe's back.

"Hello, sweet boy," Dok said softly, searching his face for any sign of recognition. "Do you remember me?"

Nothing. Not even a flicker.

The social worker shifted Gabe to face Dok. "His father said he doesn't talk. Not a single word."

David saw the way his sister touched Gabe's small hand, how she ran her fingers gently over his palm. The boy didn't pull away, but he didn't respond either. He could already see her assessing, calculating, thinking through possibilities. But he knew his sister well enough to see the truth beneath the professional veneer.

This wasn't just another child in need of care.

This was little *Gabe*. And despite everything—the uncertainty, the fear, the very real possibility of having her heart broken again—she was already lost to him.

Just like before.

Annie Fisher pulled the headset over her prayer cap and settled in behind the narrow desk in the small dispatch office at the fire station. The afternoon shift had started quietly, just the occasional buzz of the radio and the soft rustle of paperwork. The office was private, tucked near the back of the building, and she stayed plenty busy fielding nonemergency calls. It wasn't a job she'd ever imagined herself doing, but the rhythm of it had grown familiar over the past few months.

"Nonemergency line, how can I help you?" she said, her voice even, practiced.

"My neighbor fell off her back porch again," the voice on the other end said. "She says she's fine, but she's sitting on a cooler and won't let me help her up."

Annie reached for her notepad. "Is she alert and breathing normally?"

"Oh yes. She's telling me all about her tomato plants and how we're not getting enough rain this year. But . . . she can't seem to get up."

"I'll get a crew over to check on her," Annie said, making the call to dispatch.

She logged the incident and barely had time to set her pen down before another call came in—a man reporting heart palpitations who "wasn't sure if it was the spicy chili from lunch or something worse." Annie kept her tone steady, jotted down the details, and relayed the information to the medical unit. The hours passed quickly that way, one call blending into the next.

When the clock finally ticked toward the end of her shift,

another dispatcher came in to relieve her. Annie slipped off her headset, stretched her shoulders, and gathered her things. As she opened the door into the hallway, she saw Gus waiting for her just outside, leaning against the wall, hands in his pockets like he'd been there a while.

"There you are," he said, his face lighting up in that way that still made her stomach flutter. Those beautiful blue eyes of his—they were full of merriment. "You got time for supper? There's chili to spare."

Annie smiled. "I can smell it simmering on the stove. Though after a call I had earlier today, when a man wasn't sure if his wife's chili was giving him a heart attack or just stomach pains, I'm not sure it sounds very appealing."

"It wasn't the chili. It was his heart. We transported him to the hospital."

Annie followed Gus down the hall toward the kitchen. She used to hesitate at this door, back when everything here felt foreign to her. The fluorescent lights, the gray tile floor, the whiteboard covered with codes and information she still didn't completely understand—it had all seemed like a world she didn't belong in. But not anymore. It wasn't a home away from home like it was for Gus, but she'd grown comfortable here. The other first responders had accepted her Plain presence as she'd learned to navigate the dispatch system.

Gus went to the stove to dish up two bowls as Annie slid into a seat at the table. It was nice, seeing how the men at the fire station cooked, served food, and cleaned up after themselves. She'd never once seen her own father make himself a meal. He didn't even butter his own toast or fill his own coffee mug. Her parents had very clear roles—Daed was a dairy farmer who came in for breakfast, lunch, and supper. Mamm ran the house, the garden, and everything in between. Everyone too.

Gus handed her a bowl and sat across from her. "It's not bad, actually. Not as good as my Mamm's, but it'll do."

Annie smiled and took a bite. The warmth spread through her chest, and she knew it wasn't just the chili. "So, how was the woman who fell off the porch?"

Gus chuckled. "Mrs. Klemens. She was doing toe touches and got dizzy. Says it's her new fitness routine. She's ninety-two."

"Toe touches?" Annie blinked.

He nodded, his expression fond. "She had a small stroke two months ago and she's trying to bounce back. Moving too fast, though. I told her to take it slower. Talked to her about balance work—things she can do near a chair or wall."

"That's sweet of you," Annie said. "I wouldn't know where to start with that kind of thing."

"Well, I've been reading up."

She looked up from her bowl. "Reading up on what?"

"On physical therapy. Occupational therapy too. Books I've found through the library. It's fascinating—helping someone's body get back to working like it should. Guiding them through recovery. Even at ninety-two, a person can rehabilitate and gain back skills. I told Mrs. Klemens I'd stop by soon with some new exercises. She's very motivated."

Annie tilted her head, studying him. Gus's eyes lit up the way they did when he talked about something that interested him—though everything seemed to interest him. It was a quality she loved about him.

Gus reached for his glass of water. "If I weren't Amish, I think I would've gone in that direction. Maybe a physical therapist or something like that."

That caught her off guard. It was the first time she'd ever heard him say something about a life outside the Amish. "But . . . you're happy being Plain, aren't you?"

He met her eyes and reached out to give her hand a gentle squeeze. "Of course. How else would I have met you?"

She smiled, but her thoughts were turning over his words. "Still, why would you be thinking about Englisch careers?"

He shook his head quickly. "It's nothing, Annie. It's just—being Amish is all I've ever known. Sometimes I feel a little curious about what's out there. That's all. I like learning new things."

"Like about the stars," she said.

"Exactly. Speaking of, I'm looking forward to heading up to Wonder Pond tonight. I'd sure like a chance to look through Sam Mustang's fancy telescope."

"Will it be so very different from yours?"

He coughed a laugh. "Oh Annie. Wait until you see for yourself. It's like how a buggy horse must feel when its blinders come off. Like there's a world all around that it didn't know existed."

He had a look on his face like he was thinking about that unseen world, and she wasn't sure why it made her feel a little uneasy. Maybe because he'd spoken of a life outside the Amish. That was silly thinking, she told herself. Gus had been baptized long ago. He'd made his vow to the church.

"Still coming with me for tonight's stargazing?"

She nodded, though she knew her mother would fuss that she was out too late, two nights in a row. Then Annie would remind her that she was going out with Gus to stargaze, and viewing the night sky was best later in the evening. Happily, her mother adored Gus. He could do no wrong in her eyes.

Should Annie say more? Eyes on her bowl, she stirred her chili, gathering courage. "I'm . . . thinking that maybe, come spring, I could help Mamm plant celery in the garden." She kept her gaze fixed on her hands, suddenly shy. In Lancaster's Amish community, planting rows upon rows of celery was no common chore—it was the quiet herald of a daughter's November wedding. Come autumn, the stalks would be chopped, simmered, and folded into the creamy dish that always accompanied the wedding feast of chicken and mashed potatoes. Annie knew Gus was well aware of what she was trying to say. The words hung in the air between them, heavy with implication.

But before he could respond, the sharp wail of the siren echoed from the bay, cutting through the quiet lunchroom like a knife. Gus was on his feet in an instant, his chair scraping against the floor.

"You go," Annie said, already rising with her bowl. "I'll clean up."

"I'll come get you for Wonder Pond around half past eight tonight." He flashed a grateful smile before dashing off down the hall, his boots echoing behind him.

Annie stood at the sink, rinsing out their bowls, her hands moving automatically while her mind raced. Had she said too much? Not enough? The timing couldn't have been worse—or maybe it was perfect. Maybe some conversations were too important to be rushed.

She drifted to the window and watched the rescue truck leave the station, lights flashing, siren screaming into the distance. It must've been a medical call, because otherwise the fire truck would've left first. There was a specific order to everything at the fire station, she'd quickly learned. A rhythm and purpose to every movement. Not unlike the Plain life.

She closed her eyes and whispered a quick prayer—one for the person in trouble, whoever they were, and one for the man she loved. She prayed for his hands, for his mind, for his steady calm in the middle of someone else's worst day.

And she added one more prayer: that tonight, maybe while they were stargazing, they'd find the words to finish what they'd started.

Dok glanced out the window in time to catch the quick sweep of blue lights before Matt's police cruiser jerked to a stop out front. Record time, she thought, and not the least bit subtle. A moment later, he burst through the office door, car seat in hand.

"A little over the top," Dok said as he burst in. Matt only

grinned, dropped the car seat, and reached out to take Gabe from her arms. Holding him close, he tucked his chin on top of the little boy's head, rocking back and forth. *This*, Dok thought, *will be a moment I want seared in my mind forever*. Her big, tough-guy police officer husband, holding this child with such tender loving care. "Let's go home," she said.

Not much later, Matt carried Gabe into the house, holding him close against his chest. "Think he might remember us? Or the house?" Matt said, his voice hopeful. "I mean, I know he was little when he left us, but the brain is an amazing thing. It can store all kinds of information. All it needs is the right trigger. Senses, mostly. A sound or a smell or a taste, and a memory comes flooding right back."

Dok set the diaper bag on the hall floor, exhaling slowly as she watched Gabe look around the room. "Honestly," she said, "I don't know if he remembers us. I'd like to think so, but I just don't know. He was so little when he left us."

Matt shifted his hold on Gabe, rubbing his back in slow, soothing circles. "Well, if he doesn't remember, we'll build new memories. Lots of them. Right?"

Dok didn't answer right away. After Sandra had left the office and before Dok called Matt to bring the car seat, she'd given Gabe a quick physical exam at the office—height, weight, heart and lungs, a light cognitive assessment. While his growth was within normal limits, other things weren't. He wasn't talking, Sandra had said, which wasn't necessarily a red flag—some toddlers took longer—but he wasn't walking either. When Dok set him on the ground, he sat right down. She tried to coax him to come to her, but he didn't even crawl. And he didn't hold a gaze the way toddlers usually did. He seemed to look through people instead of looking at them.

She had spent the drive home from the office thinking over everything she had read in Gabe's file, then what she had observed in him. There were a dozen little things that, on their own, might not mean much. But together? Maybe they would point toward something. She just wasn't sure what.

She went into the kitchen and that's when she gasped. "Oh, Matt . . ."

He had been busy today. A brand-new high chair sat at the kitchen table, its tray gleaming. In the living room, a soft basket full of books and toys rested near the couch. Every outlet in sight had safety plugs in them. And she'd bet money there was a new crib set up in the spare bedroom.

Matt followed her into the kitchen. "What?"

"You did all this today?"

He shrugged, adjusting Gabe on his hip. "Seemed like a good idea."

It was sweet. Thoughtful. It also worried her.

Just like the first time Gabe had come into their lives, Matt was already way ahead of her. She had no doubt he'd be spearheading the path toward adoption if it came to that. Last time, she'd gotten there too—she had fallen in love with the boy, had been ready to be his mother, even at her age. Only to have their hearts shattered when his teenaged father emerged out of nowhere to claim him. The courts leaned toward reuniting a biological family, if possible. So that's what they did.

This time felt different. Gabe's needs were clearly different. And the father had started the process to relinquish parental rights because of those changing needs in his son. Very serious changes. Dok knew something wasn't right with Gabe.

Matt must have seen something on her face because his expression softened. "Hey," he said gently, stepping closer. "You're thinking way too hard."

She huffed out a small laugh. "That's my job."

"Well, take a break from it for a minute." He shifted Gabe in his arms and nodded toward the couch. "Come sit with us."

She hesitated, but then Gabe stirred, lifting his head just enough that she caught his profile. His expression was unreadable, but something about the way his little hands gripped Matt's shirt made her chest tighten. She followed them to the couch, settling beside them.

Matt bounced Gabe slightly. "Think he's hungry?"

Dok considered. "Maybe. We can try some yogurt or something soft."

Matt nodded, then turned his attention back to Gabe. "Hey, buddy. You remember us?"

Gabe didn't respond. Didn't resist being held. He didn't reach for Matt's face the way a toddler normally might. Didn't babble. Didn't look at him.

Dok swallowed.

Matt was undeterred. He lifted one of Gabe's small hands and gave it a gentle squeeze. "You're home now," he said softly. "And we're gonna take good care of you."

Four words flitted through Dok's mind: *Here we go again.*

Four

The night was cold and crisp, the kind that made the stars feel closer, sharper. Darcy wound her scarf around her neck and tucked the ends into her coat as she, Gus, and Annie stood on the shoulder of the country road, shivering, waiting for Sam Mustang to arrive. Sam was late again, which annoyed Darcy. After all, he was the one who made it sound like he would never wait for her if she was late. Both nights, she'd been waiting in the chilly February night air for him to arrive.

Finally, his truck headlights came rolling around the corner. He parked, got out of the truck and went around to the passenger side to unbuckle the seatbelt securing his telescope case, gave Gus and Annie a brief nod, locked eyes just a bit longer with Darcy (or had she imagined that?), and then off he went, through the gate and up the narrow trail.

But Sam Mustang wasn't much of a fast walker. Pretty quickly, Gus and Annie passed him and took the lead, their quiet voices carrying in the dark.

Darcy slowed down to fall into step beside Sam.

"Guessing there's something more than friendship between

those two," he said, nodding toward Gus and Annie as they climbed ahead.

She smiled. "Think so? I've never seen any PDA. Then again, Charlie told me that the Amish have a hands-free policy in courting."

Sam coughed a short laugh. "Can't imagine too many young people who follow that policy."

"You're probably right. I've only been here a little while, so I'm still learning about the Amish."

He glanced over at her.

She took that look as an invitation to keep talking. "I came for Evie and Charlie's wedding and stayed on to fill in while she was on her honeymoon. I'd just finished up a six-month traveling nurse contract in Alaska and hadn't committed to the next contract. So I was happy to fill in for Evie. She's my best friend. Plus, she'd been crazy about Charlie for such a long time and—finally, finally, *finally*—he admitted that he was equally crazy about her. I hadn't been a big Charlie fan, but my opinion is changing. Now I see that I was being overly protective of my friend. I was worried Evie would end up getting hurt. And candidly, I didn't think he was good enough for her, but I was wrong. Charlie's very good to her. Still, I think he's the lucky one, you know? I think he married up. Evie is just wonderful." She caught herself rambling and shook her head. "Anyway, on their honeymoon, Evie broke her leg while skiing—a really nasty break—so I agreed to stay on until she could get back to work."

"Then what?"

She hesitated, surprised that he asked, as if he expected her to have a plan. She really didn't.

"I'll take another traveling nurse contract somewhere," she said. "I've been thinking about going to another country, somewhere I can see the northern lights. Not just travel and hope for clear skies, but stay for three to six months, maybe longer.

That way, if I miss the northern lights one night, I'll have plenty more chances. Finland is the place I'm considering. It's supposed to be the happiest country on earth. That sounds like a good reason to go, don't you think?"

Sam didn't reply right away, and she glanced at him. His breathing was heavier than before, his shoulders rising and falling with the effort. She slowed her pace, but even still, he fell behind. Then he stopped. She walked back down the trail to where he stood, catching his breath.

Man. This dude was so out of shape. Well, Darcy wasn't going to judge him. Ahead, Gus and Annie's voices faded into the distance as they neared the top of the hill.

Rested, Sam started again and this time Darcy followed behind him, matching his slow pace. Just the two of them, heading up the hill, the night sky stretching wide above them. She lifted her head, her eyes scanning the dark sky. "Sometimes when I look up at the night sky, I feel like I'm praying."

He stopped suddenly and turned to her, an odd look on his face.

"What? Don't tell me you're one of those scientists who dismiss God as superstition. How could anyone look up at the night sky and not believe in an intelligent Creator? I mean, it practically shouts of God."

"I believe in God."

"Then what? Why are you looking at me like that?"

He turned his head. "It's just . . . someone once said the same thing to me. Long ago." He shrugged. "I'd forgotten."

She searched his face, curious now. She wondered who had said that to him.

He tilted his head back, eyes on the constellations above. A thoughtful silence spooled out between them. He didn't seem to be in a hurry to reach the top, where Gus and Annie were patiently waiting for the amazing telescope to arrive.

A thought tumbled straight out of Darcy's head before she

had time to catch it. "Do you remember that psalm that Buzz Aldrin quoted before he stepped on the moon? Something about the heavens and moon and stars? He took communion, told NASA to stop talking, and read that psalm."

"Psalm 8." A smile tugged at Sam's lips. He cleared his throat, and, in a rough whisper, quoted the verse. "'When I consider thy heavens, the work of thy fingers, the moon and the stars, which thou hast ordained; What is man, that thou art mindful of him? and the son of man, that thou visitest him?'"

"That's it!" She was impressed. "So . . . you're familiar with the Bible." She congratulated herself for catching the words "old-timey Bible, the one with all the thees and thous" before saying them.

He shrugged again. She was starting to recognize that shrug. That same low-key, evasive shrug that meant that he knew more than he was letting on. "So try to answer that last part for me."

"What part?" Darcy tipped her head. "You mean . . . what is man that God is mindful of him?"

He nodded. "God may have designed the universe, but what is man to him? Here and then gone. Maybe nothing more than dust."

"*Dust?*" Darcy let out a quick laugh. "I think you're missing the best part! God isn't indifferent. The psalmist is saying that the same God who strung up the stars like fairy lights is also the God who notices us. Who actually cares—about each one of us." She gave another small laugh, realizing she was edging into soapbox territory. "It's . . . wild, really. Beyond comprehension. God is bigger than this universe—maybe bigger than any universe we can imagine. And yet . . ." She lifted a shoulder in a half shrug. "Yet he still bothers with us. For me, knowing that, trusting that—it changes everything."

He had lowered his gaze, watching her quietly. No smile. No frown. Just a stillness that made her pulse tick a little faster.

Maybe she'd overstepped. Had she? Probably. She knew not

everyone liked to talk about God—and she hadn't meant to come on so strong. The stars just got to her, every time. "I know, I know," she said quickly, tucking her hands into her coat pockets. "I'm talking too much."

He shook his head slowly. "It's okay, Darcy."

His voice was soft, but sure. And the way he was looking at her—his attention locked on her, his gaze meeting hers with a laser-like intensity—sent warmth creeping up her neck.

Oh no. Her cheeks. Heating up.

A telltale sign.

She was starting to crush on Sam Mustang.

Annie watched as Sam Mustang set up his fancy telescope and adjusted its height lower for Darcy to comfortably peer into the lens without having to stand on her tiptoes. Sam—and Gus, too, for that matter—were on the tall side of tall, but Darcy was on the short side of short. Annie wasn't the matchmaking type, but if she were, she thought Sam and Darcy might make a match. Their oppositeness suited them. Tall, short. He was quiet, she was talkative. He was science-y, she was a caregiver. His hair was brown, his eyes as dark as his hair. Darcy's eyes were bright blue, and her hair was strawberry blond. Opposites, which was a good thing for a couple, Annie thought.

Not that Sam Mustang seemed to be interested in a match. Or Darcy either. But they both loved stars and planets and dark matter and galaxies and constellations and things that made Annie's head feel like it might explode.

Sam Mustang could seem aloof, almost detached, but the way he talked about the stars . . . it was contagious. His gruffness faded when he spoke of constellations, his voice took on an easy rhythm, and he was surprisingly patient and kind. He showed them how to adjust his fancy telescope, even Annie, and he pointed out the constellations. When Gus misidentified one, he didn't correct him outright—just angled the telescope ever so slightly and let him realize it for himself.

A nice quality in a man, Annie thought. Sam Mustang was a good teacher.

She listened to Gus and Sam chat, Darcy chiming in now and then, their voices carrying easily across the quiet hill. They spoke of stellar magnitudes and light pollution, of the Andromeda Galaxy and the orbital period of Jupiter, with the easy familiarity of those who'd spent years studying the heavens. More head exploding for Annie.

The night air was chilly, but Annie had prepared for it with a warm sweater under her winter coat and thick mittens on her hands. She tightened the knot on her woolen head scarf as she watched Gus peer into the scope, gesture toward a cluster of stars, and pepper Sam Mustang with questions.

Amazing. Gus was just amazing. He was completely at ease with Sam, confident in a way that made Annie feel even more impressed with him. She'd seen glimpses of this Gus before—when he talked about his EMT work, or when he explained something he was passionate about—but never quite like this.

She had always known Gus loved astronomy. He'd point out the night sky nearly each time they'd been together after sunset, showing her the Big Dipper during evening walks or noticing how bright Venus looked. But she hadn't realized the depth of his knowledge, the way technical terms rolled off his tongue as naturally as discussing the weather. Out here under the vast sky, he seemed to expand somehow, as if the night sky—or maybe being around Sam Mustang—gave him permission to be fully himself.

Even Sam Mustang seemed impressed, Annie thought, noting how he leaned forward slightly when Gus asked such intelligent questions. Their conversation gradually slid into an almost shorthand that included Gus and Darcy seamlessly—abbreviations and references that went completely over Annie's head. She caught fragments: ". . . seeing conditions tonight . . . that double star in Albireo . . . the Messier catalog . . ."

Soon Annie gave up trying to follow. She was thoroughly content to just lift her head and gaze at the stars. High up at Wonder Pond, in the darkness, the sky revealed itself in all its glory. Stars she'd never noticed before sparkled like fireflies, and the Milky Way stretched overhead in a ghostly river of light that took her breath away.

Her thoughts drifted to a Bible verse she'd memorized as a child, one that seemed especially fitting at this moment. "He telleth the number of the stars; he calleth them all by their names." The words from Psalm 147 kept echoing in her mind tonight. It was astonishing to think that God knew each star—*each one!*—not just the bright ones that dominated the sky, but every tiny pinprick of light scattered across the darkness. Had named each one, the way a shepherd might name every sheep in his flock. The very thought sent chills down her spine, a mixture of awe and reverence. Touching infinity, Gus called it.

That, she understood. Looking up at this vast canopy of light, she felt both infinitely small and yet somehow connected to something immeasurably large. *Such* a mystery.

Darcy's voice broke into her thoughts, yanking Annie back to the here and now. "So, Gus, how'd you get interested in astronomy in the first place?"

Gus paused in his adjustment of the telescope's eyepiece, a soft smile crossing his face that Annie could just make out in the darkness. "My mother. She used to take me out at night when I was little and teach me the constellations. We'd spread a blanket in the backyard, and she'd point out Cassiopeia, Orion, the Swan. She knew all the history that went with them too—the Greek myths, the legends. At first, I think I was more interested in those tales than the actual stars. Or maybe it was the way she told them."

Annie had only met Gus's mother a handful of times and

didn't know her well—not yet—but she hoped there would soon be more opportunities. His parents attended a different church and lived on the other side of Gap. Gus always spoke highly of his mother, describing her as a woman who encouraged his curiosity and had supported his interest in medicine—so long as he stayed within the boundaries of being Amish. He spoke fondly of his father, too, but he seemed to have a special bond with his mother.

"What started it for you, Darcy?" Gus said, flipping the question back to her.

"My middle school science teacher, Mrs. Patterson. She had more enthusiasm for science than anyone I'd ever met."

The fondness in Darcy's voice made Annie smile. The more time she spent around Darcy, the less nervous she felt. For an Englischer, she was very easy to be around, thoroughly comfortable with herself, which was a quality Annie admired greatly in others and wished she could borrow for herself. On top of that, Darcy had an enthusiasm for adventure that Annie found inspiring, mostly because she wasn't a particularly adventurous person.

"One fall," Darcy said, "Mrs. Patterson took our whole class camping overnight, just to watch a meteor shower. I'd never seen anything like it—all those shooting stars streaking across the sky like . . . like God was throwing diamonds." Darcy paused, stealing a glance at Sam, as if she seemed a little embarrassed by her poetic description. Annie found it lovely.

"Keep going," Sam said, and Annie liked him even more.

"Mrs. Patterson saw how excited I was and encouraged me to enter the regional science fair. I did a project on variable stars—spent months tracking the brightness changes in Algol. Won first place. The prize was a telescope." Darcy gestured toward Sam's impressive telescope. "Not quite like that beauty, but it was mine, and it opened my eyes to a world that I hadn't seen."

Annie could picture a younger Darcy, probably just as determined and curious as she was now, staying up late to record her observations and carefully plotting her data.

"What about you, Annie?" Darcy seemed truly interested. "How'd you get into stargazing?"

Annie froze. She wasn't good at being put on the spot, not ever, and especially not in front of an intimidating Englischer like Sam Mustang. Plus, she really wasn't "into" stargazing. She was into Gus and he was into stargazing. The quiet went on so long that even Sam straightened from the telescope to wait for her response. She had none! Her mind had gone blank.

Gus, bless him, sensed her discomfort and swooped in for a rescue. "Annie's my right-hand assistant for starry nights." Then he turned to Sam, who had turned his attention back to making minute adjustments to his equipment. "What about you? What drew you to the stars?"

Sam's hands stilled on the telescope mount, and for a moment Annie thought he might not answer, just like she hadn't. But he must have been taking his time to decide what to say. When he did speak, his voice was even quieter than usual. "Just a boy growing up on a farm with a surfeit of spare time, I suppose."

Gus laughed. "I think you've described most every male who grew up in Lancaster County."

Sam huffed a small chuckle in response, softening his serious face, making him look almost tender. Annie sensed there was a bigger story behind his simple explanation. Yet she understood it for what it was—long winter nights when farmwork slowed and there was time to wonder about the lights scattered across the darkness.

"So that," Darcy said, "must explain why the boys in Stoney Ridge are racing their buggies home on Saturday nights just before dawn. They've been stargazing."

Gus barked a cough-laugh. "More likely, they're hurrying home to do the morning milking before their father wakes up and realizes they never came home last night."

At that, Sam laughed—a full-fledged, genuine laugh. Darcy

turned toward him, startled by the sound. Her expression shifted, as if she'd just discovered something unexpected about him.

And the moment stretched a little too long.

Suddenly Sam looked away, his smile slipping off his face. He cleared his throat, as if embarrassed. The silence that followed wasn't awkward exactly, but close to it.

But in that stretched out moment, Annie caught something in Sam's eyes as he shared a laugh with them, though she couldn't say exactly what. It struck her as something like . . . longing.

Five

It was late. David had been called out halfway through dinner to meet with Johnny King, a farmer who had a dispute over land that had switched course in January's big storm. Muddy Creek had been a boundary between two farms for decades, yet had moved over fifty feet, and Johnny was worried that he'd lost valuable property.

It was only February, David reminded him. Let's hold off until spring. Johnny wasn't happy with David's solution, which he considered no solution at all. Problems don't solve themselves, he'd told David. And there was some truth in that. But many problems did resolve on their own, if given enough time. Especially when another storm might move Muddy Creek right back to where it had been.

Johnny King didn't agree.

As he left the home, David knew that he'd be the subject of some grumbling tonight between Johnny and his wife. Not an uncommon occurrence, David knew. Being bishop meant someone was always unhappy with him. He knew this was part of the role of leadership, but he also knew that he shouldn't let people's opinions sway him one way or the other. He did his best to look to the Lord for guidance, and that took time. Hearing from the Lord was not something a man could rush.

Still, it wasn't a particularly pleasant feeling to be the object of constant criticism. Normally, a deacon would handle these kinds of disputes. But Stoney Ridge's deacon, Luke Schrock, was off to Kentucky for an extended stay. A little too extended for David's liking. Conflicts and problems, bickering and grudges seemed to be piling up in the church. Unity felt like it was sorely lacking.

David's wife Birdy thought it was time to consider the lot for a new deacon. She had a hunch that Luke wanted to stay in Kentucky, helping his cousin. The opportunities were better for a young family there, she reminded David. "He won't cut the cord to Stoney Ridge without your encouragement," Birdy had said. All that Luke needed was David's blessing.

That conversation with Birdy kept nettling David. The truth was, he didn't want to give Luke his blessing to leave. He wanted to be blessed by Luke's return as his deacon.

Twenty minutes later, after settling his faithful buggy horse into her stall with fresh hay and a bucket of cold water, David walked into his house to the scent of something delicious—cinnamon, maybe? Apple butter? His whole being perked up like a bear catching a scent of honey. But before he could investigate, Birdy called him into the living room. She was kneeling beside an open box and folding small clothes into neat stacks. "I'm putting this together so you can take it to work tomorrow and pass the clothes along to Dok," she said without looking up. "So brave, what they're doing."

David leaned against the doorway, watching her. He knew this was more than just a simple act of sharing clothes. This was acceptance. Acceptance that the Lord had decided their family was complete.

Birdy had never given up hope for more children, and if she ever had the blessing of a daughter, she would've been over the moon. David, on the other hand, felt more than content with what the Lord had given to them. Two little wild boys—fast-moving, dirt-covered, impossibly loud creatures who kept him young. He was in his late fifties now, with a full house and a full heart. And grandchildren had started to arrive. David had five daughters and one son from his first marriage. Truth be told, girls were much harder to raise. So many emotions. So many words. So many tears that he could never quite figure out how to handle. His boys? They were simple—food, mischief, and the occasional wrestling match, and they were happy.

But still, he was a little sorry for Birdy's sake. She was quite a bit younger than him and would've loved a quiver full.

He glanced at his wife, aware that her movements had slowed. Birdy held up a little shirt and pair of trousers. "Remember this? Both boys wore it on Easter Sunday. They've grown so fast."

Had they? David thought they both seemed so young. Like two little colts, still kicking up their heels. Clearing his throat, he said, "Birdy, when you were part of the youth gatherings around here, do you remember anyone named Mary Zook? She'd be in her early forties by now, I think. Around your age. Maybe a little younger."

She looked up, almost laughing. "Any more information than that?"

"She would've had a baby about twenty-five years ago."

Birdy stopped folding and gave him a flat look. "Mary Zook must be one of the most common names among all Lancaster Amish, and the only detail you've added is another common event."

"You're right," he said. "But that's all the information Ruth gave me."

She shook her head, still smiling as she tucked small shoes into the box. "Why is Dok looking for this particular Mary Zook?"

David hesitated. That was a very reasonable question, wasn't it? He'd already gathered that it was important—his sister wouldn't have asked him for help without good reason. But he also knew how fiercely she guarded her patients' privacy. "I don't know much. Ruth is pretty protective of confidentiality."

"As are you," Birdy said.

David sighed, rubbing a hand over his beard. "I try to." It wasn't always easy. So often he wished he could bring his struggles as bishop to Birdy, just to hear her perspective. But more often than not, he held back. Unlike his sister's husband Matt—whose work was far removed from her medical practice—his world and Birdy's world were one and the same. He didn't want to risk coloring her view of anyone in their church community, or rob her of the joy she found among friends and neighbors.

He was glad he could cast all his cares on the Lord, because otherwise, they'd weigh him down like a yoke too heavy to bear. Still, he had learned over time that casting his cares was not a onetime event. His mind kept reeling in the worries, until he remembered to cast them out again.

Birdy sat back on her heels, studying him. "You look tired."

"I am." He nodded toward the kitchen. "What's that I smell?"

She grinned. "Baked oatmeal for tomorrow's breakfast. But I suppose I could cut you a piece now."

David's stomach rumbled in response. "I wouldn't say no."

She laughed, standing and brushing past him. "Come on, then. I can finish this up later."

He followed, already feeling lighter. Tonight, he had a warm home, a loving wife, and a slice of freshly baked oatmeal. And tomorrow—and every tomorrow after that—when the worries came creeping back, he would cast them out again to the Lord, trusting they were in far better hands than his own.

The house held that deep, settled quiet that only came in the small hours. Dok moved down the hallway on bare feet, each step placed with the kind of careful deliberation she'd perfected when Gabe first came to live with them as an infant, taking care to avoid creaky spots in the old floorboards.

Matt was working the graveyard shift, a schedule he'd volunteered for so one of them would always be home with Gabe during the day. Dok thought she might ask Annie to cover the early evening gaps when both she and Matt were at work. And then, despite Dok's reservations, Matt had persuaded her to let Charlie take over night calls. At least for a few weeks, Matt had said, until they could figure out a more permanent childcare arrangement.

Dok didn't even want to know what Matt considered to be a permanent arrangement, because as far as she was concerned, this was a very temporary situation. Emergency foster care never came with a manual. Just like before, she and Matt were figuring it out as they went along.

She eased open the door to Gabe's room, slipping inside without a sound. Moonlight spilled through the curtains in soft silver pools, and there he was—curled on his side with his blanket kicked off, one small foot poking through the crib slats.

Dok crossed the room and gently pulled the blanket back over him, coaxing his foot back inside the crib without waking him. She let her hand rest on his back, rubbing slow, gentle circles the way she used to when he was a newborn. These quiet moments had always been hers—when the demands of the day couldn't reach her, when it was just her and this beautiful little boy who'd somehow found his way into their lives. Into their hearts.

She watched the steady rise and fall of Gabe's breathing and felt that familiar knot of worry tighten in her chest. From the moment she'd first seen him in Sandra's arms, she knew something wasn't right with him. These past few days had only sharpened that instinct into certainty.

His little body felt too soft when she picked him up, muscles yielding without the natural resistance she expected from a healthy toddler. He didn't toddle around getting into everything. He made no effort to speak. No babbling. No crying. In a way, that made her sad. Crying was a way for a baby to communicate that he needed something—hunger, discomfort, love.

It was true that Gabe had been an incredibly easy baby. But what toddler was ever easy? None that Dok had seen in her practice. Gabe's passive behavior struck Dok as a warning sign. There was an unnatural calm about him, as if he'd already learned not to expect much from the world. He seemed almost . . . defeated.

Over the last week, she'd been running every test she could think of, methodically ruling out possibilities. A hearing test, a vision test, urine test, blood tests. Her entire career had been built on this kind of detective work—tracking symptoms, cataloging behaviors, following each thread until it led to an answer. But with Gabe, every lead seemed to dissolve. Nothing fit.

She'd consulted with colleagues and one word kept surfacing in their conversations: autism. She couldn't deny that many pieces fit the pattern—the lack of eye contact, the delayed speech, the way he seemed to exist in his own separate world. But something deep in her gut resisted that diagnosis. Or maybe she just didn't want to accept it.

Her hand stilled on his back. What more could she do? What other test could she consider? What was she missing? There had to be something, some key that would unlock whatever it was that was keeping him from developing normally. God must have had a reason to bring this child to her, not once but twice. What could it be?

Her brother David would remind her that God's plans were often beyond human understanding. Usually, she found comfort in that certainty. But tonight, watching this dear small child sleep, she found herself questioning anyway. Why did God bring this child into her life? It must be to help him. But what if she couldn't? What if no one could?

She brushed a wisp of hair from his forehead. The warmth of his skin under her fingers, the steady rhythm of his heartbeat—all the signs of life were there. Somewhere inside this quiet little body was a whole person waiting to emerge. She just had to figure out how to help him.

Dok straightened slowly. "Help me see, Lord," she whispered, the only prayer she could manage. "Show me what I'm missing."

She stepped back into the hallway, leaving his door cracked open. Just in case he needed her. Just in case tonight was the night he might call out for her.

Six

Darcy glanced up from the chart she was reviewing. An Amish mother sat in the corner of Dok's waiting room, her teenaged daughter beside her. They were talking quietly in Pennsylvania Dutch—Darcy didn't understand the words, but it was the tone that had caught her attention. The daughter's voice was warm, animated, with the occasional soft chuckle. The mother listened with interest, nodding gently, her hands folded in her lap. They could have been discussing chores or fabric or a boy at church. Darcy didn't know. But there was a rhythm to their exchange that felt sweet. Rare. Like they actually enjoyed each other.

Then Darcy's eyes drifted to the pair seated across the room.

A non-Amish mother and daughter—Darcy guessed about the age of fifteen—sat stiffly apart, worlds between them. The girl's thumbs flicked rapidly over her phone, eyes never lifting. The mother tried twice to speak, gave up, and settled into silence. When the girl finally looked up, it was only to snap, "Can't we just ask the nurse for the diet pills and go?"

Diet pills. For a fifteen-year-old. Darcy had to swallow the sigh that rose in her throat.

Earlier that morning, a little Amish girl had come in clutching a threadbare rag doll with mismatched button eyes and a tangle of yellow yarn hair. The kind of doll someone had probably loved before her, and someone before that. She held it close like it was the most precious thing in the world.

Right after that, a little girl in sparkly pink boots had barreled in behind her mother, dragging a backpack stuffed with Barbie dolls. She begged loudly for a stop at Walmart on the way home. "I *need* the pool party Barbie," she'd said, voice stretched sharp with whining. "*Everybody* has her."

Trying not to roll her eyes, Darcy returned to her work as Charlie came up from the downstairs office to check the day's patient list. He lifted his eyebrows. "What? Is something wrong? Did Dok head out on a house call and not tell us?"

"No, no. She's here. Why? Do I look bothered?"

"Not bothered, exactly. Well, actually . . . yes. Bothered. You look bothered."

Darcy tipped her head toward the waiting room and lowered her voice. "I've just been noticing the Amish patients. They're so . . . different from . . . us."

Charlie followed her gaze. "Different's one way to put it. Took me a while to get accustomed to their ways. Still am."

"I mean it in a good way. They seem so grounded. Even the teenagers. It's kind of amazing."

He nodded, thoughtful. "Yeah, I know what you mean. It might have something to do with growing up on a farm. These kids have a role to play. Animals count on them."

Maybe every child should grow up on a farm, Darcy thought. Where you were needed. Where your worth wasn't based on Instagram likes. Where your day ended with physical tiredness.

Charlie skimmed the patient list. "The Amish have got a lot figured out, that's for sure. But it's easy to romanticize them and overlook their shortcomings."

Darcy looked up at him. "What do you mean? What shortcomings?" She hadn't seen many.

He gave a shrug. "Their naivete, for one. They give their kids a lot of freedom. More than most non-Amish parents. Sometimes I'm not sure they realize how dangerous the world can be." He lifted a shoulder in a shrug. "And another thing . . . faith is so tied up with belonging to your family and community. You're in or you're out. That's heavy. David Stoltzfus does a good job of encouraging teens to wait on baptism until they're truly all in. Evie's heard him tell baptism classes to not get baptized until they're ready to be truly Amish, but I think he's pretty rare among Amish bishops. Sounds like it, anyway."

Darcy mulled that over.

Charlie was on a roll. "And then they've got very few choices. Sometimes I wonder if they're content or just . . . don't know any different."

"But maybe that's the whole point? If you grow up not knowing what you're missing, you're not missing anything."

Charlie gave a crooked grin. "You might be right. Maybe I just value choices because I grew up with them. If I'd grown up Amish, I might not care." He handed Darcy the patient list and called out the girl's name who wanted diet pills.

As the girl and her mother followed Charlie to the stairwell that led to the downstairs office, Darcy thought it would be interesting to see how Charlie handled this one. She glanced back at the Amish mother and daughter, still chatting softly in the corner. The mother reached over and untangled the string of her daughter's prayer cap, and the teenager smiled at her.

So maybe they weren't perfect, Darcy thought, but they seemed to have held on to something good in their old-timey lifestyle that most everyone else had let go of.

Darcy cringed. She *really* needed to stop using that phrase.

David slowed his horse at the end of the lane that led to the Grabers' woodshop, giving himself a moment before turning in. Tom Esh's words still echoed in his mind: "This one's for you, Bishop. It needs your kind of touch."

David had nearly rolled his eyes. Tom Esh was a minister, yet he had a way of stepping aside when things got messy, and the Grabers were certainly messy. Newcomers to Stoney Ridge, they had carried their comparisons with them like overstuffed suitcases. Every visit, every service, every custom was measured against the church district they had just left—and, like clockwork, dismissed as inferior. He had seen families like that before. Never rooted long, always restless. Moving from place to place, convinced the last stop had been better after all.

Still, David turned the buggy down the lane. It was his role as bishop to deal with the hard cases, and he reminded himself that these people were part of his flock, whether easy or not. But he did think again of Luke Schrock, his missing deacon.

He had scarcely tied his horse when the front door flung open and Alice Graber stormed down the porch steps, skirts swishing, cap strings fluttering in the breeze.

"It's about time someone came," she snapped, her arms folded tight across her chest.

"Hello, Alice." David pressed his lips into something like a smile and answered in the calmest voice he could summon. "Let's go inside, and you can tell me all about it." The tone was deliberate. Set calm against storm, and maybe—if God willed—the storm would quiet.

Inside, Alice did not offer coffee or baked goods, as most Amish wives would. She sat at the table and launched in without preamble. "My Billy is getting picked on at school by bullies."

David folded himself into the chair on the opposite side of the table, hands resting on his knees. He knew Billy—small for his age, quiet in a way that sometimes looked vacant, as though his thoughts floated far behind his eyes. A little unaware of others. An easy target for cruel boys.

Alice's voice tumbled on, clipped and rising, detailing every slight, every taunt. David listened, or tried to, but memory had a pull of its own.

David thought of himself at that age, all knees and elbows, watching his friends' bodies stretch tall and grow muscle while his stayed stubbornly small. Puberty had arrived for others like a sudden flood; for him, it dawdled. He was terrified it might have left him stranded. He remembered being chosen last for dodgeball games, standing with his stomach tight while the team leaders chose, until only he remained, and one of them muttered, "Guess we'll have to take Davy."

And he remembered the sharper cuts—the time a well-liked girl had leaned his way, tossing him a laugh, a flutter, though it was meant for another boy's eyes. That other boy had bristled, grabbed David by the shirtfront, and growled, "Let's fight." David had tried, but one punch had set him flat on the ground, ears ringing, pride scattered like sawdust.

He had hated those years. Hated the humiliation of being overlooked, mocked, underestimated. And yet—hadn't those same years given him the patience he drew on now? The ability to see through bluster and fury to the fear beneath?

It dawned on him that Alice had stopped talking. She was staring at him, eyes narrowed, as if she had spoken a question and waited far too long for his answer. David blinked, shifted forward in his chair. "These years can be difficult for boys," he said carefully, "but there are lessons to be learned that will benefit Billy for the rest of his life."

Alice's chin lifted. "Such as?"

"Such as empathy," David said. "Understanding."

The room went quiet but not at peace. Alice's silence was sharper than her words, her eyes speaking volumes: that David just didn't understand, that he was dismissing her son's pain, that talk of "lessons" was no comfort to a hurting mother.

David sat with it for a moment. He could not force her to see what he saw—that hardship carved a boy's character deeper than ease ever could. He could only be steady, not defensive.

At last he rose, smoothing his coat. "I'll speak to the teacher," he said.

Alice didn't move. Didn't nod. She simply stared, lips pressed tight.

David stepped toward the door, a heaviness settling on him. He had not won her over—he doubted she would ever be fully satisfied. But he had listened to her, and sometimes that was all a bishop could do.

Outside, the air felt cooler, as if the temperature had dropped during this uncomfortable errand. His horse flicked an ear, impatient to leave. David laid a hand on the reins and paused, gazing back at the house.

Billy's small, serious face floated in his mind. He prayed the boy would learn, sooner than he himself had, that the sting of being last could teach a man to see the lonely, the weak, the overlooked. It could shape him into someone who offered a hand instead of a fist.

If only his mother would allow the lesson to take root.

Darcy had never expected to feel so content in a place this small.

The ADU—technically an "accessory dwelling unit," but she preferred "cozy cottage"—was tucked behind a larger farmhouse on the edge of Stoney Ridge. She'd found it online sandwiched between listings for sterile studio apartments and overpriced cabins with "rustic charm" (read: no plumbing). This one had caught her eye with its honest description: one room, one oven, lots of quiet.

It was nothing fancy. A twin bed tucked under the window, a compact kitchenette with mismatched mugs, and a tiny table that doubled as her desk, dinner spot, and cookie staging area. It had everything she needed. Specifically the oven. She loved to bake. Cookies, especially.

Right now, that oven was working overtime on a batch of her famous oatmeal raisin cookies. The scent filled the cottage—warm cinnamon with a hint of vanilla. Mindlessly, she hummed as she cleaned up, rinsing soapy bowls, waiting for the oven timer to go off, until her phone buzzed on the windowsill.

She wiped her hands on a dish towel and checked the screen.

Clear skies tonight

No punctuation. No greeting. Just three words from an unknown number.

She stared at it, brow furrowed. It felt familiar. Not the number, but the tone. Sparse. Intentional. Like someone who didn't waste words.

She typed back:

Is this Sam Mustang or a weather app?

She hit send, then immediately regretted the joke. Too much? Too weird? She didn't know the rules with Sam. He was polite, but not chatty. Mysterious, but not unfriendly. Like a crossword clue you couldn't quite solve.

Her phone buzzed again.

Sam

Hmm. Interesting.

How'd you get my number?

Annie

Darcy smiled. That tracked. Annie, efficient to the point of clairvoyance. If Sam had asked for her number, Annie would've handed it over without ceremony.

She typed:

So is this an invitation to go stargazing tonight?

Pause. Had she scared him off? She'd nearly typed *date* . . . but had changed it to *invitation*.

Just thought you'd want to know. Jupiter's moons are visible.

Darcy blinked. That was . . . oddly thoughtful. In a very Sam Mustang kind of way.

She typed:

I've always had a soft spot for Jupiter. I'll bring cookies.

She glanced at the oven. Ten more minutes. Long, long pause from Sam. She tried not to overthink the silence.

Then:

I don't snack.

She snorted.

She typed:

You don't snack? Is that typical for astronomers? Like, you're too busy contemplating the cosmos to eat a warm-from-the-oven cookie?

Another long silence.

She sat down on the couch, pulled a blanket over her lap, and stared at the ceiling. Maybe he was regretting texting her. Maybe he was already back in his truck, driving to some remote hilltop to stargaze solo, free of chatty nurses and text banter.

Then:

I eat. Just not recreationally.

Darcy snorted.

This time, she paused, debating different ways to respond to him. To her surprise, he texted first.

9pm. Same place. I bring my telescope. You bring your cookies. Good balance.

Darcy laughed. That was practically a compliment.

She typed:

Not sure about that. My oatmeal raisin cookies will trump your flashy telescope.

She stared at her screen, wondering if he didn't get her humor. Texting could be weird that way.

Then came:

Doubtful. But snickerdoodles might tip the scales.

She grinned. He was almost, sort of, bantering with her!

She typed:

Do you ever wonder how Wonder Pond got discovered? Because during the day, it's just a big puddle. I know, because I hiked up there this afternoon just to see it in the daylight. Just a big ol' cow pond.

His end remained silent.

She folded a dish towel. Checked the oven. Took out the cookies and let them cool. Checked her phone. Still no response.

After a few more minutes, in came a text.

No

She typed:

No what?

No, I don't wonder about it.

Darcy tilted her head. Cryptic. Classic Sam.

She typed:

I do. I wonder about all kinds of things. Curious about everything and everyone. But I bake great cookies, so people tolerate me.

No reply.

She didn't really expect one, so she wasn't disappointed. Sam Mustang didn't seem like the type of guy who would volley texts back and forth. He was more like a meteor—brief, bright, and gone before you could ask follow-up questions.

He wasn't really flirting with her. His texts were the same clipped, monosyllabic replies as always. Still, as she tucked cookies into a container to take to Wonder Pond, a quiet warmth spread through her, head to toes.

She could get used to this.

Seven

The next few days brought gloomy skies and canceled plans for stargazing. Then, the grim weather finally shifted. Sunlight poured into Stoney Ridge all day long, and by nightfall, the stars were back—crisp, clear, and ready to be admired. Annie Fisher pulled her wool scarf up higher against the cold and listened as Gus and Sam Mustang spoke in a language that might as well have been a foreign one.

"Sam, I just don't get it," Darcy said, peering through the telescope.

Annie smiled. At least she wasn't the only one who had no idea what she was looking at through that narrow lens.

Darcy straightened to look at Sam. "How could you call that beautiful bright light Beetlejuice?"

Wrong. Annie was wrong. She was the only one who had no idea.

"Spelling is B-e-t-e-l-g-e-u-s-e," Sam said. "One of the brightest stars in the Orion constellation."

"Sounds made-up," Darcy said.

Sam let out a quiet laugh. "That's because you're thinking of the movie."

"Or maybe I'm thinking of the bug." Darcy scrunched her nose. "It sounds like something you'd squish under your boot."

Annie stole a glance at Sam, who was watching Darcy, amused. He had a funny way about him—gruff and detached most of the time, but every now and then, something softened in his expression, like a door cracking open just a little. And Darcy seemed to have a knack for finding those cracks.

Gus gestured to the scope. "Annie, come take a look at what Darcy's talking about."

She nodded and bent down, eye to the lens. Beetlejuice, no . . . Betelgeuse came into view—bright, pulsing red in the velvet-dark sky. It shimmered like something alive, like a heart beating light across a thousand years. Beautiful, yes, but it wasn't all that stole her breath.

Gus had leaned in beside her, reaching around her to adjust the dial. His shoulder brushed against hers. She caught the faint scent of the soap he used—clean, woodsy like fresh-cut pine, familiar. He was close enough that if she tilted her hand, she could trail a finger down the side of his jaw, feel the scratch of his evening whiskers. The thought came uninvited, soft and sudden, and she swallowed it quickly.

She turned her head slightly, hoping—maybe foolishly—to catch him looking at her the way she sometimes caught herself looking at him.

But his gaze was elsewhere.

Gus's attention was on Sam, face lit with curiosity, already brimming with another question. His focus was aimed at someone else, and she felt it like a shift in the weather.

Annie stepped away from the telescope, folding her hands in front of her to keep from fidgeting. Her mind wandered back to a few nights ago, when Dok asked her to babysit Gabe for a few hours. Annie hadn't hesitated to say yes. She'd do anything for Dok. When she mentioned her plans to Gus, he surprised her by saying he'd like to come too. He even showed up with a soft, squishy ball and a handful of wooden blocks tucked in a big paper bag.

Dok had warned them: Gabe might not be all that interested in Gus's toys. She'd told them that he might seem to be in his own world. Still, Annie wasn't prepared for just how withdrawn the little boy was. He sat on a quilt in the living room like a stone dropped in water, unmoving and silent, eating dry Cheerios from a Tupperware dish. No giggles. No curiosity. No reaching for the toys Gus set up all around him.

Annie had watched the little boy with a knot in her chest. She'd grown up surrounded by babies—being the youngest of a big family meant there were lots of nieces or nephews. Every single one of them, boy or girl, was a blur of energy, noise, and sticky fingers. Gabe, by contrast, felt like a room with the windows shut. Still and airless.

If Gus felt concerned by Gabe's lack of response, he didn't show it. He sat cross-legged on the floor beside Gabe with a calm Annie envied, his voice soft and steady as he talked to the little boy. When the toys were met with blank disinterest, Gus simply adjusted to something new. No sigh. No shrug. No giving up. Just a quiet pivot. A stuffed animal with a bell inside. A tower of wooden blocks. Or he would read from a board book, using funny voices. After a while, he lifted Gabe into his lap and gently pedaled his legs like a slow-motion bicycle ride.

Annie had sat on the sofa, watching them, and felt a sweep of love for Gus that nearly undid her. A thought crossed her mind: *This could be us. Someday we will be sitting together with our own baby.* The idea had settled in her chest, warm and certain. He had glanced up at her with a smile, as if he knew what she was thinking, and had the same hope.

But tonight, standing under the stars, with Gus so caught up with Sam and astronomy and endless questions, she rethought that moment. Had she misread that look in Gus's eyes? Was she seeing only what she wanted to see? And if the night sky hadn't been covered in clouds, would he have even offered to babysit Gabe with her?

She wasn't sure he would've.

The bell over the Bent N' Dent's front door jingled like it always did, alerting David and Sarah that a customer had arrived. David sat at his desk in the back office, squinting at a receipt that involved twelve dozen quart-sized canning jars. The Englisch woman who'd placed the order had said she needed them "pronto."

David didn't mind doing special orders for customers. Folks had all sorts of needs. But twelve dozen jars in February? Curious, he'd asked her what they were for.

She leaned in, lowered her voice, and said, "Dry soup mix. I sell them at Lancaster's Public Market. So easy. So cheap to make. And I make a killing on them."

David blinked. A killing? Over soup? He nodded politely, but in his head, he was trying to reconcile the idea of soup—something meant to nourish the soul—with the notion of it being weaponized for profit.

He returned his thoughts to the adding machine when he heard a familiar voice in the main store, one that was most dear to him. *Birdy.* David knew that voice like he knew the sound of rain on the roof or the clink of his favorite mug.

Birdy rarely dropped by the store in the middle of a morning . . . unless she had something on her mind. He set down his pencil and rose from his chair, just as the door to his office creaked open. Birdy stepped inside, her light blue cape peeking out under her dark coat. David smiled at the sight of his wife. That blue dress—it always reminded him of summer sky reflected in water. It made Birdy's eyes look like a tropical ocean, not that he'd ever seen one. Someday, he should tell her how he loved her in that blue dress.

Looking over Birdy's right shoulder was Sarah Blank, and peering over her left shoulder was Hank Lapp. Sometimes David thought he should just hire Hank Lapp to work at the store because he spent more time here than he did at home. On the other hand, having Hank Lapp as an employee sounded like a terrible idea. He'd be paying him to sit by the woodstove and eat peanuts with the other graybeards.

"Sarah," David said, "shouldn't you be at the cash register?"

Sarah hesitated a beat too long, then gave a quick nod and disappeared.

"Hank," he said, "aren't you in the middle of a checkers game?"

Hank waved that off. "I told Amos to PUT A PAUSE on it. I figured WHATEVER Birdy's here to say might CONCERN the rest of us. Especially if it's something INTERESTING."

David stepped forward and put his hand on the doorknob. "If it turns out to be interesting, I'll be sure to let you know." He gently closed the door and turned to Birdy. "I'm glad you've come. Would you like some coffee?"

"No. I just stopped by to tell you something."

"Well, at least sit down." He went around his desk and sat across from her. "What's up?"

"Have you or Dok found Mary Zook yet?"

David cringed. He'd completely forgotten about the search for Mary Zook. So had Dok, he suspected. She'd been so preoccupied with baby Gabe's arrival this last week or so that he'd hardly seen her to talk to, and when he did, all she talked about was baby Gabe. "No. No progress at all."

"I had an idea."

David's eyebrows lifted. "I'm listening."

"The Sisters' House."

Named for five elderly, maiden sisters, who all lived together in a very old house. Sadly, there were only three sisters left now. "Think one of the sisters might remember Mary Zook?"

"I don't know about that. Their memory isn't what it used to be. Or maybe it never was. But here's what they do have—*Budget* newspapers."

"Twenty-five years' worth?"

"At least. Maybe more. They've got them stacked in rows like fence posts throughout the house and in a shed out back. Tied up with string, all neat as can be."

David whistled under his breath. "So you think there might be a mention of Mary Zook in them?"

Birdy nodded. "Possibly. It'll take some digging. But you know as I do that babies are given special notices in the newspaper."

Yes, they certainly did. Even stillborn babies were acknowledged, with the comforting words that their lives were complete. David beamed. "Birdy, this is wonderful news. Thank you! Are you heading there now?"

"Me?" Birdy laughed. "Oh no. This is between you and Dok. I've got a full to-do list waiting for me today." She lifted her cape to reveal binoculars hanging around her neck. "Including meeting Micah Weaver to see a snowy owl in Ezra Miller's cornfield. Imagine. A snowy owl!"

David's smile faded quickly. Any visit to the Sisters' House was a long, drawn-out event. They were dear, sweet women, eager to show hospitality to him, but they were painfully slow and terribly forgetful. Imagine how hard it would be for him to explain that he wanted to sift through their stacks of *Budget* newspapers, and why he needed them—which he wasn't at liberty to explain. Not that he even knew the whole story. He didn't.

This would take hours upon hours. He frowned. Why was it his problem to find Mary Zook, anyway? It should be Dok's job to sift through those papers. He blew out a puff of air. But someone was out there who needed to make amends before it was too late, and David felt the burden of that. "I'll go there as soon as I can carve out a few hours." Which, quite frankly, might take him days. Weeks. This was a task he wholeheartedly dreaded.

"I told them you'd be coming by this afternoon."

What? He cleared his throat. "This afternoon?"

"Yes. I knew you'd want to see this through as quickly as possible. It's just one of the many reasons why you're such a wonderful bishop."

A nice thought, but Birdy was heavily biased. It seemed to David that opinions about him were very polarized. Half the church considered him far too progressive a bishop, the other half considered him far too conversative. No matter what, he couldn't win. He often had to remind himself that it was only God's opinion that should matter to him.

Birdy stepped toward the door, then turned back to blow him a kiss. "Blue dress today," she said softly, "just for you."

So she knew. He didn't have to tell her.

She reached for the door and nudged it open, accidentally brushing Sarah and Hank aside.

"Just dusting around the store," Sarah said, already halfway to the dry goods.

David stepped forward, eyes narrowing at Hank. "And you?"

Hank kept his gaze low. "Just helping Sarah reach the high spots."

David glanced at Birdy. She raised one brow, amused.

Then Hank added, "She's afraid of ladders."

David's eyes slid to Sarah—now perched halfway up one. "Looks like she's working through it."

Carrying a bouquet of grocery store flowers, Darcy walked up Windmill Farm's long gravel driveway, the sunlight glinting off patches of melting snow. The vast winter fields were muted and bare, the orchard stark and waiting. The windmill on the rise groaned as it turned—red blades faded by time and weather. In the distance, the shop marked Stitches in Time sat shuttered. A knit shop? She made a mental note to ask Evie about it.

There was a stillness here among the Amish farms that she hadn't expected to like, not at all. Yet she did. She liked being in Stoney Ridge, quite a lot. And it had nothing to do with Sam Mustang.

Well. Maybe a little.

She reached the buggy shop and knocked, then pushed open the door.

"Company!" Evie said, her voice full of relief. She was propped up on the sofa, her casted leg balanced on a mountain of pillows. A crocheted afghan covered her lap and a pile of books sat at her side.

"You poor thing," Darcy said. "You must be bored out of your mind." She held up the flowers.

Evie beamed. "They're perfect."

Darcy spotted a glass of water, dumped the flowers in, and scanned the room for a place to set them. A small school bell sat on a side table, within reach of Evie. "Can I move this?"

"Please. Fern's idea. In case I needed help. I rang it once and she bolted over like I'd set myself on fire. I haven't dared touch it since."

Darcy set the flowers on the side table and tucked the bell onto the floor, next to Evie. "Just in case you change your mind." She sat cross-legged on the braided rug.

Evie wasted no time. "So, how do you like working for Dok?"

Darcy inhaled. How did she like working for Dok? It felt a little like she'd found herself inside the eye of a hurricane. "She is . . . rarely still."

Evie laughed. "Aren't you learning a lot from her, though? She's letting you go on house calls with her, right?"

"Yes, I'm definitely learning a ton from her. But I have yet to be invited on a house call."

"Soon. I'm sure she'll ask you soon," Evie said. "She can be very protective about her Amish patients. Maybe a little too much. Is she letting Charlie do more?"

Darcy seesawed her hand in the air. "Not really. She still checks everything he does twice. Yesterday, he put a cast on a boy with a broken wrist and she made him redo it."

"Had he made a mistake?"

"Honestly, it looked okay to me. Sometimes, I think Dok just has something specific in mind and assumes we should be her mind readers. She doesn't seem to know how to delegate."

Evie frowned. "That's too bad. She asked Charlie to take over night calls and he was so pleased. I was hoping it might mean she's counting on him more."

"Well . . . she's got her hands full. That baby she's fostering—Gabe—is taking a lot of her attention."

"Gabe—so that's his name? Charlie couldn't remember. How's he doing?"

"Quiet," Darcy said. "Too quiet. Doesn't respond to voices or show much interest in toys. Dok's running some tests. And then more tests. She's determined to find an answer to his lethargy."

Evie's face softened. "Is she worried?"

"She doesn't say much," Darcy said with a shrug. "But she's not the chatty type. And she's always rushing from one thing to another."

"True. I don't think she'd mind my telling you that she has ADHD. She's pretty open about it. Maybe she's mentioned it?"

Darcy's eyes went wide. "No! But that . . . explains so much."

"She wasn't diagnosed until adulthood, but she works hard to manage it. Annie Fisher seemed to know intuitively how to anticipate Dok's rapid-fire methods. When she left, I took over her responsibilities and felt like I was just treading water when"—she knocked twice on the plaster cast covering her leg—"this happened."

Darcy nodded slowly, piecing things together. Dok's quick mind, her ability to pivot so quickly from one problem to the next. Trying to keep up with her was a challenge. Sometimes, being around Dok, Darcy felt like she was always jumping in on a movie halfway through, trying to piece together what she'd missed.

"Going on house calls with her will make a big difference. You'll understand her in a different way. That's when I started to see what makes her such a standout. She notices things most doctors and nurses would miss."

"What do you mean?"

"I can't quite explain how she does it . . . but you'll know what I mean when you see it." Evie wiggled her eyebrows. "So . . . I hear you're suddenly into stargazing. What's that about?"

Darcy blinked. "How do you know about that?"

"I asked Charlie where you've been lately. He said you were out every clear night." She grinned. "Since when have you liked astronomy?"

"Since I was a kid. It was my main hobby for years and years. I set it aside during nursing school, but when I moved to Alaska last summer, I picked it up again. It's a big deal up there. Kinda like birding is here."

"Charlie said you've been going up to Wonder Pond with Annie and Gus . . . and someone named Sam." She wiggled her eyebrows again, with more exaggeration. "So who's this Sam?"

Darcy shrugged. "He's just someone who knows a lot about constellations. That's all."

Evie arched a brow. "Is it? Charlie said Sam looks like the lead actor in a cowboy Western."

Darcy covered a smile with a fake cough. She'd had the exact same thought!

"Tall, dark, and handsome, Charlie said."

"More like tall, dark, and brooding."

Evie studied her, narrowing her eyes. "You like him."

Darcy groaned. "I do not."

She planted her elbows on the pillows surrounding her. "You do."

Darcy huffed. "I mention a man, and suddenly I'm smitten? Honestly, Evie. You sound like you're in junior high."

Evie gave her a knowing look. "I wish I had a mirror nearby. Your cheeks are bright red. I know you well enough to know you're embarrassed. And you're embarrassed because I'm right." She clapped her hands together. "So you like this guy! I'm so proud of you! You haven't been into a guy for . . . well, I'm not sure when. I want to meet Sam!"

Darcy stood abruptly. "This was a mistake. I should've just left the flowers outside the buggy repair shop."

"Hold your horses! You gave me years of unsolicited advice about Charlie, yet I can't give you any advice?"

"I don't need any advice!" Darcy huffed. "Besides, you were lovesick for Charlie for years. I have barely gotten to know Sam."

Evie gave her a smug grin. "And Charlie and I ended up happily married!"

Darcy went to the door. "Your leg may be broken, but your imagination is in full health. So long for now, Evie."

"Bewitched, bothered, and bewildered," Evie sang, so off key that it hurt to hear. She was seriously tone deaf—and yet it never discouraged her from singing. Whenever Darcy had begged her to stop, Evie would quote the Bible verse about making a joyful noise to the Lord. *Noise*, she would emphasize.

Painfully off key, Evie belted out another verse: "She can't sleep, she's lost her heart, and though she knows his flaws, she loves him anyway."

"Cheeky." Darcy closed the door and made it exactly four steps before Sam Mustang's stupid, perfect face popped into her head, like it seemed to be doing entirely too much lately.

Eight

David Stoltzfus stood in front of the Sisters' House, a two-story building desperately in need of fresh paint, surrounded by a small picket fence that was also in need of paint. He walked up the path to the door, steeling himself for what lay ahead. He hadn't quite anticipated the magnitude of the task until Sylvia, the youngest sister at eighty-five, had cheerfully informed him over the phone that yes, they had plenty of old *Budget* newspapers. "Every single one since 1970," she'd said with evident pride. "We keep things, you know. You never know when someone might need it."

Oh, he knew how they held on to things. Everyone knew. The condition of the Sisters' House was a topic of discussion between the ministers of the church at least once a year, when their annual turn to host church came along. Every family took a turn once throughout the year. Long ago, several people volunteered to help ready the Sisters' House for church. An impossible task. Ever since, David had decided to give the elderly sisters a pass.

He knocked gently and heard the shuffle of feet, followed by a whispered conference on the other side of the door.

"It's the bishop."

"Which bishop?"

"Our bishop. David."

"David who?"

"Stoltzfus. Our David. Our bishop."

The door opened to reveal two of the three elderly sisters, Sylvia and Fannie, beaming up at him. "Come in, come in. We've been expecting you."

He followed her into the living room where Lena, sister number three, was waiting, perched on the edge of her chair like a bird ready to take flight. David's gaze swept the room, stunned. Most Plain families had . . . well, plain homes. Rather spartan. What was that word David had heard an Englisch shopper use recently to describe an Amish home? Minimalist.

That would not describe this room. It was buried in clutter. Drowning. Filled with furniture, stacks of books, overflowing boxes. Every nook and cranny was steeped with some kind of clutter: newspapers, books, boxes filled with quilting material, baskets full of yarn, junk mail, bills.

David cleared his throat. "I appreciate you letting me look through your *Budget* newspapers. I need to research something from about twenty-five years ago."

"Twenty-five years!" Sylvia clapped her hands together. "Oh my, that takes me back. Lena, do you remember twenty-five years ago?"

"Of course I remember twenty-five years ago. I'm old, not dead."

"What are you researching exactly?" Fannie said, leaning forward with interest.

David chose his words carefully. "I'm looking for some information about births and marriages from that time period. For church records."

All three sisters nodded sagely. "Church records sound like important business," Lena said.

"Well, you've come to the right place," Sylvia said. "We have every single issue."

"Every single one," Fannie said. "Follow me, Bishop. We keep most of the ones from the last century in the spare bedroom."

Most of them? David had already noticed stacks of *Budgets* in the corners of the living room. But he followed her down a long hallway. Fannie carefully opened a door and pushed against it with all her might.

David stopped short. Newspapers were stacked floor to ceiling, so many stacks they filled every available space. Boxes of clippings sat on chairs, shelves, and even on an old sewing machine in the corner.

"Here they are!" Fannie said. "We never like to throw anything away."

"I can see that," David said in a faint voice. "But why have you saved them?" Why so many?

"Well, it had been our mother's hobby. She'd had every intention of going through them to collect the sayings, but she hadn't quite finished the project when she passed. So then it became Lena's hobby."

"How far along is she?"

"She hasn't quite started yet. Soon, though."

Lena appeared behind him, breathing heavily from the walk down the hall. "See? We told you we keep everything. Good thing too. Here you are, twenty-five years later, needing exactly what we have."

"The Lord knew," Sylvia said, joining them in the doorway.

David surveyed the overwhelming scene. "Where would I find the newspapers from around the turn of the century?"

"Oh, that would be . . ." Lena looked around vaguely. "Well, they're somewhere in here. We call it organized chaos, you know. We know where everything is, mostly."

Fannie was already navigating through the stacks near the window. "Here's 1997 . . . 1998 . . ." She picked one up to look at the date but got distracted by a headline. "Oh, this is fascinating. Look at this article about a tornado that blew a barn roof right off. Where did that happen?" She squinted. "Oh. Missouri. Terrible weather down there."

"Fannie, honey," Sylvia said, "the bishop's time is precious."

"Oh dear, you're right." Fannie moved to another stack. "Let's see. I think that turn-of-the-century time must be around this area." She waved a frail, thin arm in the general direction of the far side of the room.

David rolled up his sleeves. This was going to be a very, very long afternoon.

A few hours later, he'd found a few stacks from the 1990s. The sisters had brought him tea and cookies, then proceeded to sit nearby, offering commentary on newspaper stories.

"Oh, I remember that wedding!" Lena said as she read about a couple in Stoney Ridge. "It rained so hard the buggy wheels got stuck in the mud."

"No, that was the Blank wedding," Sylvia said, peering over her shoulder. "This was the one where the bride's dress got caught on the fence."

"There are so many weddings." Lena let out a sigh. "Hard to keep them all straight."

David smiled despite himself. The sisters might be scattered, but their hearts were in the right place. At long last, he found the year he was looking for and started a fresh stack to take home. The sun was starting to set and his eyes were getting bleary. He was ready to wrap this up for today. He'd found many mentions of Mary Zooks, but his gut told him he hadn't found the right one yet.

"See?" Sylvia said, noticing the growing stack beside David. "Haven't I always said that you never know when someone will need something? Today proves it!"

David nodded absently, turning another page. His eyes caught on a birth announcement. He read it, then held the paper close to reread it.

And there it was.

Darcy was finishing up for the day when Dok shocked her by inviting her on a house call. Evie had made it sound like riding along was a golden opportunity, and Darcy wasn't about to blow it. She sprang into action.

Ten minutes later, she was gripping the door handle for dear life as Dok took another nail-biting curve. Dok had a lead foot—and nerves of steel. Darcy had been worried about making a good impression on her first house call. Now she was just hoping to survive the ride.

The countryside zipped past her window—white farmhouses, red barns, quilts snapping in the wind like bright flags on a battlefield. Picturesque, if you could focus long enough to see it. She'd been thrilled when Dok finally asked her to come along, but she hadn't expected the scenic route to feel like a roller coaster through Lancaster County.

Dok gave her some bullet point details: Miriam Yoder had called, worried about her three-year-old son Benny. Said he was coughing like a barking seal. Classic croup. "When an Amish mother calls at the end of the day with a worry," Dok said, "I know to go."

"Why is that?"

"Because they don't panic easily."

When they pulled into the long driveway that led to a white farmhouse, Darcy noticed a line of laundry flapping in the cold breeze—sheets, diapers, tiny shirts—all hanging crisp and clean despite the gray sky.

Miriam opened the door before they knocked, the scent of eucalyptus drifting out like a welcome mat. Not unpleasant. A little like a natural medicine cabinet.

Inside, little Benny sat at the kitchen table, a towel tented over his head while steam curled up from a bowl. His cheeks were flushed, but he looked alert. Calm. The whole kitchen did, really—plain but warm, every surface tidy, a woodstove humming in the corner.

"I did what you said, Dok," Miriam said, motioning to her own throat. "I've been trying to keep his windpipes warm and moist."

"Good work, Miriam." Dok crouched beside Benny and put a hand on his forehead.

Darcy stood back and watched. This was exactly what she'd come for—the observation, the hands-on assessment, the way Dok could read a room. She moved through her exam with gentle precision: lifting the towel, checking Benny's ears and throat, pressing under his jaw, listening to his lungs. Benny coughed for her—a definite seal bark. Dok nodded and motioned for Darcy to check oxygen levels and listen in too.

"Not perfect," Darcy said, "but not dangerous."

Dok straightened and tucked her stethoscope into her bag. "Keep doing what you're doing, Miriam. Keep an eye on Benny's fever. I'm not too concerned if it stays where it is now. End of the day, temperatures tend to rise a bit, but call me tomorrow if there's no improvement."

On the way back to the office, Darcy turned over everything she'd seen—how Dok sort of slowed down. She didn't rush or talk over Miriam, she noticed and commented on what the young mother had already done.

And her thoughts wandered to Miriam. She was much younger than Darcy . . . maybe ten years or more separated them. Yet Miriam was more talkative and open than Darcy would've expected. "Miriam said her husband's an electrician," she said suddenly, glancing sideways at Dok. "But they don't even have electricity."

"That's not uncommon."

Darcy frowned, thoughtful. "Miriam said he taught himself. That's something."

There were all these little details she hadn't expected. Things that didn't fit the tidy mental picture she'd had in her head before coming to Stoney Ridge. She'd assumed the Amish weren't especially educated. Quiet, maybe even withdrawn. Stuck in the past. Old-timey. *Stop using that phrase, Darcy!* But all those assumptions went out the window with what she saw today at the Yoder farm.

"Miriam seemed so calm," Darcy said. "And Benny's her first child! She was worried, sure, but not . . . anxious."

"She caught the croup early." Dok eased onto the main road, then calmly stepped on the gas pedal and the car leaped forward. "She seemed to sense right away that Benny didn't have a typical cold."

Darcy nodded. In any other practice, Benny might've ended up with antibiotics—or worse, in the ER. But the steam trick, an old standby, had done the job. "Pretty impressive that Miriam got ahead of croup so quickly."

Dok made a sound of agreement but didn't comment. She didn't need to.

"Maybe it's because she's home with him," Darcy said. "She and her husband aren't commuting long hours and juggling day care. The Amish parents are actually raising their kids."

No response. Just the hum of the engine and the blur of winter fields outside the window.

Darcy tapped her fingers on her knee, sorting through the swirl in her mind. She had no interest in *becoming* Amish. Not a chance. She wasn't about to trade in her blow dryer and iPad for buggies and bonnets. But there was something about the way these people lived—something that kept tugging at her. It wasn't the simple living or the bucolic farms. It was their contentment. She'd seen it in nearly every Amish she'd met. A settled peace, something they just radiated.

Darcy wasn't used to that. She had become wired for forward motion—seeking adventure and new experiences.

These people worked hard, no doubt about that. But they weren't chasing something always just out of reach. They were . . . rooted. Grounded. And it was unsettling how much she admired that. She glanced over at Dok. "These Amish . . . they change how you see things."

Dok didn't answer right away. Then, "Have you been in many Amish homes?"

"No. This was the first. Besides visiting Evie at Windmill Farm."

"They're just people, Darcy. Like you and me."

Darcy nodded slowly, staring out the window. Were they just like everybody else? Maybe. Maybe not. There was still so much she didn't know about the Amish. About herself. About her future.

But it seemed that was starting to change. Ever since her brother Jonathan had died, she'd lived like a leaf caught in the wind—never still, never rooted. But now, to her quiet surprise, the wind had stilled. Something inside her had begun to settle.

David Stoltzfus gave his trademark knock on the door of his sister's office. Inside, he could hear the rustling of papers, a chair creaking. A moment later, Dok's voice rang out. "Brother or bishop?"

"Both." He pushed open the door to find her seated at her desk, peering at her computer screen, reading glasses perched on her nose. Papers were spread out in no particular order, though he had the feeling she understood the chaos just fine. A little like the Sisters' House.

She nodded toward the empty chair across from her desk. "Tell Birdy thank you for that box of clothes. And ask her if she might have a coat that the boys have grown out of."

"Hello to you too." He settled into the chair, taking his time. "How are things going with Gabe?"

"How are things going?" She squinted at him over her glasses. "We're managing childcare. Lots of juggling, but it's working."

"Any signs of improvement in him?"

"I haven't seen any. Nor have I been able to nail down any diagnosis. Not one that seems to fit his profile, anyway." She pulled off her glasses and rubbed her eyes. "Gus is the only one who seems to have a connection with Gabe."

"Gus? Annie's Gus?"

"Yes. The two of them have helped out Matt and me when we need a few hours here and there while we're both working. Gus does a lot of PT and OT exercises with Gabe."

David tilted his head in a question.

"Physical therapy and occupational therapy. I think Gus would've become a doctor or a PT if he weren't Amish."

"But he *is* Amish," David said, maybe more firmly than he needed to.

Dok gave him a *look*. The same one she'd given him when they were children and he'd lectured her about climbing too high in the apple tree. "So. You stopped by for a reason."

"Mary Zook."

Dok's eyes went round as silver dollars. "David, I have completely forgotten about her!" She clapped her hands against her cheeks. "Wait. Did you find her?"

"Possibly." He pulled a folded sheet of paper from his pocket and flattened it on the desk. "I've found ten, to be exact."

Her eyebrows lifted as she squinted at the paper sitting between them. "Ten Mary Zooks?"

"Some are too old. Some too young. One passed away, two left the Amish." He tapped the page. "That leaves six possibilities."

Dok chewed the top of her pen thoughtfully. "Tell me about them. Maybe I'll recognize someone from my practice. I only know them by their married surnames."

He went down the list, briefly describing each Mary Zook—

one from Lancaster, married with six children; another living near New Holland, running a market stand with her husband; a third who'd moved to Ohio after her husband's death.

"What about this one?" Dok pointed to the fourth name.

"Married, five children, twelve grandchildren. Lives over near Intercourse. Husband's a furniture maker."

Dok shook her head. "Doesn't sound familiar to me."

David continued down the list. Dok leaned forward, resting her chin in her hand as she listened, occasionally asking a question or making a note. He could see the wheels turning in her head.

Finally, he reached the last name. "I think this is the Mary Zook you're looking for. I doubt she'd be in your practice, though. She lives in an unincorporated area near Gap."

Dok took the paper from him, her sharp gaze scanning his neat handwriting. "How'd you find her?"

"Searching through stacks of twenty-five-year-old weekly *Budget* newspapers in the Sisters' House. That was a very time-consuming project."

Dok's eyes went wide. "Oh David, I don't know how to thank you. I'd completely forgotten about looking for Mary Zook and here you were, faithfully working away at it."

"I'm sure, in the future, there will be an opportunity to reciprocate a kindness." Though, to be honest, the scales of kindness fell heavily in his sister's favor. She had given so much to his family since she'd bought the Stoney Ridge Medical Practice. Most recently, his daughter Lydia's life had been turned around with Dok's help in managing her ADHD. He could never repay his sister for all she did for him.

But he did have a question. "What if Mary Zook doesn't want to be found?"

Dok's eyes flicked up to meet his. For a long moment, she said nothing, her fingers drumming against the desk. Then she exhaled and pushed back in her chair. "Then I'll respect her wishes." She met his gaze steadily. "But I have to try. Then we'll see what comes next."

David nodded. He trusted his sister. She might be unconventional in a hundred different ways, but she wasn't careless. If she said she couldn't tell him, he respected that.

He rose to his feet. "If you do need me involved, you know where to find me."

She gave him a dry look. "Yes, Bishop, I believe I do."

He tipped his head to her and turned for the door. But just as he reached it, he glanced back. "For what it's worth," he said, "I hope she's the one you're looking for."

Dok didn't say anything, but the way her fingers tightened on the paper told him that she thought this Mary Zook was the one.

Nine

Darcy waited by her Subaru on the road near the path to Wonder Pond, shifting from heels to toes as she watched for the familiar headlights of Sam's truck. When she saw them come around the bend, she tried to smother the happiness she felt, an ear-to-ear spontaneous smile that took over her face despite her best efforts to seem cool and aloof.

"Bewitched, bothered, and bewildered." That tune wouldn't stop playing in her head, like it was stuck on repeat.

Evie thinks I'm smitten. So ridiculous. I hardly know Sam.

Even as Darcy rolled that around in her mind, she couldn't deny it completely. She hadn't felt this kind of interest in, or even attraction to, a guy in a long, long time.

But what did she really know about Sam Mustang? Not much. Only that he was brilliant. And incredibly patient as he shared his telescope with others. And super clear in explaining what they were peering at. And crazy good-looking. And oddly clumsy. Really out of shape for a guy his age, though you wouldn't think so to meet him. He was slender, almost lanky.

Maybe Sam had a physical problem that caused pain or discomfort—something that might have caused him to trip over a rock the other night no bigger than her fist. Or maybe he had a heart issue—he always got so out of breath on the hike up to the pond. Could he be a smoker? She didn't see or smell any signs of smoking, but people could surprise you.

Maybe he had a bad back. Or a bum knee.

There was something in his eyes—some kind of ache, a shadow that flickered just long enough to make her want to reach for it. Help him. Fix it.

Not good. Not good at all. Red flags were waving in her head. Practically doing cartwheels.

She knew exactly what she'd tell Evie if the roles were reversed: *That's just your nurse brain talking. It's the reason you're a caretaker. Don't listen to it. Don't let it lead your heart straight into a mess you'll have to mop up later.*

She knew better. If a man seemed mysterious, it's because he was hiding something. Bodies in a cellar. Offshore accounts. Possibly part of the witness protection program.

Still . . . Sam Mustang had some kind of pull on her. Not loud, not obvious. But steady. Like gravity.

And Darcy, despite her normally good instincts, felt herself starting to lean.

Headlights swept over the road, and she straightened as his truck rolled to a stop. Sam climbed out and went straight to the passenger side, unbuckling his telescope. As he approached her, he said, "Where's Gus and Annie?"

"Last-minute change of plans. Dok needed babysitting help."

He held her gaze. "So it's just you and me."

"Just you and me." Did that matter? Was he pleased or disappointed? She couldn't tell. "And snickerdoodles."

Then he smiled, and her heart did a complete, ridiculous flip.

They started up the trail, with Darcy purposefully setting a slow pace. "I'm disappointed Gus and Annie aren't here. I wanted to ask them to explain a phrase an Amish patient said to me today."

"What's that?" Sam asked, already starting to breathe heavily.

So soon for him to lose his breath! Why was that? What could be causing it? Then . . . *Darcy!* she told herself. *You are not his nurse.* "He said something about jerk Amish."

Sam cut his eyes at her. "It's slang for the ones who leave the church."

"Oh." She considered that, then nodded. "I still have so much to learn about the Amish before . . ." She trailed off, realizing she didn't really want to say more on the topic.

"Before what?"

She hesitated. "Before Evie is ready to return to work and I head off on my next contract."

He adjusted the strap of the telescope case over his shoulder. "Still thinking about Finland?"

"Actually, I'm not settled on it yet. Thinking about Norway, Finland, or Sweden. But did you know Finland is the happiest country on earth?"

"I've been there. I think maybe they have a low bar." He shrugged. "Not a bad strategy for life. Keep your expectations low and you're never disappointed."

She laughed. "That's awfully cynical, don't you think?"

"Realistic."

"Well, wherever I go next, I want to see the northern lights. They're on the top of my bucket list. The very top."

"They should be." His voice softened. "They should be on everyone's."

"So you've seen them?"

He nodded. "Several times. Best viewing was in Lapland."

"What were they like?"

For a moment, his usual guardedness dropped. "Like watching God paint the sky." Then he cleared his throat, as if embarrassed by the admission.

They reached their usual spot on the top of the ridge,

overlooking the pond, and he set down the telescope. Again, it struck Darcy how he handled it with such care, almost reverent.

"Sam, how long are you staying in Stoney Ridge?"

"As long as it takes."

"Because of this project you're working on?"

Setting the legs into position, he glanced up at her. "Yes."

She unzipped her backpack and pulled out the container of snickerdoodles, holding it out to him. As he took one, she blurted out, "So then, guessing you're not married?"

He stilled, and she immediately regretted the question. It popped out of nowhere. And why did she ask him as she handed him cookies? How pathetic was that? Like she was trying to lure him to the altar with a cookie. And she wasn't! Unfortunately, mortification didn't stop her from talking. Just the opposite. Embarrassment ramped up her chatter. "I just wondered. I would think you've got a wife or girlfriend anxious for you to return home."

He took a bite of the cookie. "You don't know me very well."

What was *that* supposed to mean? *Could* he have a dark side? Was that what he was hinting at?

She just didn't buy it. "I don't mean to pry. I just wondered, that's all. So . . . no one is expecting you home soon, then?"

"No." He polished off the cookie and took another. "They're good. Almost as good as my mother's."

"Send me her recipe and I'll try to duplicate it."

"Can't. She's passed."

Oh. That meant that the snickerdoodles were a memory to him, which meant she'd never be able to replicate them. Nor should she.

Standing now, he peered through the lens and adjusted dials. She assumed the subject of romantic involvements was closed until he said, "I suppose I could ask you the same thing."

Was he asking? She wasn't sure. She looked up at the sky. "Not married. Not involved."

"Why not?"

She jerked her chin down. "Because . . . I just . . . haven't met the right man."

"Not so easy to do when you're constantly moving from place to place."

"Well, I have my reasons." All it took was a side-glance from him. An invitation to talk. "I had an older brother. Jonathan. I adored him. When he was thirteen years old, he was diagnosed with Juvenile Huntington's disease. Incredibly rare. It's an inherited neurological disorder."

"I know of it."

"Really? Most people have never heard of it. Anyway, Jonathan died when he was twenty. The earlier the onset, the faster it progresses." Pausing, she looked up at the sky, trying to keep her emotions in check. As a rule, she didn't talk about Jonathan. Too hard. But here, in the dark, it was easier. "It was like he disappeared before our eyes. It was terrible. Truly awful. My parents split up soon after Jonathan died. Sold our home and found new partners. I went to college . . . and I've never gone back."

Sam didn't say anything. Just watched her. Unfortunately, now she had shifted into overthinking, which also made her overtalk. "Jonathan is the reason I became a nurse. I learned how to care for him." His illness had shaped her, deepening her compassion for anyone facing hardship. "Still, I wish I could have done more. It never seemed fair that I got the good genes and he got the bad. He never saw the ocean. Never climbed a mountain. Never stood in front of the *Mona Lisa* at the Louvre. Before he died, he made me promise to live life to the fullest—for both of us."

Sam nodded, as if he understood Jonathan's limits . . . or the guilt she still carried.

And that slight gesture gave Darcy permission to keep on talking. It was like a switch flipped in her head and she couldn't shut it off. "So that's why I'm a traveling nurse. Jonathan wanted to see the world. I'm trying to see as much of it as I can, for him. For both of us, but mostly for him."

Sam had tipped his head to look up at the sky and she wasn't sure if he was still listening. Not until he said, "So adventure is your strategy to cure a broken heart."

Ouch! That smarted. Was he trivializing the loss of Jonathan? It felt like it. She'd shared a very private part of her life and he responded by belittling her. "I shouldn't have said anything. Let's just get back to stargazing." She turned away, stung.

"Hey." He put a hand on her shoulder. "I'm not trying to be dismissive. Adventure is not a bad strategy. To be honest, I wonder if it's working. If you'd recommend it."

She turned to face him. "What makes you ask?"

"I just . . . have never had much success trying to outrun grief."

Hold on. Was Sam Mustang expressing insight? Wisdom? Possibly some private information about himself? Inviting more discussion? Before Darcy could pry open that door, he bent over and was rubbing his calf muscle.

"You okay?"

He didn't answer for a while. "Just a cramp."

"I get those when I don't drink enough water. They hurt."

"Yeah." He winced. "They do."

It seemed to pass, because he stopped rubbing his leg and lifted his heel, then the toe of his boot, stretching out his leg. Satisfied, he returned to the scope, bending over it, adjusting the knobs, his hands slow, deliberate. Then, suddenly, he stilled. "There it is. The Orion Nebula. It's a stellar nursery. A place where new stars are being born. A cosmic cradle." He straightened. "Did you know that there are hundreds of millions of stars born every day? Every single day." He stepped back. "Here. Take a look for yourself."

Darcy leaned in, pressing her eye to the lens.

"See those wispy clouds of gas? They're glowing because of those four bright stars in the center. They're called the Trapezium."

She saw them! A gasp escaped her lips. "Sam, it's absolutely stunning. Breathtaking."

"*That* it is."

She blinked, lifting her head, and found herself inches from him. He didn't move. Neither did she. The night air seemed to hold its breath around them. Then he reached a hand to push a strand of her hair off her cheek, and before she could think—before she could overthink—his lips grazed hers in the softest, lightest touch.

Warmth flooded through her as she slowly wrapped her arms around his neck. His hands slid around her waist, pulling her close. And then, just as suddenly, like he'd been stung by a wasp, he pulled away. "Sorry." He turned from her, hands on his hips. "That should never have happened."

She watched, stunned, as he started packing up the scope.

"Why shouldn't it have happened?" she asked, her voice quiet. "Because of me or because of you?" When he didn't answer, she tried again. "You said you weren't involved with someone. Are you?"

"No." His voice was rough. "Let's forget it."

She put the lid on the cookie container and slipped it into her backpack, zipped it up, and slid it on her back. "It's not like I'm the clinging type. I have plans, you know." Lots of them. Nothing nailed down yet, but she was thinking about what came next. She folded her arms. "Just tell me why."

Now he seemed annoyed. "Look, when you said you wanted to stargaze, the deal was no talking."

"So . . . I talk too much?" She let out a short laugh. "That's a pretty lame excuse, Sam Mustang."

He exhaled, long and slow, gripping the edge of the telescope case. She caught something in his expression—something unspeakably sad. He shook his head. "You just . . . don't want to get tangled up with me, that's all." He started down the hill.

Watching him go, one thought ran through her mind: *The problem, Sam Mustang, is I think I already am.*

Annie Fisher watched from the rocker as Gus patiently worked with little Gabe, holding him under his arms, helping him to take a step. Gabe would straighten his legs for a moment, hovering between standing and squatting, before plopping back down onto his bottom.

"You can do it, little guy," Gus said, adjusting his hold. "You're stronger than you think."

Gabe blinked, his chubby fingers curling into the fabric of Gus's shirt. It seemed as if he didn't quite trust his legs to hold him up to walk. He preferred the security of the floor. Over and over, Gus encouraged him to try again, his voice low and steady, murmuring soft encouragements.

The patience in his hands, the gentleness in his voice—he would make a wonderful father someday. The thought sent warmth rushing through Annie, right up to her cheeks.

The grandfather clock in the hallway chimed, shaking her from her thoughts. "Time for bed," she said, standing. "Dok said to give him a bath and read a story."

Gus hoisted Gabe onto his hip, and Annie reached for him, expecting him to hand the baby over to her.

"Let's go," he said.

She glanced at him, surprised. "You're coming too?"

"Why not?" he said simply.

She hesitated before following him up the stairs, her mind spinning. She didn't remember her father ever being involved in childcare. Not once. Daed was a dairy farmer—he rose before dawn, went to bed early, and was always, always exhausted.

He loved his children, she had no doubt, but this—Gus—was different. He seemed to enjoy just being with Gabe.

In the nursery, she filled the small tub with warm water while Gus knelt beside her, holding Gabe steady. Annie added some bubble bath and swirled the water. When she poured a little water over his hands, he tried to slap at the bubbles.

"I think he likes the bath," she said, smiling.

Gus was watching Gabe, his expression thoughtful. "Do you ever wonder . . ."

She turned to him. "Wonder what?"

"I just wonder what's going on in Gabe's mind," he said, his voice quiet. "Why he doesn't always look at us when we talk to him. Why he's reluctant to walk." He hesitated, then added, "I'm going to do a little research. See if there's anything more I can do to help."

Annie's eyes stung with unexpected emotion. She felt so much love for Gus in that moment that it nearly overwhelmed her. She looked away quickly, but not quickly enough. Gus reached out and brushed a tear from her cheek.

"What is it?" he said.

She put her hand over his. "You're so good with him." That wasn't all she wanted to say. She wanted to tell him how much she admired him. How she had never imagined a man being so naturally gentle and patient. How she couldn't stop thinking that he would be a wonderful father one day.

Gus gave a small, almost bashful shrug. "I look forward to having children someday. Gabe is giving me practice." He grinned. "Giving *us* practice."

Annie's breath caught. He said it so casually, as if it was a given. As if he saw a future with her—a family with her. *Someday.*

Her heart raced. *When will that* someday *happen, Gus Troyer?*

Before another thought filled her mind, Gabe splashed his hands, sending a spray of bubbles flying into their faces.

They both jolted back in surprise. Gabe's eyes widened, then he let out a giggle. And then—seeing their reaction—he splashed his hands again.

Gus wiped a hand over his face, shaking his head with a laugh. "Annie," he said, his voice full of wonder. "Do you realize what just happened?"

Yes, she thought. *You mentioned us getting married. Having children of our own. You said "someday."*

But Gus's eyes were locked on Gabe, full of realization. "This is a breakthrough moment," he said. "He saw us react and did it again. He has a real connection to us."

Annie looked at Gabe, who had gone back to patting the bubbles. She wasn't as convinced as Gus that this was a breakthrough moment. Nothing seemed all that different, other than the fact that she now had bubbles on her prayer cap. But Gus clearly saw something she didn't, and she wasn't about to dampen his excitement.

Her mind, however, was elsewhere. On what Gus had just hinted at.

When would *their* someday get here?

Dok had been tossing since just after four, thanks to the wind slapping the leafless branches of the maple tree against the bedroom window. By five, she had given up. No point lying there staring at the ceiling. She slid out of bed quietly, careful not to wake Matt, and padded into the kitchen. The floor was cold, the kind that made you think about booking a trip to Hawaii, and the air had that dry, bitter edge February always brought. She flicked on the light, started the coffee, and leaned against the counter, already thinking about Gabe. Last night Gus had been so sure, so utterly convinced that Gabe had experienced some kind of breakthrough. A connection with him and Annie. A cause-and-reaction moment, so much a part of a child's experience as he learned about his world.

She wanted to believe it. She *really* did. It's why she couldn't sleep.

But by seven o'clock, over breakfast, she'd seen nothing new in Gabe. Same lack of eye contact and social engagement. Most toddlers resisted being held after a while, wiggled when they were getting their diaper changed, squirmed in protest when they were dressed. Gabe didn't. He had low muscle tone, which could explain his reluctance to take steps. Like he didn't think his legs could bear his weight. And he slept so soundly, both naps and bedtime, like he was always tired, just exhausted. What toddler ever welcomed bedtime?

She thought back to those first few months when Gabe was with them as a newborn, so quiet and content. She remembered thinking that it seemed as if he knew he was a houseguest who had overstayed his welcome. At the time, she and Matt thought they were lucky. He was just an easy baby. A dream to take care of.

Now she wondered. Had she misread his calm nature when he was an infant? Had she missed something crucial?

And if so—what?

She sighed and rubbed her forehead. Matt was like Gus, always hopeful, always seeing the bright side. And for the most part, she loved that quality in her husband. But when it came to Gabe, she didn't have the luxury of optimism. She had to deal with what was in front of her.

By eight thirty, she had kissed Matt and Gabe goodbye for the day and headed to the office. She nodded hello to Charlie, filled a mug with coffee, and went to her desk to review the patient list for the day. But her mind was still at home. *What* was she missing with Gabe?

A knock on the door interrupted her thoughts. She looked up to see Darcy standing there, looking oddly uncomfortable.

"Sam Mustang is here," Darcy said. "He doesn't have an appointment. He says he just needs a minute of your time."

"Sam Mustang? No kidding? I've been trying to figure out how to get in touch with him."

"You should've just asked me."

Dok lifted her eyebrows. "You know Sam?" That might explain why Darcy had such an odd look on her face. "Are you dating him?" She lifted her hand. "Never mind. Not my business. I shouldn't have asked."

"Not dating. Not at all." Darcy shook her head firmly. "Annie Fisher and Gus Troyer and I have been going stargazing with him up at Wonder Pond. He has this high-level telescope—you can practically see someone waving from the space station." She hesitated, as if she hoped Dok might jump in and volunteer as to why she wanted to get in touch with Sam. Then, when the silence spun out a little too long, she said, "So I'll just show him to an exam room?"

"No," Dok said. "Just to my office."

Darcy paused, frowning. Then spun on her heels and left.

A moment later, Sam came in and sat down. "Have you found her?"

No pleasantries. Well, Dok didn't mind. "I think so. Possibly. But first, I'd like you to talk to my brother, David Stoltzfus."

"The bishop," he said in a flat tone.

"That's right." She tipped her head. "Sounds like you've had some experience with Amish bishops."

"I have. Not good ones."

"Well, David isn't your stereotypical bishop."

Sam had a skeptical look on his face. "How so?"

"He listens. He cares. He's a wonderful problem solver. And I'm not just saying that because he's my brother. He's a remarkable man. Quite learned." She thought of what Darcy had just revealed. "David likes to study the stars too."

One of Sam's eyebrows lifted, which Dok took as a sign of interest.

"Look, if you're going to disrupt a woman's life after all these years, not to mention her child's life, don't you think it would be wise to talk to someone, first? Even if your intentions are honorable—"

"They are."

"Even still, you are about to drop a bombshell into this woman's life. You can't just show up and say you're sorry and think it's going to be easy for her."

Sam watched her for a while, as if it hadn't occurred to him that he would be upsetting an apple cart.

Dok tried to hide what was running through her mind: Why were most men so especially obtuse?

"I'll think about it."

That's really all Dok could ask for. She handed him a piece of paper with Mary Zook's phone number on it.

"Thank you, Dr. Stoltzfus." He got up to leave.

She studied him for a moment, noticing something about the way he moved—jerky, stiff.

"Sam, sit down."

He hesitated but stopped.

"Tell me more about your ALS diagnosis."

He let out a breath, clearly annoyed. "Dok, I appreciate it, but I've seen plenty of doctors in Houston. I'm not here as your patient."

"Sit," she repeated.

He did.

She folded her hands on her desk. "Start from the beginning. Symptoms. Timeline. Diagnosis."

Sam exhaled, then relented. "It started last summer. Weakness in my legs. Tripping over things. Fatigue that wouldn't go away. I saw a bunch of doctors, including a neurologist, and went through a battery of tests. Nerve conduction studies, EMGs, blood work. They all said it pointed to ALS."

"And what about treatment?"

He shrugged. "I'm on meds. Riluzole, a couple of others."

"Are the medications helping at all?"

"Not really," he said.

Tapping a pen against her desk, Dok watched him, a hundred questions running through her mind.

As he held the paper in his hand, it was shaking. Tremors. She'd also noticed that he had a habit of rubbing his knuckles, the way older people with arthritic aching hands did.

Something about this wasn't adding up to her. "I'd like to run a panel."

Sam shook his head. "Dr. Stoltzfus, please don't take this personally, but I work at NASA. I have excellent medical care in Houston. There's nothing more you can do for me. But thank you for asking. And thank you"—he rose, lifting the paper with Mary Zook's phone number—"for this."

She watched him go.

Nothing more I can do?

She wasn't so sure about that.

Darcy had already led Sam Mustang into Dok's office, though she had no idea why he was there. He hadn't been on the schedule and he clearly wasn't here as a patient. He didn't offer an explanation and she didn't ask. Last night, at Wonder Pond, his lips had met hers, just for a moment, and then he pulled away like he'd been singed by fire. "That should never have happened," he had said, voice rough with something she didn't quite understand.

Ten minutes later, as Darcy stepped out of an exam room, she nearly collided with Sam. She sucked in a sharp breath, barely stopping herself from stumbling back. Sam tucked a folded paper into his back pocket—a little too quickly, like he didn't want her to notice.

She folded her arms. "You heading up to Wonder Pond tonight?"

His gaze flicked past her, like he was considering the best escape route. "I haven't decided yet. Might rain."

She gestured toward the window at the clear blue sky and huffed. "There's no rain in the forecast. It's a perfect night for viewing the Andromeda Galaxy, Sam." But only with his high-tech telescope.

His jaw tightened, but he didn't move.

"Look," she said, voice steady. "I love learning about the stars. You know everything about them. That's all this is."

His mouth pressed into a thin line. "That's all it was supposed to be. I'm not sure that's all that it is."

She scoffed. "Wow. You're pretty full of yourself, aren't you?"

He exhaled sharply, shaking his head. "Darcy—"

"I'll be there tonight," she said, not letting him off the hook. "Same time as usual."

He studied her for a long moment, then muttered, "Fine. But don't even think about kissing me."

"Me?" She blinked. "*Me*?! Kissing *you*?"

But he was already walking away, heading for the door.

Ten

David Stoltzfus walked along what had once been the quiet boundary between the King and Lapp farms—a shallow, familiar creek bed that had marked the line between properties since before Johnny King or Bill Lapp was born. But Muddy Creek had its own ideas of where it wanted to wind and, to David's disappointment, no new storm had reversed its course.

So now he stood in mud and late winter's chill, listening to two men argue over whose land was whose.

"That creek's been the boundary since 1952," Johnny said. "My father said so. My grandfather said so. Just because a storm threw a tantrum doesn't mean we toss out seventy years of common sense."

Bill Lapp gave up an indifferent shrug. "But the deed don't say 'where the creek used to be.' It says 'bounded on the east by Muddy Creek.' And Muddy Creek is over there now." He nodded toward the new waterway, lazily threading its way through what had been considered Johnny's field.

David folded his hands. "I can see how this is difficult. Johnny, you've worked that field your whole life. And Bill, you're looking at the creek as it now stands."

"I'm looking at a field my grandfather cleared with a mule and a plow," Johnny said, scowling, hands on his hips. "Why are you plowing so early in the year, anyway?"

"I always plow eight weeks before Easter," Bill said. "Always."

What?! David sucked in a breath. Easter was only eight weeks away? How had he missed that?

His mind jumped ahead, tallying the preparations that needed doing to prepare the church for the holy season. Attnungsgemee, a significant time to bring peace and unity to the church and, two weeks later, spring communion, a day that bound members together with sacred ties. A dull pinch tugged at David's gut, the familiar warning of an ulcer that never quite healed, only waited for stress to feed it.

Easter wasn't on Johnny's mind. "I don't know why you thought it would be a good idea to start plowing this field. You knew we had to work this out."

Again, Bill only shrugged. "I needed to start somewhere."

A sharp voice called out across the slushy yard. "Well, you can start somewhere else, if it's all the same to you."

David turned to see Cathy King striding across the field, her apron flapping in the breeze.

"Your plow team passed within three feet of my clothesline, Bill Lapp," she said. "Three feet. And that fresh manure you worked in has made my fresh laundry smell like it belongs in a barn."

Bill raised both hands. "I didn't move the creek, Cathy. It moved itself."

Just then, Myna Lapp joined them, her cheeks pink from the cold. "The field belongs to us now. He's got the right to work it." She glanced at Cathy, then the laundry flapping stiffly near where the creek used to run. "I always did think you should move that clothesline closer to the house."

Cathy lifted a brow. "It's put there to get a full day's sun."

Myna pursed her lips but said nothing.

David's voice rose a notch. "Friends. The creek moved. No one's to blame for that. But until we sort this out—no more plowing. I'll come by in a few days and we can talk it over."

There was a long pause. Cathy and Myna gave each other one last look that could curdle cream, and the men nodded stiffly.

"In the meantime," David said, "try to see the situation from each other's point of view."

Cathy stared at David like she was thinking he was useless as a bishop. Right now, he felt a little useless. This job belonged to a deacon, but his deacon, Luke Schrock, wasn't here.

As David turned to walk back toward his buggy, he heard Johnny and Bill start their bickering again. The storm may have moved the creek—but it had also swept away neighborly peace.

The call center was quiet today, the kind of lull that made the minutes stretch. Annie sat at her desk, absently tapping a pen against her notepad. The biggest emergency so far had been a lost dog that turned out to be napping under its owner's porch. She didn't really mind the downtime, though—it gave her a chance to think.

This morning, Gus had picked her up in his buggy to head to work together. He'd been unusually quiet for most of the ride, the kind of quiet that meant he had something on his mind. Finally, as they pulled into the fire station's parking lot, he'd turned to her and said, "Annie, lately I've been giving something a lot of consideration."

Her heart started to pound. This was it! The moment he was going to ask her to marry him. It wasn't how she'd imagined it—a Sunday afternoon walk, or maybe a sunset at Blue Lake Pond. But she was ready. More than ready. "What is it?" she said, trying to sound cucumber calm.

"B-12."

She'd blinked at him. "B-12?"

"The vitamin. For Gabe."

Oh.

She looked away, trying to rein in her disappointment. With Dok's and Matt's unpredictable schedules, Annie had been filling a lot of childcare gaps. Gus helped, too, whenever the night sky was cloudy. They were both glad to provide a steady presence for the boppli and had grown increasingly attached to him. Maybe Gus more than Annie.

She reminded herself that it was kind of him to care so deeply, to think through every possible way to help. That was Gus—steady, thoughtful, loyal. But still, she couldn't shake the feeling that somewhere along the way, she'd been quietly moved to the side. Like a chair no longer needed at the table.

"Some of his symptoms—low muscle tone, the way he tires so quickly—might be from a deficiency. I read that B-12 can help." Gus helped her step down from the buggy, still talking about Gabe. "I know Dok's on top of things, but . . ."

Annie sighed. "I'll mention it to her," though, knowing Dok, she'd probably already considered it. Probably already tested for it. Still, it was touching, the way Gus cared about Gabe.

She hadn't needed to mask her disappointment when Gus brought up getting vitamins instead of getting married—he hadn't even noticed. Not the way her voice had quivered. Not the way her hands had gone still in her lap. He'd just kept talking about Gabe and B-12 like that was the only thing on his heart.

And maybe it was.

She stared at the console and tried to shake the feeling that she'd been left behind in a conversation she thought they were both having. She wasn't upset, not exactly. Just . . . unsettled.

The closer she felt to making a commitment, the further Gus seemed to be. It had something to do with Sam Mustang.

If Gus wasn't puzzling over possible diagnoses about Gabe, he was meeting up with Sam Mustang to stargaze. Sam said this. Sam thinks that. Lately it felt like Sam was the one on Gus's mind—and Annie wasn't sure where that left her.

She'd always enjoyed stargazing with Gus, but Sam and his fancy telescope took it to a whole different level. When Sam started talking about interstellar something-or-other, and Gus or Darcy jumped in with a question about gravitational waves, Annie was completely lost.

Before Sam and his telescope came to Stoney Ridge, there had been a different rhythm. One where it was just Annie and Gus, walking together after supper, standing beneath the stars and talking about things that mattered to them. The sky hadn't changed. The stars were still out there, same as ever. But she had gone from being Gus's stargazing partner to a silent bystander.

What had happened to the way he used to hint at their getting married? Almost every other day, he'd say something like, "We should go looking for places to live that are closer to Lancaster, for when you'll be working as a dispatcher." Or "I want at least five acres to raise a family. Don't you think so?"

She squeezed her eyes shut. *Don't be so selfish, Annie Fisher!*

The switchboard lit up, jolting her from her thoughts. She straightened, flipping on her headset.

"What's your emergency?"

A deep, booming voice filled her ear.

"I found a bottle of KETCHUP in the fridge."

Hank Lapp. He called at least twice a week.

"Says it EXPIRED four years ago. Eddy says it's just FINE. She isn't one to WASTE food, but I also don't wanna get myself POISONED. You think it'd KILL ME if I ate some?"

"This isn't the poison control line."

"So it *is* poison?"

She sighed, rattling off the number for poison control, purposefully not identifying herself.

Hank paused. Then, in his booming voice: "Why . . . Annie FISHER? Is that YOU? Eddy, ANNIE IS ON THE PHONE."

Annie pinched the bridge of her nose. "Hank, do you feel sick?"

"No, because I ain't EATEN the ketchup yet. That's why I'm askin'."

"Then call poison control, not emergency services."

Another pause. Then, a bit huffy, "FINE. But don't BLAME yourself if I DIE."

"Pretty sure you'll survive, Hank. And don't call this number unless it's a true life-and-death emergency."

"DEATH is what I'm TRYING to PREVENT." The line clicked off.

Annie exhaled, shaking her head as she scribbled *Hank Lapp—ketchup emergency* in her log. Gus would get a kick out of this one.

As Annie finished her morning shift, she stood and stretched, rolling out the tension in her shoulders. She grabbed her coat and stepped outside, hoping she might see Gus over by the fire trucks, but instead, she spotted Dok leaning against the hood of her SUV, a brown paper bag in her hands.

"I brought lunch," Dok said, holding up the bag. "I thought we could eat together."

Annie stopped short.

Was Dok feeling okay? She was well aware of how much strain Dok was under. The stress of making sure Gabe got the care he needed, the worry of trying to figure out what was causing his delays, her long workdays.

"Don't look so shocked," Dok said. "We've had lunch before."

No. They hadn't. Annie had worked for Dok for over a year, and never—not once—had Dok suggested sitting down for lunch together. Dok was always eating on the go, powering through her day with a granola bar in one hand and a medical bag in the other.

Dok gestured toward the picnic bench near the station, bathed in a patch of pale winter sun. "Come with me. Let's sit and talk. Before the sun disappears."

Annie followed, still trying to figure out what this was about. They sat down, the wooden bench cold against her legs, but the lack of wind made it bearable.

Dok handed her a sandwich wrapped in butcher paper. "Annie, I wanted to get your opinion on something."

"Oh, I'm so glad you asked! Yes! Definitely yes!"

"Yes . . . to what?"

"Give Charlie more of your patient load."

Dok's eyebrows lifted. "Charlie? Why bring him up?"

"Because . . . you look so tired. I thought you might be thinking of taking some time off. Charlie could do so much more for you."

"Charlie's gaining experience, I'll grant you that. He's making progress." She took a bite off the corner of the sandwich. "But that's not what's on my mind."

Annie raised a brow as she unwrapped her sandwich. Had Gus called Dok this morning? "So is this about B-12?"

Dok frowned. "What?"

"B-12," Annie repeated, pausing mid-bite. "For Gabe. Gus read that some of his symptoms could be caused by a deficiency, and he thought maybe we should—"

Dok held up a hand. "Already tested for that. Not an issue."

Annie knew it. Dok was more on top of things than anyone realized.

Dok leaned forward slightly. "I want to ask you a few questions about Sam Mustang."

That caught Annie completely off guard. She sat back, wiping her hands on her apron. "What about him?"

Dok hesitated, then said carefully, "Darcy mentioned that you and Gus have gone stargazing with him."

"Yes. Quite often these last few weeks."

"Have you noticed anything that concerns you about Sam? Anything physical. Anything that seems unusual for a man his age."

Annie considered that. "Well, now that you mention it," she said, thinking back, "his hands shake quite a bit."

"Consistently?"

"Er ziddert wie an Laabblaat."

"He trembles like a leaf?"

Annie nodded. "Yes. Last time, he needed Gus's help to focus the dial on the telescope. He said it was because of the cold . . ." She trailed off, meeting Dok's gaze. "I don't know if that's what you mean."

Dok gave a small nod, her expression unreadable. "Yes. That's what I meant."

A strange feeling settled in Annie's stomach. She didn't know much about Sam, but this—whatever it was—felt serious.

Dok sighed and glanced toward the parking lot. "Please keep this conversation between us."

"Of course," Annie said. That went without saying. "But have you asked Darcy? She's spent more time with Sam than I have."

Dok tipped her head. "Because . . . they're involved? Romantically?"

Annie had her opinion, but she knew better than to voice it. She wasn't her mother, after all, who kept nothing to herself. "They both love the night sky."

Dok's lips pressed into a thin line, her expression shifting slightly into worry. She packed up the rest of her sandwich, barely touched.

Annie couldn't say for certain, but she felt as if she had just handed Dok another heavy stone to carry.

Darcy pulled her coat tighter around her as she sat on the cool boulder, waiting. Sam was late. She checked her phone—

not that it would do any good. No texts, of course. She huffed out a breath, sending a little cloud of vapor into the night air.

Maybe she'd scared him off.

But then again, Sam Mustang didn't really seem like the type who could be easily scared off. He was the most perplexing man she'd ever met—quiet, brooding, yet surprisingly tender.

And that kiss. Ohhh, that kiss.

It had been . . . unexpected. Soft, but firm. A kiss with weight, with meaning. A kiss that changed things.

Then he had to go and ruin it.

Shouldn't have happened, he'd said, like he'd just backed his truck into a pole instead of kissed her breathless by Wonder Pond. Told her to not even think about kissing him again, like she'd been the one who'd leaned toward him. She hadn't! Or had she?

Here she was, waiting for him. With a container of her incredible chocolate chip cookies in her backpack.

Why? Well, because she liked him. Quite a lot. Because there was something about Sam—something she couldn't quite pin down. And if he didn't feel the same way? Fine. She was leaving soon for another adventure, anyway. This was just a moment in time. A really lovely, frustrating moment in time.

Headlights crested the ridge, and she sat up straighter, smoothing her hair down on instinct.

Don't talk, she told herself. *Don't talk too much tonight.*

His truck rumbled to a stop, and he climbed out, giving her a quick nod in greeting. Not much, but enough. The streak of red crawling up his neck and into his cheeks? Very interesting. If Sam was anything, it was careful—about his words, his movements, and especially his emotions. He hid everything. But that blush? That was evidence.

You like me, don't you, Sam Mustang?

She barely bit back a grin as he moved to the passenger side of the truck and reached for his prized possession—the telescope—but as he hoisted it, he took a step back and stumbled, nearly dropping the case. "Slipped," he said, quickly adjusting his grip.

She arched a brow but didn't say anything. He was always slipping. The clumsiest man she'd ever met. She had theories about that—mostly that his big brain was too busy contemplating the cosmos to pay much attention to his own two feet.

They started up the hill, the soft crunch of grass beneath their boots the only sound for a while. "So," she said, forgetting her promise to stay quiet, "what's a day like for an astrophysicist?"

He glanced at her, clearly thrown. "You want to know about my work?"

"Well, yeah. Don't you get asked that a lot?"

A long pause. Then, finally, "No."

That came as a surprise. No one? How could anyone not be fascinated by the work of an astrophysicist? What did people talk to him about, then? Weather? Crops? The price of gas? "Well, I'd really like to know what you do. You're here for a project, right?"

"I'm here *on* a project, yes." He adjusted the telescope strap on his shoulder, his voice quiet but steady. "Most people think the night sky is still, but it isn't. Everything's moving—planets, stars, galaxies. Even the light we see is traveling, sometimes for millions of years, before it reaches us. My work is about studying those movements, mapping out what we can barely see through the best telescopes afforded by modern technology. But the more we discover, the more we realize how much we don't know. Space isn't just vast—it's infinite. It's continually expanding. The deeper we look, the more it reveals something far greater than man can comprehend."

Darcy stopped walking. Just—stopped.

He turned, confused. "What? Did that not make sense?"

She stared at him, at this exasperating, fascinating man who spoke about stars like they weren't just burning balls of gas but something more. Something profound.

Her heart was in trouble.

"You made sense," she said, voice quieter than usual. "Sam, that's beautiful."

He shrugged, but his ears had gone pink now too. "You asked what I do."

She exhaled, trying to slow the rush of emotions inside her. She was *not* falling for Sam Mustang.

Absolutely not.

Except, she kind of was.

Eleven

Dok Stoltzfus eased her SUV down the narrow two-lane road, the late afternoon light slanting across the fields in long, pale streaks. In early March the countryside held shades of gray and brown, the snow mostly melted except for stubborn patches clinging to the edges of fence posts and shaded ditches. The sky was the color of tin, and the air held that damp chill that made her wish she'd worn her heavier coat.

She kept one eye on the road and the other on the thermometer on the dash—34 degrees. Black ice territory. Normally, she considered speed limits to be suggestions, but today she let the car hum along at a cautious pace.

Her thoughts kept circling back to Charlie King. He was trying—really trying—and she could see the potential in him. But he needed so much experience. She'd given him a verbal instruction for an antibiotic for the Troyer boy's tonsilitis, and he had written down ampicillin instead of amoxicillin. An easy mistake to make when a doctor was inexperienced with children, and she'd caught it, but only because she double-checked everything he did. Charlie, like always, had been grateful, not at all defensive. That counted for something. Quite a lot, in fact.

Still, she'd been hoping to pass more responsibility to him

and yet she couldn't quite do it wholeheartedly. With Gabe in their home, Matt had been insistent that she let Charlie take over night duty. "He won't learn if you don't let him try," he'd said, while rinsing out Gabe's sippy cup and giving her that look that meant he was right.

The idea of handing over night calls to Charlie made her stomach knot. If Matt hadn't been so adamant, she couldn't have agreed to it. And there was a small part of her that wanted to let go. She was tired! Night calls were a wipeout.

Still, this was *Charlie* covering for her. Not a comfortable thought.

Happily, the Lord must've agreed with her, because so far, there'd been no calls. No emergencies. Just quiet nights. A miracle.

She rounded the bend near an old stone barn, the road dipping slightly where the creek ran under it. A thin sheen of ice glinted on the shoulder, and she tapped the brakes gently, steering wide. A few cows stood in a distant field, unmoving, like they'd given up on the idea of spring.

Dok sighed and rubbed her thumbs along the steering wheel. She wasn't going to give up on Charlie. He had the makings of a good doctor—a kind heart and the humility to learn. But she couldn't afford mistakes in her practice. Not with the trust the Amish placed in her.

She flicked on the wipers as raindrops began to pepper the windshield. The SUV climbed the last hill before home, the trees thinning to reveal the outline of their house, porch light already glowing. She felt the tension in her shoulders begin to ease. She smiled faintly. Maybe letting go a little wasn't the same as letting go completely.

The car rolled into the driveway and Dok whispered a quiet thanks—for catching Charlie's prescription error, and then a request—*Please, Lord, another night without any calls.*

Dok set her medical bag on the kitchen table and glanced

around. "Matt?" Usually, he was here, stirring something on the stove, a dish towel slung over his shoulder, waiting to ask how her day had gone.

"In here."

She followed his voice into the living room, where she found him sitting on the floor with Gabe, side by side, back against the sofa. Blocks were stacked in front of them, a little unsteady but standing. Matt reached out and knocked them down with a grin, then looked expectantly at Gabe.

A typical toddler would've squealed and knocked them down first, without waiting for permission. But Gabe only stared at the blocks, lifting a hand halfway before dropping it again, as if even that small effort was too much.

Dok's heart clenched.

Matt looked up, rubbing his hands on his jeans. "Gus said he knocked them down this afternoon." His voice was even, but there was something behind it, something tight. "It's like he does things for Gus that he won't do for me."

She almost thought he sounded a tiny bit . . . jealous. "It might be a time-of-day thing." She dropped onto the sofa with a sigh. "More energy at different times."

Matt let out a soft snort, shaking his head. He ran his fingers through Gabe's fine, dark hair—the only feature of his that hinted at his mother, Matt's missing cousin. So Matt said, anyway. Dok had no idea what she looked like, other than a few childhood pictures.

Dok reached over to move a block closer to Gabe, holding it out to him. He lifted a hand to take it, but she had to place it right in his range for him to grasp it. Had Gabe's motor skills declined since he had come to them? She thought maybe they had. "I want to run a few more tests."

At that, Matt stiffened. His jaw set, and before she could say another word, he scooped up Gabe in one swift motion and stood. "No more tests."

Dok blinked. "Matt—"

"All you do is look for data." His voice was sharper than she'd ever heard it. "It's like he's a puzzle to you, not a little boy."

She stared at him, stunned. "That's not fair. I'm not looking for data—I'm looking for answers. How can we help him if we don't know why he is the way he is?"

Matt's grip on Gabe tightened, and the little boy rested his head against his chest, his small hands curled into fists. "Why can't you just accept him as he is?" His voice was quiet but laced with frustration. "Why can't you just love him?"

Dok recoiled. "I do love him!"

Matt shook his head. "Ruth, you never hold him. You don't play with him. You're constantly analyzing him." He exhaled, and when he spoke again, his voice was tired. "Enough. He is who he is. The child God made and the child God put into our lives—again."

He turned and walked toward the door. "I'm taking Gabe out for a walk. Get some fresh air."

"A walk? Now? It's starting to rain. And it's cold!"

"We'll bundle up."

The door shut behind them with a soft thud, leaving Dok alone on the sofa, feeling like the wind had just been knocked out of her. She clenched her hands into fists, staring at the empty space where Matt and Gabe had just been sitting. Did Matt really believe that she didn't love Gabe? That she didn't accept him?

She felt like she was trying so hard—trying to find out what was wrong, trying to figure out why he was always tired, weak, why he often seemed distant, why his little hands trembled when he reached for things. She was trying to fix him.

But Matt didn't think there *was* a fix. He just wanted to . . . let him be. She closed her eyes and leaned back against the cushions. Maybe that was the difference between them.

He thought her need to find answers meant she wasn't satisfied with Gabe as he was.

But she thought her need to find answers was proof of how much she cared.

Annie Fisher kneaded the dough with slow, steady motions, her palms pressing into the soft lump before folding it over again. Normally, she loved kneading dough, preparing it to rise overnight and baking it in the morning. This evening, it only reminded her how tightly her thoughts were wound.

"I think I should call Gus," her mother said from across the room.

Annie paused, her hands resting lightly on the dough. "Mamm, Gus is an EMT, not a doctor."

Her mother examined the pale pink patch on her forearm as though it might be the start of a terminal disease. "But he'll know if it's something serious."

Annie offered a quiet, practiced smile. "It's probably just a mild rash."

Sally didn't disagree, but her frown lingered. "Still, it's spreading. What if it's poison sumac? I read that can travel through the bloodstream."

Annie didn't correct her by reminding her that sumac bloomed only in the summer. There was no point. Her mother's worries came like the tides—predictable, impossible to stop. "You could make a paste of baking soda and water. That should stop the itching."

Sally sighed. "I called Dok's office, but she's gone home. I could see that young boy—"

"That young *man*. His name is Dr. King." Her mother didn't think Charlie looked old enough to be a doctor.

"—but I just don't think he'd know what to do. Each time I go in, he needs to look up my symptom in a big medical textbook. Dok never needs to consult a book. Nor does Gus. That's why I thought Gus might be able to help. He never seems to mind when I ask for his advice." She sighed a long-suffering sigh.

Annie folded the dough and pressed again. Gus had a better way of managing her mother than she did. He said that when she was spiraling, like now, there was no point in using logic. Instead, to let her latest worry run its course.

"Since we're talking about Gus," her mother said, lowering herself into a chair, "isn't it time you two start making plans? It's getting to be that time of year. If you're planning a wedding next fall, I need to know. The celery will need to be planted in time to use it for a proper wedding meal."

Annie didn't answer. She kept kneading, pushing and pulling, pressing out air, trying not to let the question settle in her chest like a stone.

Mamm carried on, oblivious to Annie's discomfort. "And your daed won't paint the house unless he has a reason."

Annie rolled out the dough, pressing a little harder than she normally did. "Gus and I haven't talked about anything like that."

"It's high time. Everyone says so."

The words made Annie's stomach tighten. *Everyone says so*—a phrase her mother loved to use when she wanted something to sound like common sense instead of her opinion. Annie didn't ask who everyone was. And honestly, it wasn't the comment itself that stung—it was the feeling behind it. Like she was failing at something.

"I know you don't like to speak up, Annie, but maybe you ought to ask Gus what he's thinking about the future. You don't want to be wasting time if he's not interested in getting married. Maybe you should find out. Better to know now than later."

Annie brushed flour from her fingers and reached for the pan. She didn't trust herself to speak. Because the truth was, she *had* been wondering if something had changed with Gus. Had he lost interest in her?

His attention had definitely turned elsewhere from Annie. Last night, when Gus brought up meeting Sam at Wonder Pond, Annie declined, saying she had a lot to catch up on and needed a night at home. He didn't try to dissuade her, not at all.

He could've tried a *little*.

When Annie and Gus had first started spending time together, he'd helped her study for her EMT classes, walked her home even when he was dog-tired, and searched high and low for a remedy to ease her motion sickness so that they could be EMTs together. He'd been heavily focused on her. Now, that focus was on the stars. More particularly, on Sam Mustang. She thought she caught the tiniest bit of longing in his voice as he spoke of Sam's higher education, of his work at NASA.

She could feel her mother watching her. "Everything's fine, Mamm. Just busy lately."

Sally tilted her head. "Busy is one thing. But if you wait too long, the season slips past. Sometimes, you have to plant the celery when the soil's ready."

"Right now, the ground is frozen solid," Annie said, lifting the pans gently and setting them to rise. "Sie druwwelt sich alles." *You worry about everything.*

"You sound just like your father." Sally examined her arm again. "I'm going to bed. I just hope I'll be able to sleep with this terrible rash."

When her mother left the kitchen, Annie leaned both elbows on the counter and stared out the window into the dark night. She knew better than to let her mother's nagging get under her skin—but it did. Lately, with all this stargazing and time spent with Sam Mustang and his talk of the wider world . . . she couldn't help but wonder.

Was Gus starting to get a glimpse of a life outside of the Amish?

And if he was—where did that leave her? Because she wasn't going anywhere.

Darcy had been up before dawn plenty of times in her life, but never for stargazing. Standing here in the chilly air, waiting for Sam to arrive, she hoped it was worth it. A few nights ago, they'd been texting, something they were doing more of, and he had mentioned that he'd been going up to Wonder Pond predawn.

She called him immediately. "Why do you go out in the morning?"

"Who is this?"

She rolled her eyes. "You know it's me. Why do you go stargazing in the morning?"

"The cold morning air makes for crisper seeing conditions for deep-sky observing."

"How so?"

"Cold air holds less moisture, which creates less atmospheric distortion."

What?! How had she never known that? "So you've been going up to Wonder Pond in the mornings?"

"Yep."

And he'd never said a word about it! "I'm coming too. Tomorrow morning."

"Not going tomorrow. Clouds are already gathering."

"Then . . . next time you go, I want to go too."

He coughed a laugh. "Darcy, I'm talking five in the morning. On the trail. Pitch dark. Freezing cold. No coffee."

"I'll be there."

"Five a.m. I'm not waiting for you."

"I'll be there," she said, more firmly.

Last night, after checking the weather app, she saw a clearing in the skies between three and six a.m., so she texted him that she would be waiting for him at the trailhead to Wonder Pond at five in the morning. He didn't text back.

Still, she went. And she was freezing, though she did bring coffee in a thermos. She shoved her hands deeper into her coat pockets, waiting for Sam's truck. When he finally pulled up, she watched as he unbuckled his telescope. No hello for her today, no pleased look in his eyes that she was here, waiting for him. Frankly, he just seemed . . . off. "Are you feeling okay?"

"I'm fine."

"Something on your mind?" she asked, tilting her head.

He barely glanced at her. "No more than usual."

That was a lie. But she let it slide, following him as he set off toward the trailhead.

They hiked in silence, their breath puffing in the crisp air as they climbed toward Wonder Pond, following the beam of his flashlight. It was still dark enough that the stars stretched wide and endless above them.

After a while, Darcy spoke. "One of my Amish patients, Micah Weaver, told me about an eagle's nest up here. As big as a buggy, he said. I'm hoping to see it if we're still here when the sun comes up."

Sam grunted, which she assumed meant he was interested.

"He's really into raptors," she said. "Apparently, he's the go-to guy for birds of prey. People come from all over to ask him questions."

Sam said nothing.

"They're always surprising me."

"Who?"

"The Amish. I used to think of them as old-timey."

At that, Sam shot her a look. "Old-timey?"

"Yes. Old-fashioned. Outdated." She exhaled, watching her breath fog. "I'm embarrassed to say that I had even tried to talk Evie out of coming here to work. But after going on some house calls with Dok, and meeting a lot of Amish patients, my opinion is changing."

Breathing heavily, his steps slowed and he turned to look at her. "How so?"

"Seeing the way families work together. They really enjoy being together. And they're not distracted by modern stuff. Have you noticed that? No cell phones. No TVs or computers. Their kids are able to just be kids."

Stopping, Sam smirked. "An Amish farmer would correct you on that. You just called his children goats."

"Noted," Darcy said with a laugh, then her smile faded. "But it's more than just their lifestyle that impresses me. It's how they handle *life*. The other day, I was taking the history of a new patient—an Amish woman—and she mentioned she'd lost her son in a tragic accident. I paused and told her how sorry I was, that my brother had been the same age when he died. I said grief was the hardest thing I've ever faced . . . and honestly, I'm still facing it." She tilted her head slightly. "You know what she said to me?"

Sam didn't answer, but Darcy wasn't really expecting a response. "She looked at me, calm as anything, and said it must have been her son's time to go. That God's timing is never wrong. And she meant it—you could see it in her eyes. That kind of faith . . . it shook me. I've never thought about Jonathan's death like that. I've always felt like he was cheated out of life, like he had so much more ahead of him. But what if . . . what if his days were already counted? What if heaven was always waiting for him at a specific moment?" She let out a slow breath. "It's strangely . . . comforting."

She was on a roll and couldn't stop. Thoughts tumbled out, unfiltered. Unconcerned if Sam was even listening. "I'm just amazed by how the Amish face hard stuff. It's like they understand the world is broken and instead of trying to fix every wrong, they somehow . . . accept it. I can't stop thinking about what that mother said—about God's timing. They really believe he's in control. Even of the worst things."

Suddenly aware that she had been fire hosing poor Sam with her jumbled musings, she glanced at him and saw something shift in his expression. A flicker of something she couldn't name. Then, just as quickly, it was gone.

Without a word, he started up the trail, and she wondered if he was annoyed with her for talking way too much. Had she taken up precious predawn time with her monologue? Or maybe she'd said something wrong. Broody was normal for Sam Mustang. Extra broody was not.

When they reached Wonder Pond, Sam set up his telescope, and as he leaned over the lens, she noticed a change. The tension in his shoulders had eased. The brooding melted, just a little.

He was in his happy place, she realized. Maybe that was why he came up here so often.

Whatever was troubling him, it left him alone here. She took a thermos of coffee out of her backpack and filled two paper cups, handing him one. Then she surprised him by bringing out a container filled with two homemade cinnamon rolls. A pleased look filled his eyes as he took a bite out of one. "Very good, Darcy."

"Do you come here most mornings?"

He took a sip of coffee to wash down the roll, which he'd finished in three bites. "When I need to."

For work? Or for whatever it was that seemed to be troubling him? Darcy didn't ask which. Instead, she turned her attention to the sky. The stars were starting to fade, swallowed up by the coming dawn.

"We should go," Sam said, swallowing the last of the coffee. "Clouds are starting to gather."

She glanced over at him. "I was telling an Amish patient that I love to stargaze. He told me something I'll never forget. 'The sun tells the time, the moon tells the day, the stars tell the month. We live inside the most beautiful clock ever made.'"

Sam looked at her for a long time.

"What? You've heard that saying?"

"Stop it."

"Talking?" Her eyes widened. "I only talk when I just can't help myself!"

"No." His brows furrowed together. "Stop being so wonderful."

And just like that, he bent down to pack up his telescope, leaving her completely confused. Completely bewitched, bothered, and bewildered.

But then she smiled.

She *was* getting to him.

The rain that had begun as the day started showed no sign of letting up. All morning long, it had pounded the roof. From his small office at the back of the Bent N' Dent, David Stoltzfus could hear the squeak of shopping cart wheels along the store aisles, the murmur of conversation, and the occasional creak of laughter from the corner where the graybeards were gathered around the woodstove, playing checkers and cracking peanuts. Those sounds pleased him. They reminded him why he'd never been drawn to farming.

On a wet day in March like this one, a farmer would be staring out the window, fretting about the fields that needed plowing and the work that couldn't yet be done. But David wasn't a farmer—never had been, just as his father before him had always run a store instead of a plow. Farming had its gifts, but it was lonely work. Long days out in the field, behind a horse or mule, with nothing much to fill a man's mind.

David needed people. He thrived on the steady hum of voices, the flow of customers in and out, the sense of being part of the rhythm of their daily lives. This was his soil, his harvest—neighbors and friends stopping in, trading news, and leaving with a bag or two of groceries.

He heard the jingle of the front door open and close. A moment later, a knock came on his office door. Sarah poked her head in, eyes practically dancing with curiosity. One hand was on the door handle, the other on her jaw, nursing a toothache. She'd complained about it for weeks, and David kept telling her to go see a dentist. "Someone wants to see you," she said in a stage whisper. "An *Englischer* someone."

"Sarah, haven't you gone to the dentist yet?"

"I tried! But I didn't have enough cash to pay for the visit."

David cringed. He should've thought to help her with that. Without insurance, the Amish negotiated for a cash discount for health care. Sarah lived with her maiden aunt Faith, who was pleased to tell you that she'd never been sick a day in her life and somehow managed to avoid going to dentists or doctors. Sarah just didn't know how to go about it. Well, that could be remedied. He'd call the dentist himself. Or . . . maybe Birdy wouldn't mind calling. He set his pen down and gave her a measured look. "Let the Englischer in."

Sarah stepped aside but didn't move far. A man entered, tall, lean and lanky, with dark hair. His expression was unreadable, his posture carefully composed. David had a pretty good idea who this man was, as his sister had told him to expect a visit.

"I'm Sam Mustang," the man said.

David stood and extended his hand. "David Stoltzfus." They shook firmly, and then David glanced toward the door, where Sarah lingered. "Sarah, please close the door when you return to the customers." He turned back to Sam. "Have a seat."

Sam lowered himself into the chair opposite the desk, resting his hands on his knees.

The door opened and Sarah's head popped in. "Would you like coffee?"

David sighed. "No, thank you."

Sarah frowned but finally stepped back and pulled the door shut, though not without an exaggerated pause. David listened for the sound of footsteps slowly shuffling away. How many times had he warned Sarah about her nosiness? Too many to count. David waited a beat, then asked, "How can I be of help to you?"

"I've been looking for someone," Sam said. "A woman named Mary Zook. I came to make amends for a very big mistake I once made."

David raised an eyebrow but said nothing, letting the man explain at his own pace.

In a bit of a wooden tone, Sam explained that he and Mary had been involved, as teenagers, and that when he found out she was pregnant, he abandoned her. Rather dramatically, David learned, by faking his own death by drowning. Even his own mother presumed him to be dead.

David waited until Sam had finished his tale. "May I ask you a personal question?"

"Let me guess." Sam leaned back in the chair. "You're shocked. You wonder how I could have done such a thing."

David almost smiled. "No, actually. I'm not." You couldn't be a bishop for ten-plus years and be shocked by the choices people made.

"Okay, then. You want to know why I ran."

"I think I understand why you ran. You were a boy yourself. You panicked. And you bolted. What I was wondering was why you stayed away? What made you not want to ever return? You must have thought about it over the years. It's not easy to be raised Amish and try to find your way in the world. If thought to be dead, that meant you were truly all alone out there. No relatives to rely on. No one to call for help."

Sam tipped his head, gazing out the far window. "It wasn't easy. Especially at first. I had just enough bus fare to get all the way to Houston. There, I found a job as a dishwasher in a restaurant. Someone had told me that was the best way to guarantee one good meal a day. Then my luck started to change. The owner of the restaurant saw that I was a hard worker and took an interest in me. Helped me get my high school GED, then pushed me to go to junior college. I had a knack for science and ended up with a scholarship to finish up at a four-year university. From that point, I found my way. Graduate school, and then a job at NASA. I've been there ever since."

"So that's why you never came back?"

"No. For that, I'd have to say it had to do with one word."

Shame, David thought.

"Questions."

So he was wrong. Not even close.

"I had so many questions. About the world, about how things were made, about everything. I still do. But growing up, I was never encouraged to ask questions, to find answers. I'm not saying that's true of all Amish churches, but it was true of the one I was raised in. Mary Zook was full of questions too. It's what drew me to her. But I knew she wouldn't leave the Amish and I knew I couldn't stay. So I ran. And once I had a taste of science, I couldn't go back. Science is all about asking questions."

"I've always considered Scripture to be full of questions. God asking man. Man asking God."

Sam shifted in his seat to face David. "I think, perhaps, a bishop like you might've made it easier for someone like me to grow up. Maybe things would've turned out differently." He took in a deep breath. "Dr. Stoltzfus, your sister, helped me find Mary Zook."

Actually, David thought, *I was the one who helped with that particular discovery*. But it didn't need to be said.

"Mary lives in Gap, married to a man who used to be my best friend." Sam's tone was even, almost detached, but David didn't miss the way his hands curled slightly, as if bracing himself. "I always thought Marcus was sweet on her."

"So why now? What brought you back now?"

Sam hesitated. "I need to meet with Mary before it's too late."

David frowned slightly. "Too late?"

Sam's gaze was steady. "I've been diagnosed with ALS." There was no self-pity in his voice, just a quiet resolve.

David sat back, absorbing that information.

"You know of it? Sometimes it's called Lou Gehrig's disease."

"I know of it." He knew what it would mean for Sam.

"Bishop, I wonder if you'd be willing . . ." Sam winced. He rubbed his forehead as if he had a headache. "Sorry. I have a bear of a headache."

"Can I get you something?"

"No." Sam shook his head. "I've been getting these headaches a lot." He dropped his hand and started again. "Would you mind reaching out to Mary for me? See if she'll meet me? And then, um, do you think you could be there when . . . if . . . we do meet?"

David studied him. Sam's expression was neutral, his voice steady, but something about the way he asked made David realize—he wanted him there for Mary's sake, yes, but also for his own sake. "Of course, Sam. Of course."

Sam nodded once, though his shoulders eased just a fraction.

"I'll do my best to set up a meeting," David said. He wasn't quite sure how he would approach Mary and Marcus, what he'd say, or not say.

"Thank you." He handed over a slip of paper.

David recognized his own handwriting, though Sam wouldn't know that. On it was Mary's name and phone number. "Where would you like to meet?"

Sam glanced around the store. "Maybe . . . could we meet here?"

David tapped his fingers against his desk thoughtfully. The

store was a neutral place. Quiet. No expectations of hospitality, no audience.

"It'll have to be before or after hours," David said. "I'll speak to Mary and see if she's willing."

Sam let out a breath—not quite relief, but close. "Thank you."

"Sam, you mentioned luck. Do you still think that's what brought you here?"

Sam lowered his gaze, letting the silence hang for a beat. "A few months ago, I'd have told you my luck ended the day I was told I had ALS." His voice was steady, but the words landed heavy between them. He stood then, slow and deliberate, meeting David's eyes. "But I think I know what you're getting at, Bishop . . ." A faint curve touched his mouth—not quite a smile. "And for both our sakes, I hope you're right."

As Sam left, David folded the note. As light as a feather, as heavy as a stone.

Twelve

Darcy adjusted the rearview mirror of her Subaru and squinted through the windshield. The clouds had been hanging low for days, thick and stubborn, like someone had pulled a gray wool blanket over the sky and forgotten to take it off. No stars. No Sam.

She hadn't heard from him in three days. Not a text. Not a "Hey, cloudy again" or an amusing meme about constellations shaped like goats. She'd texted once or twice but never heard back from him. Nothing. And it was starting to gnaw at her.

The folder on the passenger seat caught her eye again—in it was a contract printed out from a hospital in Finland. Six months in Helsinki, working in a pediatric unit. The happiest country on earth. That contract was everything she'd planned for as a traveling nurse: new places, new people, a sense of motion. But now, it felt like a test. Like it was scolding her: "Well? Would you really stick around for a moody guy who barely talks to you? Or are you going to get back on track—travel the world, find new adventures?"

She sighed and turned into town, the Subaru humming quietly beneath her. She didn't have a plan, just a vague hope that maybe she'd see Sam this week, even if there were cloudy skies.

Maybe she'd stop feeling like she was dangling off the edge of something.

And then—there. Parked a little crooked in front of the pharmacy, like it had been abandoned mid-thought, was Sam Mustang's truck. She recognized the faded bumper sticker that said *I brake for meteors*. Her stomach felt a weird little ping.

She pulled into a spot across the street and watched as Sam stepped out of the truck. He looked tired. Not just "I didn't sleep well" tired, but worn down, like something was pressing on him from the inside. He glanced around quickly, then ducked into the pharmacy.

Darcy opened the door but then hesitated. This was probably a bad idea. Was it? On the other hand, she was tired of waiting. Tired of cloudy skies and silence. She crossed the street and pushed open the pharmacy door. She spotted him immediately, standing in line at the back of the narrow store as he waited for the pharmacist, hands shoved into the pockets of his jacket. His shoulders were hunched slightly, like he was trying to shrink into himself. The sight of him hit her harder than she expected. Three days of silence, after weeks of texts and stargazing and that one kiss that had felt like the start of something. Then—*poof*. Cloud cover and radio silence.

He hadn't seen her yet in the store. She considered ducking out, pretending she'd never come in. She could do it. Save her dignity. But her feet moved forward anyway, like they hadn't gotten the memo.

Sam turned just as she reached the shelves near the counter. His eyes widened, then narrowed, like he was trying to decide whether to smile or bolt. "Darcy," he said, voice low. "What are you doing here?"

"Well, I—uh—I came to pick up something." She glanced around wildly, scanning the shelves. Her eyes landed on a bright yellow container. "Athlete's foot powder," she said, instantly regretting it. *So gross!*

Sam raised an eyebrow. "I didn't take you for an athlete."

"Oh, I am. Crazy about sports. I'm very athletic. I play everything. Baseball, volleyball, soccer, tennis, football . . . you name it, I play it." *Bald-faced lie.*

"You play football?"

"I have. Not recently." *More like when I was six years old.*

He turned back to the counter, where the pharmacist was bagging something. Darcy couldn't see the label, but Sam reached for it quickly, stuffing it into his jacket pocket like it was contraband.

"Everything okay?" she asked, softer now.

"Everything's fine," he said, a little too fast. "Just picking up something for a friend."

Darcy nodded slowly. "Right." He had no friends in Stoney Ridge other than her. "I haven't heard from you in a few days."

"Just have a lot going on," he said.

She waited. And waited. That was it? That was the explanation for disappearing? He didn't answer. The silence stretched between them, awkward and brittle. "So that's why you're ghosting me?"

Sam scowled. "I'm not ghosting you."

"What do you call it when you don't return my texts?"

Sam looked down at the bag in his hand, then back at her. "Darcy, things are just . . . complicated."

Darcy gave a short laugh, not because it was funny, but because it was either that or say something she'd regret. "Right. Complicated."

He looked at her then, really looked at her, and she saw something flicker across his face—fear, maybe. Or guilt. Or something heavier. "I already told you," he said quietly. "You shouldn't get tangled up with me."

The pharmacist cleared his throat. "Miss, do you want to pay for the athlete's foot powder?"

Darcy turned, cheeks flaming. “No. Thank you, but I think I’ll just . . . let my feet fend for themselves.”

She walked out without looking back, the bell chiming again behind her. Outside, the clouds were still heavy, the sky a dull slate gray. No stars tonight. No stars for days.

She climbed into her car and stared at the folder on the passenger seat. Finland. The contract. Six months in Helsinki. A clean break. A new chapter.

She hadn’t responded yet. But maybe she should.

Whatever complication Sam was dealing with—whatever was in that bag—it wasn’t something he wanted to share. And she was tired of trying to read between the lines of a man who spoke in ellipses.

She started the engine, the folder shifting slightly on the seat in the breeze from the vent. The contract was calling to her. Maybe it was time to stop waiting for clear skies. Maybe it was time to go where the stars were visible again.

She didn’t drive off right away. Just sat there, watching the pharmacy door, half hoping he’d come out and stop her. Say something. Anything.

He didn’t.

The Bent N’ Dent smelled of woodsmoke, burnt coffee, and the faint sweetness of day-old honey buns stacked by the register. David had arrived early, stoking the woodstove until it gave a steady heat, putting on coffee, setting things in order more out of nervous energy than necessity. Birdy had asked him why he needed to be down at the store so early, and he’d wanted to tell her the truth. Only he couldn’t, because he didn’t know it himself—how this morning would unfold, what words might be spoken once Mary Zook walked through that door. What he did know was that this conversation would be heavy, thick with the weight of years, regrets, and lives altered by one man's—a very young man's—reckless choice.

Sam Mustang sat stiffly in the rocker near the woodstove, rubbing his hands slowly—whether from nerves or the creeping grip of ALS, David wasn't sure. Maybe both. Two mugs of coffee cooled on the counter between them, and Sam had a look of dread on his face.

"Mary doesn't know why I've asked her here," David said at last. "I only told her I wanted to meet with her at the store, and that I'd hoped she would bring her husband." He paused, feeling the weight of his own words. He knew she'd come, because you didn't say no to a bishop, even if he wasn't your bishop. "I expect her husband will be with her."

"So she doesn't know it's me?"

"No. When I spoke to her on the phone, she had a child with her. Maybe two. She was very distracted, in a hurry, and there just wasn't time to explain anything more to her."

Sam gave a slow nod, his fingers continuing their restless motion. He looked as if he wanted to say something, but the squeaky sound of buggy wheels approaching cut through the quiet.

David stood first, and Sam followed, rising to his feet just as the buggy came to a halt outside. A moment later, he saw a glimpse of Mary Zook's black bonnet through the window, and then her husband stepping down from the buggy, tying the reins to the hitching post, then helping his wife climb out. "Sam," David said, "why don't you wait in my office until I get them settled?"

Sam quietly walked to David's office.

David moved to the door, his expression neutral, welcoming. He pulled it open and stepped back from the threshold.

"Good morning," he said, offering his hand first to Marcus, then to Mary. "I'm David Stoltzfus. Thank you for coming. Please sit down." Before he took Marcus's hat and Mary's bonnet to hang on a wall peg, he motioned to the rockers by the woodstove.

"So," Marcus said warily, "you didn't say why you wanted to meet with Mary."

"No, I didn't," David said, sitting across from them. "There's someone who's come a long way, who has something important he wants to tell you. I hope you'll listen to him."

At that, the door to his office opened and Mary's eyes shifted beyond David. The second she saw Sam, a soft, strangled gasp escaped her lips. Her fingers clung to the arms of the rocker. Marcus's own face paled, and he reached out to cover his wife's hand.

Sam approached slowly, shifting his weight, his hands clenching briefly before falling to his sides. "Mary," he said softly. Then, glancing at the man beside her, "Marcus."

"Sam?" Marcus stared at him, his brow drawn, as if trying to make the pieces fit. "Sam Smucker?" The name left his mouth slowly, like he couldn't believe what he was seeing. His gaze swept over Sam, taking him in, trying to absorb the fact that he was standing here at all. "We thought you were dead. We never found the body so we buried an empty coffin for you." His voice was quiet, almost stunned.

"I've come to explain." Sam's eyes stayed on Mary. "And to ask forgiveness."

Marcus's expression tightened, the quiet disbelief hardening into something sharper. "Forgiveness?" He rose from the rocking chair, his voice gaining weight. "So you let us believe you'd drowned—deliberately. Nicht wahr?" *Isn't that true?*

Marcus let out a short, disbelieving breath. "You vanish for twenty-five years, show up with an apology, and think it makes such a thing right? People grieved for you, Sam. Your mother . . ." His voice cracked, just for a heartbeat. "She was never the same."

"I know," Sam said, and his voice, too, was fraying at the edges.

Mary, still shaken, looked between the two men, her confusion evident.

"Mary, we should go," Marcus said, reaching for her arm.

But she hesitated, her gaze still locked on Sam, as if struggling to reconcile what she was seeing.

David spoke up, his voice steady but firm. "I know this is a shock, but I ask that you let Sam speak. Hear him out."

"Please," Sam said.

Marcus hesitated, then exhaled sharply before dropping back into a chair, though his posture remained tense.

Sam ran a hand over his mouth before speaking. "I couldn't face being a father. Not at sixteen years old." He swallowed. "I didn't know what else to do."

Marcus stiffened. "So you left a fifteen-year-old girl to face it alone?"

Ever so slightly, Sam's eyes narrowed, like that remark made him cringe. "I'm not saying it was right. It wasn't. I've regretted it every day of my life."

For a long moment, no one spoke. Then Mary, her voice almost tentative, said her first words. "Why now?"

Sam met her gaze. "I came to apologize to you."

Marcus stood abruptly. "So you did. Now leave us alone."

David raised a hand. "Marcus, please. I know this is difficult. But I'd like you to hear the whole story."

Marcus glared at Sam for another long moment before sinking back into the chair, arms crossed tightly.

Sam drew in a breath. "I've been diagnosed with ALS. My time is limited."

The weight of the words settled over the room like a stone.

Another long silence.

Finally, Sam spoke again, his voice rough. "I also came because . . . I'm hoping . . . I'd like to meet my child."

Mary's head jerked up, eyes wide. Marcus went still beside her. They exchanged a stunned, almost horrified glance.

Marcus shot to his feet again, his anger now in full force. "You can't just arrive in town and upset a child's life!"

David, sensing things were about to unravel, stepped in. "If this happened twenty-five years ago, he or she is hardly a child." Then a thought struck him. His gaze flickered to Mary. "You never told your child the truth."

The silence stretched unbearably.

Finally, Marcus spoke, his tone clipped. "We decided not to. We decided it together. A child needs security."

"Yes," David agreed. "But a child needs the truth too."

Marcus exhaled sharply and turned on his heel, striding for the door. He yanked it open and stepped out, slamming it behind him.

Mary sat still, her hands folded tightly in her lap. After a long moment, she finally spoke. "Marcus raised our son as his own."

Sam swallowed, his voice barely a whisper. "A boy."

Mary nodded. "A fine boy. Now a young man. You should know that not a day has gone by when he wasn't loved as Marcus's own. There's never been any difference in how he treats our children. They're all his." She hesitated, then looked at Sam directly. "I think I always knew this day would come."

Sam blinked at her, surprised.

"On the banks of Blue Lake Pond," she said, "you left a hat and coat on the shore." Her gaze shifted to the floor beyond Sam, as if she was peering back in time. Her voice took on a soft note, almost a whisper. "You were an excellent swimmer. A rowboat overturning on the pond wouldn't have been a problem for you. It didn't make sense to me that you'd taken off your coat to go rowing. Not on a day in November." She turned back to Sam. "But it was the hat that made me doubt you'd drowned." She tipped her head thoughtfully. "It wasn't your favorite hat."

"No. I took that one with me," Sam said.

"I think, deep down, I knew you hadn't drowned. I think I knew you'd run off." Mary nodded, as if that confirmed something deep inside her. After a long moment, she rose to her feet, gathering her composure. At the door, she turned. "Please let Marcus and me have time to talk and pray before we decide if Gus should be told about you."

Sam's face paled. His breath hitched slightly. He rose and went to the window, watching her walk to the buggy. "Gus?" His voice was hoarse. "Did she say . . . Gus?" He turned sharply to David. "There's no way. She couldn't mean . . . the Gus who . . . the one who goes stargazing with a girl named Annie?"

David felt a twinge from his stomach ulcer. Gus Troyer. Annie Fisher's Gus.

And suddenly, he realized—Sam's son.

Thirteen

Darcy turned her car onto the long, winding driveway of Windmill Farm, the bare branches overhead tipped with the first hints of green. She could almost picture it a month from now—pastures as lush as velvet, the orchards full of pale blossoms, the air soft and warm. By April, this farm would be as pretty as a postcard.

April.

April meant decisions. Evie would be back at work by April. April meant Finland—or not.

Darcy cut the engine, jammed her hands into her coat pockets, and stepped out of the car. Out of nowhere, Fern Lapp appeared from behind her, leading a goat by a short rope toward a pen. She'd met Fern once or twice during her weekly visits with Evie. Fern reminded Darcy of a songbird: small, fast, intent, not a single ounce of wasted motion.

"Evie's not here," Fern said. "Gone to the bone doctor for a checkup on her broke leg. She's hoping the cast will come off."

Darcy bent to pat the goat, a plump, friendly looking creature with ears that stuck out sideways. "Well, aren't you adorable," she said. The goat flicked an ear, sniffed her, and before she could move, gave a quick, decisive chomp. Darcy yelped, jerking back. "Hey! Did it—" She looked down in horror. The goat had neatly severed the button from her coat and was chewing it like a jawbreaker.

Fern's lips twitched. "It did," she said, unlatching the gate to lead the goat inside the fenced areas. On the far side was another goat, waiting and watching. For a very long moment, Fern remained still, staring at the goats as they moved closer toward each other. "Okay," she said, satisfied. "They're making friends with each other. Come inside, and I'll find a button to sew back on your coat."

"Why two goats?" Why any goats at all? But Fern wasn't paying her any mind. Darcy followed behind, tugging her coat together with one hand.

Inside the farmhouse kitchen, the air smelled of coffee and chocolate. Fern shooed Darcy toward the table, then set about gathering thread, needle, and a tin of buttons. "Pick the one that's closest to the one the goat ate."

Darcy looked through the tin of buttons while Fern threaded a needle. "This one is close enough," she said, handing a button to Fern. She pulled off her coat and draped it across Fern's lap, watching her sew the button on with neat, efficient stitches. This woman could teach Charlie a thing or two about stitches, she thought. His stitches were a little uneven.

She wished she could take a picture of this moment and show it to Sam. He'd get a kick out of the button-eating goat.

Sam. His name was a constant echo she tried to silence—an impossible man, with impossible walls. She dragged her thoughts elsewhere, to safer territory. "I stopped by to tell Evie that I received a nursing contract for a hospital in Finland," she said as Fern snipped a loose thread. "Six months. Good pay. I could leave as soon as she's ready to return to work."

Fern said nothing, just kept to the sewing.

Darcy kept talking, because silence made her squirm. "Seems like a good opportunity. Evie will be healed up pretty soon and back to work. And I should move on. It's important to be independent. To take care of myself."

The grandfather clock ticked away. Fern's needle flashed. Darcy wondered if she'd said too much, or not enough.

At last, Fern finished sewing and glanced toward the window. "That one goat," she said, almost absently. "The one that ate your button. She's new to me."

Darcy blinked. "Oh?"

"You asked why two." Fern tied off her thread and pressed the button firm. "Funny thing about goats. A goat alone doesn't thrive. Some even die young. They need a companion. It makes them better goats. Better together than alone, that's for sure." Fern set the coat across the back of a chair and moved on to filling a plate with brownies as though nothing more needed saying. She slid the plate across the table to Darcy without comment.

Darcy reached for a brownie. She bit into it and her eyes widened. "Oh my goodness. These are incredible. Did you"—she leaned in for another bite—"did you add coffee to the batter?"

A slight smile lit Fern's eyes.

Darcy sat quietly, chewing, swallowing slowly, trying not to read too much into Fern's words, but the meaning pressed down all the same.

Because a goat on its own doesn't thrive.

Sam's face flared in Darcy's mind, stubborn jaw, steady eyes, the warmth of that kiss he insisted had been a mistake. She had told herself she was fine without him, that Finland was another adventure. But Fern's words burrowed under the surface.

Because Fern wasn't talking about goats. Not really.

The Bent N' Dent held its late afternoon hush like a quilt held warmth. Sarah had left early for a dental appointment for her aching tooth, the graybeards had gone home, the store had nearly emptied out. Peaceable, David thought. Or near enough. He lifted a case of pickle jars from a box and set each jar gently on the shelf, careful not to let glass kiss glass.

From the next aisle, two voices edged into the calm. "Nine is too young," said one woman, low but pointed. "Levi's legs still swing when he sits. He should be with you a while longer."

"And twelve is too old to cling to his Mamm," the other said, sharper. "Joseph ought to be on the men's side by now."

David kept his eyes on the labels—Dill Spears, Sweet Gherkins, Bread & Butter—while his ears did what ears will do. He knew both women; he recognized most voices in his church by their first word. Alma Kline and Julia Miller. They were sisters, inseparable in every way, including their opinions. One would begin a sentence and the other would finish it, often with twice the sting.

"Levi isn't even ten yet," Julia said. "And he sat like a little man last Sunday."

"Little man," Alma snorted. "He knocked the Ausbund off the bench. Did you see all those swallows take flight?"

David couldn't help but smile. Ah, that crossing of the aisle—every boy's graduation. Better even than finishing grade eight. How he had swelled with pride that first time, still small in his best broadfall trousers, when he stood in line with the men to go into church—after being heavily warned by his mother to behave.

He could feel the firm handshakes even now—the bishop's, the ministers', the deacon's—each one clasping his small hand for a sober second. He had sat next to his brother Simon, unaware of the frog, slick as soap, in his pocket. Simon gave him a nudge and slid that frog onto David's arm just as the first hymn rose. It wriggled up his sleeve and David bit his lip till he tasted blood, shoulders shaking, the whole bench vibrating with his silent laughter—and then not so silent.

The next Sunday he'd been back on the women's side.

The two sisters' voices carried on, sharp as geese in spring. "Levi behaves better than some others I could name," Julia said.

Alma sniffed. "If you mean my Joseph, he listens just fine."

"Listens? He's only staying on the women's side to moon over the girls!"

"He's just not ready yet for the men's side. He feels he doesn't belong there yet. Not everyone is in such a rush."

David lifted the last jar into place and straightened the row, the green glass bright. *Not ready. Doesn't belong.* Such light words that bore such heavy freight.

The sisters rolled on, carts squeaking like the wheels themselves disapproved.

"And did you try the bread at the fellowship meal?" Alma said, lowering her voice in a way that somehow made it louder.

"Terrible."

"Truly terrible. Was it even baked all the way through?"

"I always know Birdy's bread."

Alma cackled. "And know to stay away from it!"

David pressed his lips together. Such pettiness! But they weren't wrong. Birdy's cooking wasn't her greatest gift.

But the sisters weren't finished.

"Did you hear Hank Lapp's snoring during the bishop's sermon?" Julia said.

"Can you blame him?" Alma said. "It went on forever. My Milo said we should hand out dictionaries with the Ausbunds, just to understand our bishop's preaching."

Their laughter clattered around the corner—and straight into David.

They saw him and both women gasped, hands flying to their mouths as if to catch the words that had escaped. Julia's eyes widened, then darted to the floor. Alma's color climbed, then stalled halfway up her cheeks.

"Hello, Julia. Alma," David said mildly. "Fine day we're having."

"We, uh—" Alma coughed. "We thought Sarah was working today."

"She left early. I've been stocking shelves."

"You?" Julia's voice quivered. "That was you? All this time?"

They didn't say anything David hadn't heard before. He smiled, letting annoyance and irritation stay tucked under his beard where they belonged. "Let me know if you need anything." He picked up his empty box and carried it back to his office.

At the end of the day, David guided the reins with one hand and kept the other loosely on his knee as the horse clopped along the familiar back road. He'd just come from another contentious meeting about the rogue creek that lay between Bill Lapp's and Johnny King's properties. Neither man would budge an inch. Neither wife would look at each other.

The trees still held the dull gray bark of winter, but the scent in the air had changed—wet earth, thawed mud, and something faintly green. Maybe he was being overly optimistic? He inhaled and exhaled through his nose, slow and thoughtful. It was there, ever so slightly. Spring was coming, and with it, Easter. The most wonderful time of the year.

Council Meeting Sunday, Attnungsgemee, would come first. A time of preparation, a time to make things right. Confess wrongs. Ask forgiveness. Clear the air. Pay off debts, if possible. It was a cleansing ritual—for the soul. Clean hands, clear hearts, one mind before the bread and the cup.

It was a time to foster and affirm unity. Each member would be asked whether he or she was in agreement with the Attnung, whether he or she was at peace with the brotherhood and sisterhood, and whether anything "stood" in the way of entering into the communion service. Two weeks later, communion would follow, Lord willing, with the church united. And then came Easter. A day of rejoicing.

It was the rhythm of the church. The rhythm of the Plain People.

David gently pulled back on the reins as a car passed the other way. He tipped his hat to the driver, who nodded back. The mare kept a steady pace after that, hooves sure on the road home. To the barn, to her supper of hay. David barely noticed. His thoughts were too loud.

Attnungsgemee meant something deep. It was a spiritual reckoning, a way to clean out the heart before sharing the bread and cup. But over the last year or so, he'd noticed that fewer people seemed to be doing the hard work of repentance.

He thought of Eli Zook and Les Esh—neighbors for thirty years, and still not speaking after that ornery bull got loose and wrecked Les's fence line. That was months ago. They nodded stiffly to each other at church, but David knew there'd been no real forgiveness. Just smoldering silence.

And then there was Sally Fisher and Edith Lapp. They'd been the best of friends yet they'd gone the whole winter without sharing a word. Something to do with a borrowed pie plate that had been returned with a chip. Petty, yes. But their injured feelings had grown roots.

And then there was Alma and Julia's nitpicking of others that he'd overheard in the store this afternoon, himself included.

David sighed and shifted on the hard buggy bench.

He missed his deacon.

Luke Schrock had a gift. Somehow, Luke could walk into a messy situation, speak plain truth—Uff en grower Block, gheert en grower Keidel. *A thick log needs a coarse wedge*—and still leave people feeling heard and hopeful. Maybe it was because Luke himself had lived on the edge of ruin. He knew what restoration cost. He didn't skirt around grudges—he waded into them with eyes wide open and a deep belief that Gelassenheit, humility, was possible when Hochmut, pride, was laid down.

David swallowed hard.

The problem wasn't just out there in the congregation. The problem was sitting right here on this buggy bench.

He'd been telling himself for months—maybe longer—that people would see for themselves the importance of keeping short accounts with their neighbors. That a soft answer turned away wrath. That sometimes things healed on their own. But that wasn't what Council Meeting was for. It wasn't meant to be a polite suggestion. It was a call to clean house. Not just sweep the corners, but to get down on hands and knees and scrub what had settled deep.

He had failed to lead them there.

The truth was, David was a top-notch conflict avoider. He'd been avoiding the hard conversations. Skirting around the shepherd's work. Waiting for Luke to return to handle problems. "I've been the worst excuse-giver of all."

His mare flicked an ear at the sound of his voice but didn't break stride.

The truth pressed heavier with each turn of the buggy wheel. He couldn't keep waiting for someone else to reset the spirit of the church. It had to begin with him. He was the bishop.

David looked up at the dull clouds and wondered if he would get home before the rain started. He could feel it building, that soft heaviness in the sky. Just like something was building in him too.

The coffee in Dok's mug had gone cold. She hadn't taken a sip since pouring it, and now the bitter smell of it was making her stomach turn. Across from her, Matt sat stiffly at the kitchen table, fingers curled around his own mug, though he hadn't touched his coffee either. The early morning light filtered through the kitchen window, catching in the fine lines of his face, making him look older. Tired.

She understood. She felt it too.

"I have a friend at the police station—his kid has autism. Sounds a lot like Gabe."

Dok swirled the coffee in her mug. "In what way, exactly?"

Matt shrugged. "I don't know. The staring, maybe."

That wasn't helpful. At all.

"So I've been reading about autism," he said, breaking the silence. "Everything I've found says early intervention is key. I thought we could look into some pediatric occupational therapists. You must know a few, right?"

"I do," Dok said. "But first we need to know exactly what we're dealing with."

Matt exhaled through his nose, rubbing a hand over his jaw. He sighed.

Dok narrowed her eyes. "What is that sigh for?"

Matt looked at her then, his gaze steady, but there was frustration behind it. "I feel as if you're wasting time that Gabe doesn't have to waste."

Dok set her mug down with a little more force than necessary. "I don't see it that way."

"I do." He leaned back in his chair, arms crossed. "I think we need to accept reality and get going with treatments."

Dok pressed her lips together, inhaled slowly. "I want to get him tested for lead poisoning."

Matt let out a sharp breath. "And then what?" His voice was tight, the frustration in it evident. "It would just lead us right back to here. He needs treatment, not tests, Ruth." He leaned forward on his elbows. "Sandra has called twice. She wants to know if we're ready to start adoption proceedings."

Dok rose from the table, heading to the coffee maker and returning with the coffeepot to refill both their mugs. A deliberate pause. A moment to gather her thoughts before she said something she couldn't take back. She sat down and looked straight at her husband. "Matt, I know you feel a huge sense of responsibility for Gabe. But he may need more than we are able to provide."

Matt went still. The tension between them, already taut,

stretched even further. "A year ago, we were ready to adopt him." His voice was quiet but edged with something sharp. "Both of us. We were this close." He pinched two fingers in the air.

Dok swallowed. "That was over a year ago. When his future looked very different than it does now."

Matt's jaw clenched, and for a moment, neither of them spoke. The hum of the refrigerator was the only sound in the room.

Finally, she softened her tone. "Look, can't we both agree that we want the very best for Gabe? The best care, the best family to care for him."

Matt pushed back from the table abruptly, the chair legs scraping against the floor. He stood, his fingers tented on the tabletop as if grounding himself. "Sounds like you've already made a decision."

"I haven't."

He shook his head, then turned and walked out.

Dok's chest ached. "I really haven't," she repeated. But she was trying to gather the right information so they could make the right decision. For Gabe. For them.

If only Matt could see that.

Gus had been acting strange all day at work. Distant, preoccupied, serious. His usual easy smile was missing. Then when he told Annie that he wanted to talk to her tonight, just the two of them, she'd been sure—so sure—that this was finally it. The proposal. The one she'd been waiting for. Praying for.

Her heart had pounded when she heard his buggy turn into the driveway that led to her house, the steady *clip-clop* of his horse's hooves matching the rhythm in her chest. But the moment he climbed out of the buggy, she could tell that something was wrong.

Normally, he leaped out of the buggy and bolted toward the farmhouse to see her. Normally, he would greet her with a teasing remark, a sideways smile. Normally—

But tonight, she sensed right away, was not normal.

Gus stood by the buggy, hands shoved deep in his pockets, staring off toward her father's dairy barn. She walked outside to meet him and saw how tight his face looked. How troubled.

"Let's go for a drive," he said, opening the passenger door of the buggy.

She hesitated. "Where to?"

"Blue Lake Pond."

Gus flicked the reins, urging the horse forward. Silence sat heavy between them, heavier than Annie had ever known. A knot formed in her stomach, twisting tighter with every passing minute. She wanted to ask. *What is it? What's wrong?* But something in his posture warned her not to push. Not yet.

They reached the pond just as the sky deepened to twilight. A sliver of moon reflected off the water, rippling when a light wind stirred the surface. Gus climbed down first to secure the horse's reins. She expected him to come reach for her hand like he usually did, to help her down. He didn't.

She stepped out on her own, brushing her skirt straight. Gus was already walking toward the shoreline. She hurried to keep up. They walked in silence for what felt like an eternity.

Finally, Gus exhaled hard and made an abrupt stop. "Annie, my parents told me something shocking last night."

Annie stayed quiet.

"They said . . ." He hesitated, then took off his hat and ran a hand through his hair. "They said the man I have thought to be my father for twenty-five years . . . isn't my father."

Annie's eyes widened.

Gus turned to face her, his eyes dark in the fading light. His voice was flat, like he still didn't believe it himself. "Apparently, when my mother was fifteen, she had a serious boyfriend. They thought they were in love, and my mother ended up pregnant. With me. But that boyfriend wasn't the man she hoped him to be. He didn't want to be married, he didn't want to be a father. He didn't want to be Amish. But he didn't tell her any of that. Instead, he faked his own death and disappeared." He turned and pointed to the water. "Right here. Right on this pond. He made it look like he had drowned. The rowboat was overturned. His coat and hat were found on the shore. But the truth was, he ran off to live his life. Left his fifteen-year-old girlfriend to face everything alone. Left my mother."

No wonder Gus looked like the wind had been knocked clear out of him. His entire world had just been shaken. Even Annie felt lightheaded by this news.

"Marcus Troyer offered her a way out of disgrace. She accepted his offer." He blew out a puff of air. "And suddenly, twenty-five years later, this horrible man has come back."

"Why?"

"He wanted to apologize to my mother for deserting her . . . and he wants to meet me."

Oh boy. Annie studied Gus in the soft moonlight, wondering what was running through his mind. He was trying to act like he had it all together, but she knew him too well. His hands had curled into fists at his sides. His jaw was tight.

She tried to imagine how she'd feel if she were in his place and she really couldn't even get her head around it. Gus's whole life had been upended. "How do you feel? I mean . . . what are you thinking?"

"I don't know what I'm feeling," Gus said, his voice hoarse. "I don't know how I'm supposed to think about this. Any of it. The life I thought was true . . . wasn't true at all. I've been told a lie about who I was and where I belonged, for my entire life."

She held out her hand, but he didn't take it. A flicker of fear touched her heart.

She had hoped tonight would be their night. The night he'd

ask her to spend the rest of her life with him. But now—now he was a man who had just learned that his sense of who he was, was different than he thought. And maybe that meant his future was different too. Including the future she'd imagined with him.

Annie forced herself to breathe. *Stop being so selfish, Annie Fisher.* Gus needed her right now, not a flood of emotions he wasn't ready for. She dropped her hand. "Gus, do you even want to meet this man?"

Gus didn't respond. He just kept staring at the water, silent and distant, the ripples reflecting the night sky.

He turned to her, releasing a large sigh. "That's just it, Annie. I already have."

Fourteen

The sun was barely up, low on the horizon, painting the sky with hues of rose and gold as David Stoltzfus stood on the porch of the Bent N' Dent. Beside him, Sam Mustang shifted from foot to foot, either from the cold or the biting wind . . . or just nerves. A pair of cardinals flitted through the leafless branches of a nearby maple, their color sharp against the muted morning. Somewhere down the road, a crow called once, then again, like it was keeping watch. Birdy, David thought, would enjoy seeing the cardinal couple. The crow she could do without.

"You're sure you got the time right?" Sam said.

Nodding, David glanced at him. "They'll be here." Mary Zook Troyer had called David yesterday, asking to meet again. David suggested seven in the morning, well before the store opened, long before Sarah arrived. After calling her dentist to work out a payment plan, he'd given her the morning off to get her toothache taken care of. No chance she'd come in early today. A quiet smile tugged at him. Double insurance for privacy.

Sam rubbed his hands together, then shoved them deep into his coat pockets. Not before David had noticed his tremor—

that fine, visible shaking. It wasn't just the cold that made the man shiver. Nor was it nerves. "Do you want to go inside to wait?"

"No," Sam said. "But I have two questions for you." Without looking up, his voice rough, he said, "Do you think God gave me ALS as a punishment? For what I did to Mary?"

David turned slightly, studying Sam's face. The man looked worn out—not just by illness, but by something older. Regret, maybe. Guilt that had settled deep and stayed. He placed a hand on Sam's shoulder, steady and warm. "'For the mountains shall depart and the hills be removed,'" he said quietly, "'but my kindness shall not depart from thee, neither shall the covenant of peace be removed, saith the LORD who hath mercy on thee.'"

Sam let out a breath, slow and shaky. "So," he said, clearing his throat, "is that your way of saying no?"

David offered a small smile. "It's not my way. It's his. We live in a broken world, Sam. That includes broken bodies. But God's mercy doesn't break."

Sam took that in for a while.

"You had another question?"

"I do. Do you think God can—" He clamped his mouth shut as the sound of an approaching horse and buggy caught his attention. Whatever else was on Sam Mustang's mind was put on hold.

Mary Zook emerged from the buggy first, her husband Marcus next, moving with less resolve as he tied the horse's reins to the hitching post.

"She's still a beauty, isn't she?" Sam said quietly, watching them.

David cast a side-glance at Sam, not sure if he knew he had voiced that thought aloud.

Coming up the steps to the store, Mary dipped her head in greeting. Following behind, Marcus gave a small grunt of acknowledgment.

David offered a warm smile. "Let's get out of the cold."

Inside, they settled into the graybeards' rockers. Mary took off her bonnet and set it on the ground. Marcus followed, putting his hat right on top of hers. An awkward hush hung between them. David prayed silently. *Lord, bless this important conversation.*

Mary lifted her chin. "Sam," she said quietly, "I've been thinking a lot about your circumstances. I have to say . . . it's brave, what you're doing. Coming here to face me because you're dying." Her hands lay still in her lap. "And in a strange way, you've given me a gift."

Sam's Adam's apple moved with a swallow.

Mary's voice was low but sure. "What if I had died—and Gus somehow, some way, found out that Marcus wasn't his father? How would he have ever forgiven me?" She glanced at Marcus. "We've had close calls. Gus had an accident once. He fell from a tree"—she dropped her eyes and gave a slight shake of her head—"he was always climbing trees. This was a bad fall."

"Needed surgery." Marcus pressed his fist against his abdomen. "Lost his spleen."

Mary nodded. "He'd lost enough blood that the doctor thought it best to give him a pint of blood. That's when we found out he didn't match my blood type. Or Marcus's. Thankfully, Gus was too young to realize what that meant." She looked away. "But the doctor knew."

A breath escaped her lips, weary but steady. "Living with a lie—it eats at you. You patch it, you work around it, but it's always there. Leaking through the seams."

David didn't speak, didn't move. Nor did Sam. It was like they both sensed she needed to say every word.

"We've lived with a lie for twenty-five years. I used to tell myself it was for Gus's sake. But I always knew—deep down—he had a right to know the truth." She paused. "With you coming . . . I have a chance to make it right. To tell the truth." She turned to Sam, meeting his eyes. "So, the other night, we told him."

Sam's eyes shimmered. He nodded, wordless.

"We told him everything. Even what happened at Blue Lake Pond." She knotted her hands together. "He can decide for himself whether he wants to meet you."

"But, Mary—" Sam began, voice tight, but she lifted a hand.

"Please, let me finish." There was no anger in her voice. Just grace. "I want . . . I need . . . to stand before the church and confess. I want to speak the truth."

Surprised, David leaned forward, as if he hadn't heard her properly. A public confession wasn't ever easy, nor was it necessary—that church was long gone and Mary attended a different one now. But she knew all that . . . and asked for it anyway. When had anyone ever asked to sit on the sinner's bench and make a public confession? No one that he could remember. It was always the deacon who would lay the need for confession on someone. In all David's years in the church, he had rarely, if ever, seen such humility and maturity. *Lord*, he prayed, *you have listened and answered my prayer in a remarkable way. Bless this woman.*

After a moment, he remembered there was another person to consider. He turned to Marcus. "And you? What do you think of Mary's decision?"

"What do I think?" Marcus echoed. He had been looking out the window as Mary spoke, the light casting faint shadows across his face. He turned back to David. "I think my wife has always had a better sense of the right thing to do than anyone I've ever known." He turned back. "She believes this is the best way forward for everyone." His voice dropped. "I love my wife. And I love our son. I raised him like my own." His voice cracked. "So I support her decision, even the public confession."

Again, David felt nearly overcome.

In the quiet, he heard a faint creak come from his office. He cocked his head. A door? He had come in through that back door and, if it weren't shut tight, the wind could push it open. It was a breezy March morning. He listened, but there was nothing. No one else seemed to notice.

Sam spoke next, in a raspy voice, like he was trying to keep his emotions in check. "Mary, if you're both going to confess to the church . . . then I'll stand beside you. I'll confess too. I did . . . a terrible thing, Mary. You were fifteen years old, and I left you alone to face an unwanted pregnancy. I ran, and I never looked back."

Mary straightened her back and lifted her chin. "Not unwanted. Just unexpected. Gus has been one of the greatest gifts of my life."

Marcus reached for her hand. "And mine."

Mary gave him a tender smile, then turned to Sam. "While I appreciate the gesture of standing alongside me, you had never joined the church. You were never baptized. There's no need to confess publicly."

"There's a great need," Sam said, pressing a palm to his chest. "I need it."

David felt the moment settle over them like a hush. Like he was on holy ground. "I'll speak to your bishop for you, if you'd like me to."

"Yes," Mary whispered. "Yes, that would be very helpful." She looked away, blinking quickly, but not before David saw the shine of tears in her eyes.

They rose to leave. David opened the door and Marcus stepped out first to head down the stairs. Mary paused at the door's threshold. "I've been thinking that . . . maybe we should all live like Sam."

"How's that?" David said.

She glanced back at Sam, who remained in the rocker, chin to his chest. "Live like we're dying."

David watched as she joined her husband in the buggy. As he closed the door after them, he noticed Sam now had his elbows on his knees, head in his hands. *Yes*, David thought. *Yes, that's the right response to this astonishing conversation.*

A creak echoed from his office. Leaving Sam to his silence, he crossed the room and stood by his office door. He listened, then pushed it open.

The back door was wide open, banging in the wind. He stepped inside and crossed the room, shut the door hard, turned the lock, and started back to return to the main room. At the door's threshold, he stopped.

Sam Mustang's shoulders were shaking. Heaving. He was weeping.

Darcy glanced at her watch. It had been a nonstop morning. Dok had needed time off to get her little foster boy somewhere for a test, so Charlie was covering for her. An hour ago, he'd headed out on a house call and Darcy handled the last few patients of the morning alone. And now, she had just enough time to dash to the Bent N' Dent, buy a yogurt and apple, hurry back and eat a quick lunch before afternoon patients began to arrive. As she pulled her wallet out of her purse, the door blew open.

"EDDY needs to see DOK!" Hank Lapp marched through the threshold. Following behind was his wife Edith, her expression tight, like she had a popcorn kernel stuck between molars. "We don't have an APPOINTMENT," Hank said, "but I KNEW Dok would SQUEEZE Eddy in. She's ITCHING like a cat with fleas."

Edith stood beside her husband like a storm cloud brewing under her big black bonnet.

Darcy let her wallet drop back into her purse and set it back in the drawer. "Dok's out on a house call, but I can take a look."

Hank was already ambling down the hall to an exam room.

"I TOLD Eddy it's her nerves. Or maybe SOMETHING she ate. Like Sadie Glick's PICKLED BEETS. They give me INDIGESTION something fierce."

Edith snorted. "Never stops him from eating them, though."

Darcy followed them both into the exam room. Hank took the only chair and Edith, with Darcy's help, perched on the exam table.

"She can't SLEEP, neither," Hank said, thumping a hand on his knee for emphasis. "Scratching ALL NIGHT LONG. Sounds like someone SANDING furniture. I keep JOLTING AWAKE, thinking there's a RACCOON in the room." He jerked his body like he'd been shocked, to help Darcy understand the gravity of the situation. Edith shot him a glare that could've curdled milk. What was it Charlie had once remarked about Edith Lapp? *"She didn't need to say a word because her eyes spoke paragraphs."*

Darcy did her best not to laugh. "Let's take a look, Edith."

Edith rolled up the sleeve of her dress, revealing the red, irritated patches of skin at the bend of her elbow. The skin looked dry, inflamed, but not infected. Darcy examined both arms and asked a few questions about soaps, new foods, changes in routine. Edith answered in short, quiet, punctuated phrases: Yes. No. Nothing.

So Hank felt the need to fill in the blanks. "She's been using that NEW SOAP that Sally Fisher made. Smells like LEMON PIE. I told Eddy NOT TO TRUST anything that SMELLS like dessert but you can't EAT it."

Darcy nodded thoughtfully. "When you have sensitive skin, sometimes strong fragrances can aggravate it. I'd recommend switching to a soap without fragrance. I can give you a few samples to help with the itching. And I'll write down some over-the-counter products at the pharmacy that should help."

As Darcy jotted down some notes, Hank leaned back in his chair with a loud and satisfied sigh. "I TOLD Eddy we oughta just COME IN to see Dok. I know all about SKIN TROUBLES. I had POISON IVY once so bad I had to sleep standing up in the barn for three nights. THREE LONG NIGHTS."

"That happened hundreds of years ago," Edith said. "You were just a boy."

"And I STILL remember it CLEAR as day."

Darcy turned back. "I'll get Dok to call in a prescription to the pharmacy. Hank can get it later today. There's an ointment that will help calm things down."

Edith's shoulders had eased a bit. Hank stood, clapping his knees like the visit was a grand success. "SEE? I knew we should COME IN and get you FIXED, Eddy. She's got a BIG birthday coming up. Her son JIMMY FISHER is heading HOME for it. Can't have her ITCHING like a HEN wearing WOOL SOCKS at her own BIRTHDAY PARTY."

Wow. What an image. "No, we certainly can't." Darcy opened the door for them, trying not to smile too wide. "If things don't improve, call in and I'll make an appointment with Dok."

Edith walked straight out the door without a word, chin high. Hank followed. "I'll keep you POSTED on the ITCHING!"

Darcy leaned against the doorframe for a moment, watching them, chuckling quietly to herself. Hank Lapp was one of a kind. Her stomach rumbled and she glanced at her watch. Still just enough time to dash over to the Bent N' Dent. She bolted to her purse and pulled out her wallet.

Just then, the door opened and in came the first patient on the list for the afternoon, followed by the second. With a sigh, Darcy dropped her wallet back in her purse.

The March sun sagged low, casting golden light through the trees as David turned his buggy toward home. The mare was tired, same as he was, her hooves steady on the road. It had been a long day—longer still for the thoughts he hadn't shaken since morning.

Live like you're dying.

Mary Zook Troyer's phrase had lodged itself in David's mind earlier that day, and it hadn't let go. It was a curious idea—one that made him wonder what he might do differently if he knew his time was short. Not in a dramatic way, but in the quiet corners of life. What would he change? What would others?

Just past the covered bridge, another buggy approached, and David recognized the outline of the driver right away. Hank Lapp. He slowed the horse as Hank reined in and pulled over with his usual boisterous grin.

"DAVID!" Hank said in that unmistakably loud voice of his, as though they were two fields apart instead of ten feet.

David pulled alongside. "Hello, Hank. You heading home from town?"

"Eddy needed SOMETHING from the pharmacy. She's ITCHING like a CAT with FLEAS." Hank scratched himself under his arms, as if David might not understand. Then he leaned out slightly, resting an elbow on the side of his buggy. "Just heard some TROUBLING NEWS."

Oh no. David lifted the reins of his mare to get going home. "Never a shortage of troubling news in this world." He lifted a hand to wave goodbye.

Hank didn't catch on. "This PARTICULAR trouble is closer to home."

David cringed. He didn't want to hear whatever it was Hank had on his mind.

"I NEVER was a fan of secret-keeping. Sooner or later, they ALWAYS get found out."

That, David thought, was because Hank couldn't keep a secret if his life depended on it. "Birdy's expecting me home. Good night, Hank."

"This is about our ANNIE's boyfriend. GUS TROYER."

David's shoulders tensed before the words had a chance to land.

"His FATHER isn't his REAL father. It's that STARGAZER. Sam Mustang. That's his REAL father."

Bristling, David looked away toward the horizon, where the sun melted behind the ridge. "How did you come to hear that?"

"You know how NEWS flies in this town. FASTER than a FLOCK of BIRDS."

"Actually, Hank, you just described gossip."

Hank, naturally, missed David's point. "I hear there's GONNA be a CONFESSION over at the Gap church. If that's SO, Eddy and I might just PAY a VISIT."

David turned to look at the horse's swishing tail. A young man's whole world had shaken loose, and the community buzzed like it was a barn raising. The thought made his stomach roil.

"BETTER get this SCRATCH medicine home to Eddy." Hank lifted one hand and shook the reins with the other. Off he went, his buggy creaking as it rounded the bend.

David sat still for a moment, staring at the road. A breath of wind swept through the trees, and with it, he remembered the sound he'd heard in his office this morning. He'd told himself it was just the door slamming in the wind. So maybe it hadn't been the wind.

The walk down from Wonder Pond was slow and easy, Darcy's and Sam's footsteps crunching softly on the cold dirt path. The night still hummed with the echoes of the meteor shower they had just watched, a spectacular display neither of them had expected to be quite so breathtaking. It wasn't meteor season yet, not like the Perseids in midsummer, when the night sky would be full of bright flashes of light with their glowing trails.

She glanced over at him. Out of the blue, he'd texted to meet up and, remembering Fern's goat story, she'd agreed. And now she would catalog this night as one of the best—one where conversation flowed, where his smile had come easily—and wondered if he felt the same way. He'd even laughed a few times! Whatever was bothering him this last week seemed to be resolved. If not resolved, it wasn't weighing him down like it had been. He seemed lighter, younger.

Then, just as they reached the fence that ran along the road, Sam stopped abruptly. His breathing hitched. A sharp inhale. A pause. Another uneven breath.

Darcy turned to him. "You okay?"

He nodded, but his hand shot out, gripping Darcy's shoulder as if the ground beneath him had tilted.

Her stomach clenched. "Sam?"

He was still upright—but just barely. His chest rose and fell too quickly, his breath uneven, shallow. She stepped closer, placing a steadying hand against his chest. *Oh no.* His heart was hammering—wild and erratic, like a bird trapped in a cage. A heart attack? She met his eyes, her voice firm. "We're going to the hospital."

"No." His protest was weak, but the stubborn set of his jaw was familiar.

"Sam—"

His knees buckled.

She caught him just in time. That was it—no more arguments. Bracing against his weight, she helped him walk to her car. With one hand around his waist, she opened the door with her other hand. "Get in."

This time, he didn't fight her.

Fifteen

The harsh fluorescent lights of the ER had none of the warmth of the starlit sky. Sam lay on the hospital bed, an IV taped to his arm, a heart monitor beeping steadily beside him. His color was better now, though that stressed look had returned, pulling at his features. Darcy sat in the chair beside him, arms crossed, her worry still pressing hard against her ribs. Now and then her eyes flickered to the monitor. This wasn't good.

The attending physician studied the monitor. "Your EKG's picking up an irregular heartbeat. Has anyone ever told you that you have arrythmia?"

Sam let out a slow breath, glanced at Darcy, then answered the doctor. "No."

"Any fainting episodes?"

"A few."

"Have you seen a doctor about them?"

"Yes."

"What did they find out?"

Sam hesitated so long that the doctor looked up. "After a battery of tests, I was diagnosed with ALS."

Darcy froze. The words hung in the air, heavy and final.

The doctor paused, typing some notes into his chart. "When were you diagnosed?"

"Last summer."

Darcy gripped the chair's armrests, frozen. ALS—last summer? The words kept spinning in her head—impossible and undeniable, all at once. And yet it fit. The stumbling, the tripping, the tremors, the bone-deep exhaustion—it had all been there. She was a nurse and didn't see the signs of disease. Or maybe she just refused to see them.

The doctor's pager went off and he excused himself, saying he'd be back in a bit. A beat of silence stretched between them before she asked, softly, "So this is why you regretted kissing me."

"I didn't regret kissing you," he said, his voice low. "I regretted getting you tangled up in my mess."

"ALS is more than a mess." She swallowed. "So why are you here? It's not because of some NASA project, is it?"

He gave a slight shake of his head. "I came here to make amends with someone."

She tilted her head. "Who?"

He lifted his eyes to glance at her. "Has anyone ever told you that you're nosy?"

"Yes." He had. Evie had. Lots of others too. Darcy had always been told she asked too many questions. But as far as she was concerned, asking questions was the only way to get answers. "So why are you here?"

A muscle flickered in his jaw. Then, quietly, "Because I was raised Amish and got my girlfriend pregnant. Then I ran away so I didn't have to marry her. Faked my own death."

Darcy felt as if she could hardly breathe. What kind of man was he? She thought he was such a good, kind person. He was *horrible!* What was *wrong* with her man-radar? What was wrong with *her* that she let herself get emotionally involved with a guy like him?

Sam didn't look at her. His gaze was distant, fixed on some invisible point beyond the hum of the monitor. "I came back to apologize to her. And maybe . . . to meet my son while I could still stand on my own two feet. To see him. Just once, that's all."

He drew in a breath, slow and careful, as if weighing his next words. "Darcy, I want you to think of the night sky. You're always talking about God. Well, I want you to picture those stars. They represent all my sins. Too many to count. Pride. Betrayal. Cowardice. Selfishness. Lack of concern for my girlfriend, none for the baby she was carrying. My child. The list goes on and on." He turned to face her now, his dark eyes holding hers, raw and unguarded. "Now do you see why I haven't wanted a nice girl like you to get tangled up with someone like me?"

A long pause.

Before she could answer, the doctor came in to go over some test results with Sam, and she rose from the chair, grabbed her coat, and slipped past the curtain. She could feel Sam's eyes on her with every step.

It was late, the kind of stillness that made every creak of the old house sound louder. Birdy and the boys had been asleep for hours. Restless, David dragged a rocker close to the woodstove and fed it a few sticks of kindling—enough to keep the chill off, but not enough for a lasting blaze. He knew he should go to bed soon. Heat washed over him, yet his thoughts wandered far beyond the room.

"When are you coming to bed?"

He turned to see Birdy at the door. That look on her face—like she was waiting for him to say it, like she already knew. "So," he said, voice low, "you've heard."

Birdy nodded and came in to sit on the couch. "Sally Fisher came by this afternoon. Said she wanted my recipe for peach chutney, but she didn't even make it to the kitchen before she blurted it out." She leaned against him. "So this is why you spent hours at the Sisters' House searching through old *Budget* newspapers. Gus Troyer's father . . . isn't who he thought he was."

David's mouth tightened. He crossed his arms. "Birdy, this is a delicate situation."

"Sally says she's going to insist that Annie break things off with Gus."

David sighed.

"She was quoting Scripture—the sins of the father spreading to three generations."

"I hope you dissuaded her."

"I did my best to try," Birdy said. "But you know Sally. Once she gets her teeth into a thing, there's no getting her to let go."

David rubbed the back of his neck. "What I know," he said, "is that Sally Fisher is missing the forest for the trees. The next verse says that God will show mercy unto thousands who love him and keep his commands."

Birdy tilted her head. "Sally isn't entirely wrong. Sin does have ripples, David. You've said so yourself."

He looked over at her. "Sam Mustang came here to make amends. Because he's dying, Birdy. And because he's finally facing the things he ran from. He has a disease called ALS. His time is limited, and in that time, he's chosen to tell the truth. To apologize to Gus's mother for leaving her like he did."

Birdy didn't say anything. The grandfather clock ticked on the wall, loud in the stillness of the night.

David's voice softened. "Mary—Gus's mother—has responded to Sam in the most remarkable way. She showed incredible maturity. She could be so angry with Sam. What he did was terrible. You can make all kinds of excuses for him being just a boy himself, but it was still terrible. Yet she's forgiven Sam, and she's owned her part in this story. She told Gus the truth. She wants to go a step further and offer a public confession to the church."

"A very wise move."

"How so?"

"Because a public confession will put an end to all gossip for her son."

David tilted his head. He hadn't thought about that, but Birdy was right. Once a sin had been confessed, it was to be spoken of no longer. "She's making herself so vulnerable."

Birdy smiled. "Mothers do that kind of thing for their children."

"I wonder if Gus will understand what his mother is doing for him."

"How did Gus respond to the . . . news about Sam Mustang?"

"I didn't ask. All I know is that Mary and Marcus are letting him decide if he wants to meet Sam."

Birdy cringed. "And word is already out."

David sighed. "So it is. I passed Hank Lapp on the road this afternoon and he shouted it out to me." He blew out a puff of frustration. "During the meeting with Mary and Marcus and Sam, I thought I heard a sound coming from my office. After everyone left, I went in and found the back door wide open. I thought the wind had done it—you know how bad that lock is. But now I wonder if Sally might have been listening to us."

"When did you have this conversation?"

"Early this morning, before the store was opened."

"Then it definitely wasn't Sally. She and I were together, helping Karen and Amos Lapp get their home ready for church this Sunday. Quite a few women were there. Sally didn't say anything. If she had known something, that would have been just the time for her to spread her news." She tipped her head. "Sarah seems a likely candidate."

"I know for a fact that Sarah was at the dentist. That's why I had everyone come to the office at that time. I knew she would be fully occupied." He sighed. "Well, whoever overheard it, it seems to be spreading fast through the rumor mill."

Birdy reached for his hand and he let her take it. "There's something else on your mind. I can sense it."

She knew him so well. He squeezed her hand. "The closer we get to Council Meeting, the less prepared our people seem to be for the holy season. I fear a big wake-up call will be required."

"I can think of one big wake-up call."

"What's that?"

"You plan for a lot to get a deacon to replace Luke."

Oh. *That*.

"David, I realize how fond you are of Luke. But you need help in this role. You're not meant to carry so much alone." She rose from the couch to kiss him on the top of his head. "Come to bed."

"Soon," he said, giving her a tender smile. When she was gone, he fed the fire a few thin sticks—just enough to hold the warmth a little longer. The embers glowed, then dimmed. He knew Birdy was right—he needed help. He needed a deacon. But his reluctance to replace Luke wasn't just because he was fond of him. It was because Luke was his friend. And a bishop didn't have many friends.

ALS.

Darcy had heard the syllables come from Sam's mouth like they belonged to someone else. Three letters, and yet they cracked something open in her chest. The realization had sent fear slicing through her. And now, standing outside the hospital in the cold, those three letters wrapped around her like a shroud.

ALS.

Darcy pressed her palms against her forehead, eyes shut. Off in the distance, she heard an ambulance siren on its way to the hospital. Normally she'd have noticed that. Normally, she'd have wondered what the emergency was about, whose lives might have just changed. Whenever she thought to, she would even say a prayer for those lives.

But not tonight. Nothing was normal about this night.

Sam Mustang had ALS. He also had a son. And a girlfriend he'd left behind, a pregnant fifteen-year-old girl—alone, grief-stricken, probably terrified. *How do you walk away from that?* Even if he was just a teenager, an Amish teen to boot, how did he come up with the idea of faking his own death and then disappearing? She'd listened as Sam had told her, his voice low and tired, eyes focused on a spot on the floor. Not trying to defend himself. Just laying it all out like he didn't expect her to stick around.

And maybe he was right.

Maybe she shouldn't stay.

She'd only known him a few weeks. That was nothing. A blink. A brush of wind. She could still get out now, before sorrow took root. Before she let the longing she'd begun to feel for him get carried away.

Before he died.

Darcy let out a shaky breath. She couldn't do it a second time. It was Jonathan all over again. Different, but the same—a terrible disease that stole a life inch by inch, stripping away the person long before the body gave out. She could still see her brother near the end of his life, so frail, slumped in the recliner, his once-quick smile gone, his words reduced to sounds she had to guess at. She'd been a young teenager when much of her brother's care fell to her—her mother had to go to work to help pay off mounting medical bills, her father traveled heavily in his sales job, though Darcy felt he wanted to be anywhere but in that room. So she was the one who stepped in.

Seeing her devotion to her brother, the visiting nurses taught her some basic caregiving for Jonathan. Later, hospice arrived and she learned more skills. By the end, he couldn't feed himself, so she had learned how to thicken liquids so he wouldn't choke, how to coax a spoon past lips that no longer obeyed him. How to steady his jerking limbs during a spasm. How to read the flicker in his eyes when he was in discomfort or pain. How to be his voice when he had none.

And now, with Sam's diagnosis echoing in her ears, different from Jonathan yet much the same, she knew exactly what the future would bring. She could see the road ahead as clearly as if she'd already walked it. There was no winning. No remission. No miracle.

She couldn't do it again.

She should back away now. Be smart. Be safe.

But when she pictured herself packing up and leaving, off to a new traveling nurse contract—when she imagined slipping quietly out of Sam's life—her chest ached in a different way.

There was just something about Sam Mustang.

What was it that drew her to him, from the moment she'd met him? What made him different from other men she'd known? She squeezed her eyes shut, trying to answer that question. Sam was incredibly smart but didn't need to make sure everyone knew it, like a lot of guys did. Doctors, especially. His was a quiet, unshowy intelligence—the kind that revealed itself in patient explanations, not loud opinions. He'd taught Gus to align the telescope himself. He'd showed Annie how to find Saturn's rings. Darcy had grilled him with every space question under the sun and he hadn't once lost his cool.

Unlike other men, he seemed to enjoy her questioning mind. He'd made her feel smart. He'd made her feel special. His gruff exterior was such a facade. Scratch beneath the surface, and Sam Mustang was the most tender, most kind man she'd ever met.

And he was going to die.

Tears stung her eyes. *No. Don't you dare.* She pressed a palm over her eyes, willing the tears not to come.

The automatic doors sighed shut behind her, and the faint tang of antiseptic clung to the night air, sharp enough to pull her backward in time. Instead, she should be thinking about what came next—where she'd go after Evie's leg healed. That had always been her method: Keep moving. Keep going. Don't stop.

She had promised Jonathan that she would see the world for both of them. His eyes had followed her voice even when his head no longer could, his fingers twitching against the blanket she'd tucked around him. As his world had shrunk to a bed by the window, she tried to fill his mind with images of the world outside: the scent of baking bread in Paris, the tropical blue ocean in Fiji, the red dust of the Australian outback. He couldn't answer, but she'd seen the flicker of longing in his gaze.

Movement honored Jonathan. Stillness felt like a betrayal. She'd promised him she would live a full life, for both of them.

But tonight, standing out in front of the hospital, she didn't feel like she'd been living a very full life. Interesting, adventurous, exciting . . . but not full. Not deep. Rather shallow, if she were honest with herself. Rather self-serving.

She opened her eyes and looked up at the stars in the sky. Sam would probably know their names. He always did. And somehow that thought made her smile. Just barely.

Why Sam? Why her? Was God playing a cosmic joke on her? Trying to see how far she'd get before she shattered into a million pieces? Because she was pretty close.

"Are you Darcy? Sam Mustang's friend?"

She turned around to see the nurse from the emergency room station. "Yes. That's me."

The nurse held Darcy's purse out to her. "Sam asked me

to tell you to go on home. He said he'll take an Uber when he gets released."

"Oh. Okay." She took her purse from the nurse. "Thank you for finding me."

Sam had sent her away. Darcy felt both hugely relieved and hugely disappointed.

Sixteen

It had been a slow day at the Bent N' Dent—quiet enough to make David restless. Quiet enough that Mary Zook Troyer's phrase—*live like you're dying*—kept returning to his mind. What might that phrase mean for him? What more could he do to prepare his church for the important Council Meeting?

Late in the afternoon, a group of older men came to the store. David welcomed the familiar clatter of checkers and the crunch of peanut shells from the front room, even if the graybeards never bought much of anything. They were a pleasant distraction.

Toward closing time, Hank Lapp appeared in the doorway of David's office, looking for the broom. It was his turn to clean up the graybeards' mess: a scatter of shells carpeting the wooden floor, courtesy of the old men's attempts to pitch them into the yawning oven door of the woodstove. They missed more than they hit. Months ago, Sarah, fed up with the daily debris, had laid down a rule—if they wanted to snack like squirrels, they'd have to sweep up after themselves. Today, Hank drew the short straw.

David handed him the broom from the corner, then asked,

almost absently, "Hank, if you knew you were dying, what would you do differently?"

Hank paused, one hand on the broom handle. He blinked at David, then looked down at the broom. After a beat, he handed it back.

"Well," he said, "I wouldn't BOTHER sweeping."

David gave a quiet laugh. "Fair enough."

Hank shrugged. "Seems like a POOR USE of my final hours."

He turned and headed out, leaving David holding the broom. The door swung shut behind him with a soft thud.

Later that night, as David lay beside Birdy in the hush of their bedroom, he turned the question over once more and spoke it aloud. "If you knew you were dying," he said softly, "what would you change?"

Birdy shifted, rolling toward him. Her eyes found his in the dim light. "You mean, what would I change about my life?"

He nodded.

She was quiet for a moment. "I feel very happy with most of my life."

"Most?"

She rolled onto her back, staring up at the ceiling. "Yes. Most."

David turned slightly, propped on one elbow. "What would need to change to make it all of it?"

She hesitated, then said it plainly. "Another baby."

That caught him off guard. He turned fully to face her now. "Birdy . . . if you knew you were dying, would you really want another child?"

She looked at him, her expression calm. "But that's not what you asked. You asked what would need to change to make me feel happy with *all* of my life."

"Oh." He let the word settle between them.

She turned on her side, facing away from him. The room fell quiet again. Outside, the wind moved gently through the trees, and the old house creaked in familiar ways. David thought she might have drifted off, but then she sighed—a long, soft breath that felt like a prayer released into the dark.

He reached out and rubbed her back in slow, thoughtful circles. "Birdy," he said, his voice low, "we could keep trying."

She turned toward him, and in the faint light, he saw her smile.

The low-lying sun had just slipped behind the Fishers' dairy barn. Annie could tell that Daad had made his way from one cow to the next, fastening the milkers to each teat, because the lowing, the cows' fretting, had ceased. The barn had quieted.

Not so for the kitchen. Annie's mother hadn't stopped repeating herself since yesterday, circling the same point, her voice wound up like a ticking clock that wouldn't stop. "You need to end things with Gus Troyer, Annie. I'm serious. This is not a small matter. End it today."

In the kitchen, Annie kept her head down as she made her sandwich to take to work. She spread two slices of homemade bread with a thin layer of mayonnaise, laid a slice of cheese onto the bread in front of her, added lettuce and sliced turkey, then pressed the sandwich together with more force than needed.

"Mark my words. Sam Mustang will persuade your Gus to leave the fold."

In truth, her mother knew only two things about Sam Mustang. He'd been raised Amish and he had left. That was enough, apparently.

"Sam has never expressed any intention to persuade Gus, Mamm."

"Sam Mustang has lived a worldly life," Sally said. "No one can deny that. And you think Gus won't do the same?"

Annie felt it again—that flicker of unrest, low in her chest. Just like it had stirred when the story had spilled out of Gus when they were at Blue Lake Pond. His voice had trembled as he spoke, and as much as she had tried to remain utterly calm, she felt unsteady, like she was trying to walk on uneven stones over a rapidly rushing creek.

Sam Mustang is Gus's biological father. So hard to believe, yet something in Annie had accepted it instantly. Like a door had opened in her mind she hadn't known was there, and now that she did, she couldn't shut it. She could see so many similarities—the high forehead, the shape of his jaw, the angled cheekbones. Even his hands were like Sam's.

But Gus tilted toward Sam in ways that went beyond bone: Their intelligent minds. Their hunger to learn. They had the same desire to understand the vast night sky.

Her mother was still talking, still running Sam Mustang down, still pointing out his many flaws.

"But you've never even met Sam Mustang," Annie said, when her mother finally took a breath.

"He was Amish and he left. That's all that matters."

Annie folded her sandwich into wax paper, pressed the edges closed. "Sam Mustang was a boy when he made a mistake. A terrible mistake. But he'd never been baptized. And he's come back to apologize. You can't fault him for that."

"It does not excuse twenty-five years of absence." Sally sniffed. "Mark my words, Annie. Gus will have one foot out the door before you know it."

Annie turned. "So you're saying that Marcus and Mary Troyer have had no influence on Gus? That twenty-five years of being loved and supported by his parents has not shaped him and made him the man he is today?" Without thinking first, she said, "This is the same man you call on for advice each time you have a little ache or pain or rash? This is Gus, Mamm. Why can't you believe the best in him?" Something snapped in Annie. "Why can't you *ever* believe the best in others?"

Too much. From the deeply offended look on her mother's

face, she'd gone too far. Her mother spun on her heels and left the room in a huff.

Annie dropped her sandwich into a cloth bag and tied it closed. She held the bundle against her chest. Her hands felt cold. Her stomach churned.

What if her mother was right?

What if Gus already had one foot out the door?

David placed the receiver in the phone cradle and stood for a long moment in the hush of the phone shanty, the line gone quiet, his thoughts anything but. He hadn't expected much from the bishop in Gap, but he had expected understanding. Compassion. He received neither.

The bishop in Gap had been pleasant enough, but firm. This was something, he'd said, that could stir up more trouble than peace. The sin, after all, had happened long ago. Mary had not been baptized then. Neither had Sam. It had happened before either of them had made their vows before the Lord and the church. And Sam never had, he pointed out. He owed nothing to the church.

"Mary Troyer is a married woman now, with other children to think of," the bishop told David. "She's a member in good standing. Best to let the past stay buried, if it's already been confessed in the heart. Some things are best kept private."

David understood the bishop's logic. It wasn't without wisdom. But it wasn't the whole story either. Mary and Sam had lived with that hidden thing for years. Maybe they had thought they could carry it to the grave. Maybe they'd even tried to forget it themselves. But the truth had a way of pressing up from the soil, no matter how deep you buried it. And now Sam, knowing his days were numbered, wanted to put it right. That mattered, didn't it?

Spring communion was coming. That special Sunday was

only a little over four weeks away. The thought brought a quiet weight. Not just the communion meal itself, but the preparation for it—how the church gathered to make peace with one another, to lay bare what was hidden, to walk into the holy season of Easter with clean hearts. It was never about ritual for ritual's sake. It was about readiness. Wholeness. A community united in its need for Christ.

David had always loved that about the season—the way it drew everyone back to the center. Just plainspoken words, honest reflection, and the sacred hush of forgiveness. And here were Mary and Sam, choosing to step into that space fully. Willingly. Not because anyone demanded it of them, but because they felt that they owed it to God.

David straightened a little, stretching, pressing his hand into the small of his back. If the bishop from Gap didn't want the confession in his church, fine. But it would not be swept away like a mess under a rug. Not here. Not in Stoney Ridge. David would welcome their confession. Not as a spectacle. Certainly not as gossip. But as an act of spiritual courage.

Mary's baptism may have covered that long-ago sin, yes—but there was something holy in her and Sam choosing to name it aloud now. In front of witnesses. In front of their son.

David's stomach tightened slightly at that thought—Gus.

Just a few months ago, Sarah Blank had told him to expect both Gus and Annie to be getting married this fall. She had it on good authority, she'd said, which meant very little to David. Sarah often spoke as if she had everything on good authority. But David had seen Gus and Annie together, numerous times, and he had a hunch that, for once, Sarah's gossip might be true.

David didn't know Gus well, but from what he could tell, he was an admirable young man. He wondered how his parents' revelation, his mother's public confession, might affect Gus. It had the makings of rocking one's foundation.

And he couldn't forget about sweet, shy Annie Fisher. How

was she handling the news? Her mother, Sally, came to mind. After Mary's confession, any discussion of this matter would stop among church members. That would be beneficial for all. Gus, especially.

David stood up from the little shanty chair, thinking about Gus's well-being. He would pray this revelation about his biological father wouldn't break something in the young man, but that it would build something new. Something stronger. Something better. For Annie too.

And, after observing Mary Zook Troyer's humility in a public confession, he would pray that the church remembered who they were—a sinful people in need of a Savior.

David stepped out of the phone shanty and let the door swing shut behind him. The air carried the scent of turned soil and damp grass. Spring was almost here.

He walked toward the house, toward the light in the kitchen window, where Birdy would be setting out breakfast. And in his heart, David offered up the prayer that had been rising in him lately: *Let our hearts be ready, Lord, for the coming of Easter.*

Darcy shook her head. She'd been staring at the same name on the patient list for nearly a minute. For two days now, focus had been slipping through her fingers. She moved on autopilot—vitals, notes, a quick smile—while Sam's face kept intruding, along with the words he'd told her. ALS. A slow, merciless disease. He would die from it.

She hadn't heard from him, and she hadn't reached out. She didn't know what to say. She didn't know what to think. She only knew she wasn't sure she could face what was coming.

Couldn't imagine staying.

Couldn't imagine walking away either.

On the third morning, when Charlie told Darcy that he needed to run back to Windmill Farm to get his forgotten medical bag, she jumped at the chance to do the errand for him. "Two patients just canceled, and Dok is on a house call. If you don't mind handling the office, I'll go for you." He didn't, so she made a dash out the door and to her car.

Ten minutes later, at the buggy shop at Windmill Farm, Darcy knocked lightly on the door before letting herself in. "Evie?"

"Right here."

Darcy stepped into the cozy space, with morning light streaming through the window where Evie sat, painting.

"You're watercoloring?" Darcy said. "You?"

Evie looked up, a brush in her hand. "I know. Who am I?"

Darcy smiled and wandered closer. She couldn't figure out what Evie was trying to paint. A bird, maybe? A barn? "It's . . . coming right along."

"Thanks." Evie looked out the window. "Sheep are very hard to paint. They keep moving."

Sheep? That's what it was?

"I've never made time for hobbies. But now, apart from a broken leg . . ." She gave a wry smile. "I'm kind of enjoying the time off." She pointed her paintbrush at her leg. "You didn't even notice."

Darcy glanced at Evie's leg. "The cast. It's gone."

"I've graduated from crutches to a walker."

Darcy's mind started to spin. This meant that Evie would be ready to return to the office sooner than she'd thought. It meant Darcy would be free to move on. For the second time in just a few days, she felt a sweep of conflicting feelings—both relief and disappointment. She shook off that thought and moved to the stove. "Charlie forgot his medical bag so I came to get it. But I do have a few minutes to spare, if you do."

"Why, in fact, I do."

"Mind if I make us some tea?"

"I'd love it."

Darcy set the kettle on, then rummaged through the cabinet for two mismatched mugs and a tin of loose-leaf. Soon, the warm, slightly floral scent of tea filled the small space.

When they were both settled—Evie still by the window, Darcy in the rocker nearby—she took a sip and said, "So I've been spending time with Sam Mustang."

Evie put down her brush, glancing over. "Don't tell me. You're starting to fall for him, and him for you . . . and that makes you freak out. So you're considering how far away you can go with the next contract."

Darcy blinked. The answer was yes, yes, and yes. "Why in the world," she said, a little defensively, "would you think that?"

"Because you have a classic case of grief in disguise. I just read a book about it. I've had rather a lot of spare time, as you can imagine."

Darcy looked down at her teacup, as the dark tea leaves infused the hot water. *Grief in disguise.* Wow . . . what a tidy label for such a complicated subject.

"I'm sorry. I didn't mean to be so blunt. But . . . you are freaking out, aren't you?"

Darcy hesitated. "I am, but there's more to the story."

Evie watched her over the rim of her mug. "Okay. Rewind to before I interrupted you. You've been spending time with Sam."

Darcy nodded slowly. "I only have time to give you the CliffsNotes version. Sam was raised Amish. There was a girl—she got pregnant. And he left when he was sixteen. Abandoned her."

"Wow." Evie's lips pressed together.

"He never contacted her. Just . . . left her to handle it on her own. She was only fifteen."

Evie didn't answer right away, only leaned her head back and looked out the window. "That's a lot to carry."

"Twenty-five years later," Darcy said, "he's come to make amends. Meet the son. Apologize."

"Well, I guess that's something."

Darcy hesitated. "He's doing it because he's dying."

Evie's eyes darted to her. "What?"

"ALS. I just found out a few days ago."

Evie set her tea mug down with deliberate care, as if any sudden movement might shatter something more fragile than porcelain. "Oh, Darcy. I'm so sorry."

Those words carried everything—sympathy, understanding. Darcy's chest tightened, her throat closing around the grief that had been building since she'd heard the diagnosis. She pressed her lips together, fighting the tremor that threatened to betray her composure.

"I've seen what a disease like this will do to a person. The way it strips someone down, muscle by muscle, until only their mind is left trapped inside. It's—" Darcy stopped, unable to finish. Cruel seemed too small a word for what she'd witnessed with Jonathan. The slow theft of everything that made him *him*, while his eyes remained bright and aware, watching his own body become his prison.

Evie didn't speak for a long moment, and Darcy was grateful for the silence. It gave her time to swallow back the sob that was clawing its way up her throat.

Finally, Evie said, "And you don't think you can watch it happen again."

The quiet observation hit like a physical blow. Darcy's gaze drifted to the watercolor painting Evie had been working on. She still couldn't see the sheep Evie claimed were there, just blurred shapes that might have been clouds or stones or nothing at all.

But Evie was waiting for a response, one that was painful to give. The truth scraped against her like broken glass. No, she didn't think she could survive watching another person she loved disintegrate, piece by piece, until death finally came as a mercy.

"Oh, honey," Evie said. "You love Sam Mustang."

That deeper truth crashed over Darcy like a wave, stealing her breath. She was falling in love with Sam. Had been falling, maybe, since that first time he'd shown her binary stars—two points of light that were inseparably cosmic partners. The realization should have been joyful, should have felt like coming alive. Instead, it felt like standing at the edge of a cliff, knowing the ground was about to crumble beneath her feet.

"I can't do this again, Evie. I just can't." The words slipped out before she could stop them. Her hands trembled around her mug. She swirled the tea in her mug, watching the liquid catch the light filtering through Evie's window. Jonathan's face flickered in her memory—not as he'd been at the end, but as he'd been before, laughing at something stupid she'd said, ruffling her hair.

After a long moment, Evie said, "Darc, I'm not trying to tell you what to do. I know I'm not in your shoes, but I've had moments like this—times when I'm standing at a fork in the road. And here's what I've learned during those moments. It's not really about the circumstances. It's about believing in God."

"I believe in God."

"I know you do. But it really comes down to what you believe *about* God. Especially when life gets overwhelming." Evie leaned back in her chair, her expression soft with understanding. "My grandmother used to quote a Bible verse when things felt too big. 'My grace is sufficient for thee: for my strength is made perfect in weakness.'"

Darcy lifted her eyes, blinking back tears she refused to let fall. "Meaning?"

"Meaning that God can do amazing things when we stop pretending we're strong." Evie's smile was gentle, sad. "When we finally admit we're not."

The words settled over Darcy like a blanket—not comforting, exactly, but somehow grounding. She held her mug a little tighter, feeling the warmth seep through the ceramic into her palms. She already knew she wasn't strong. Not really. She might seem strong to others, might have built her life around being the one who held everything together, but inside she was exactly what Evie had said. She was grief in disguise, held together by the desperate hope that if she just kept moving, kept functioning, the cracks wouldn't show.

Maybe Evie was right. Darcy believed in God . . . but did she believe God would truly be enough for her? Would he be strong enough, big enough, caring enough? Could he carry her through loving Sam, knowing what was coming? She might have a better idea of what lay ahead for Sam than he did. Could God help her choose love over fear?

She didn't know. She just didn't know.

Seventeen

Annie stepped out of the fire station and tugged her bonnet strings tighter beneath her chin as the breeze caught the hem of her apron. The air still carried the bite of winter, that sharp in-between season that couldn't make up its mind. Gus stood waiting by the buggy, shoulders hunched against the wind, hands buried in his coat pockets. He looked up when she came, barely offering a smile that didn't reach his eyes. Those beautiful blue eyes of his—they'd lost their twinkle.

"Sorry to keep you waiting," she said. "The dispatcher who covers the next shift was running late."

He nodded, silent as he helped her up into the buggy. Once they were seated and the horse started off, she thought he might ask her about her day, like he usually did. But he remained quiet. The usual ease between them had stretched thin lately, like thread worn smooth. Annie tried to stitch it back together with small talk—mentioning the rain due in that afternoon, the blossoms spilling over the trees above—but Gus only gave the barest nod, his gaze fixed on the road ahead.

Finally, she looked at him. "So have you decided yet?" she said in a gentle voice. "About talking to Sam?"

"I've decided." Gus didn't even look at her. "And the answer is no."

She waited.

"There's nothing to say."

She couldn't disagree more. There was so much to be said. And Sam, at least, was willing to start the conversation.

"Your silence is loud, Annie. I know you disagree, but my mind is made up. Sam Mustang or Sam Smucker or whoever he is, walked away from me twenty-five years ago."

"Sam might not have been with you each day, Gus, but he's still part of you," Annie said, her voice low but sure. "You look like him. You laugh like him. You even walk like him. Did it occur to you that Sam might be why you've always loved stargazing?"

He flinched, just barely. "My DNA," he said, with a bitter edge.

"Possibly." She turned toward him. "So you're not going to see him. Just pretend he doesn't exist?"

"I can't really do that, can I?" His hands tightened on the reins. "My parents have lied to me for twenty-five years." He snapped the reins with a jerk, causing the horse to lurch forward. "Sorry."

They fell into silence again, the clip of hooves marking time. Annie watched Gus's profile, sharp against the slanting afternoon light. He looked so angry. So hardened. Nothing like the Gus she knew.

"This whole thing," Gus said, his voice low now, like it hurt to talk, "has turned me upside down. Everything I ever thought about myself—what made me who I am—it all seems fake."

Annie's fingers twisted the edges of her apron. She didn't know exactly what he meant by that. Was he only talking about his family? Or was this deeper—shaking loose everything, even them? She wanted to ask, but she wasn't sure she wanted to hear the answer.

He turned down the lane that led to the Fishers' dairy farm. When he reached the house, he pulled the buggy to a stop but didn't move to get down.

Annie could see her mother's figure at the kitchen window, peering at them. "Will you come in?"

He shook his head. "I bumped into Dok earlier today and she asked if I could watch Gabe for a few hours tonight."

The day was sunny, the night would be clear. But she didn't have to ask to know he wouldn't be stargazing. "I'll join you. Give me a minute to run in the house and tell Mamm—"

Gus stopped her. "Annie, you don't need to come along. I know I'm not much fun lately."

Annie shifted on the bench to face him. "Gus," she said, soft but firm, "what is it about Gabe . . ." She trailed off, unsure how to finish. Ever since he found out about Sam Mustang, his attachment to Gabe had gone to a new level. Even the way Gus looked at little Gabe had changed—what used to be a look of fondness was replaced with this fierce, aching tenderness. Like being with the baby seemed like the only place he felt comfortable, at peace. "I'm not sure I understand why you feel such a strong burden for him."

"At first, I suppose I felt sorry for him. I wanted to help him. But that's changed." Gus looked down at his hands. "Gabe and I, we're alike. We're both the product of two teenagers—"

Annie's head snapped up. "A child isn't a product. It's God's work."

"You know what I mean. Gabe will never know how his life might have turned out if different decisions had been made."

Suddenly she understood—he'd tied his own story to Gabe's. "Gus, has your life been so very bad?"

"No. No, of course not." He ran the back of his hand down her cheek. "Don't mind me. I'm just . . . trying to sort things through." He let his hand fall to his lap, thumb worrying the seam of his pants as his gaze drifted toward the windshield. "Do you think I should see Sam?"

Well, he did ask. "I do. You have a chance to know your birth father before . . ."

"Before it's too late," Gus finished.

The finality in his tone sent a chill through her. Annie watched him a moment, her chest tight. He was looking straight ahead, not at her, not at the barn. Just somewhere far off, where she couldn't follow.

The door opened and her mother started toward them.

"Oh boy." Gus reached for the reins again. "I'm sorry, but I just can't handle your mother right now." He didn't look at her. "You go on in. I'll be fine."

Annie nodded slowly and stepped down. She stood there, watching the buggy disappear down the lane, her heart heavy.

The rain that had been threatening all day finally broke—first a scatter of sprinkles, then a steady, drumming downpour. When Sarah's aunt Faith stopped in for a few things, David sent Sarah home early. She'd walked to work and was glad for the ride; besides, David knew few customers would venture out in weather like this. A few did, though—Sally Fisher among them. She swept into the store with an air that suggested her errand might be as much about conversation as it was about the sugar, flour, and small bottle of vanilla she set on the counter.

"I was hoping Gus Troyer might be heading into town," she said, placing her groceries near the register. "I thought he could pick these up for me, but he dropped Annie at the house and took off like he was chasing a fire."

David had a fair idea where the conversation was headed—straight to Gus Troyer and Sam Mustang—so before she could draw breath, he rang up her groceries and asked, "Sally, what would you do differently if you knew you were dying?"

Her eyes went wide, the color draining from her face. "Dying?" It came out like a squeak. "What exactly did Dok say? I knew it! I just knew it. She's not telling me something."

Before he could explain, she hurried for the door with surprising speed. Through the window, he watched her march across the lot toward Dok's office, skirts swishing, bonnet strings flying. He sighed, gathered her groceries into a bag, and wondered how long it would take before Dok could convince her she was fine, just fine, and send her back to the store.

Not much later, Fern Lapp strode into the Bent N' Dent, water dripping from the edge of her black bonnet. She moved with purpose, her sneakers squeaking faintly on the linoleum.

David handed her the spools of thread he'd ordered. "Fern, if you knew you were dying, what would you do differently?"

She didn't miss a beat. "I'd better finish that quilt before the Lord calls me home," she said, already halfway to the door.

The bell jingled as she left, and David stood there, watching the rain trail behind her like a second thought. A very different response than Sally Fisher's.

Dok sat cross-legged on the floor, a cushion tucked beneath her, as she read aloud from a picture book about barnyard animals. Gabe sat propped up against pillows in front of her, his head a little wobbly. Was it wobbling more than yesterday? She thought maybe so. "'. . . and the pig said oink, oink,'" she finished, tapping the page with her finger.

Gabe didn't respond, but she thought she caught the faintest twitch at the corner of his mouth. A tiny smile. Maybe? She closed the book and leaned closer. "You're just keeping me guessing, huh?" she said, brushing his cheek with her fingertips.

She heard a knock at the door and rose to her feet—a little slower and creakier than she wished. She bent down and picked up Gabe. That, too, took a little more effort than she expected.

Goodness, she was feeling her age lately. She'd turned sixty a few months ago and, ever since, seemed to be aware she'd turned a page. Or maybe a chapter? Matt would say age was just a number . . . but the numbers were starting to add up.

The door opened and Gus stepped inside with a gust of wind. "Hi, Dok. Hey there, buddy," he said to Gabe, taking off his hat and shrugging off his coat.

Gabe's whole face lit up at the sound of Gus's voice. His arms waved, and he let out a squeal. Gus's grin followed, and in two strides, he was across the room, scooping the baby from Dok and into his arms. "Well, aren't you full of smiles today?" Gus said. Full of smiles might've been a stretch, but he did burrow into Gus's chest with a soft, contented sigh.

Dok stayed quiet, just watching—Gus holding the child like he was made for it, Gabe melting into him like he knew he belonged there.

No wonder Matt had said something the other day, in passing, about how it sometimes made his stomach knot up to see the way Gabe reacted to Gus. There was nothing wrong about it, he told Dok, other than feeling a little left out of the club. It just seemed there was something unique between the two of them. A thread, maybe, or a resonance. Dok thought Matt might be oversensitive, but today, she saw what he meant.

"I've got a new PT exercise I want to try today," Gus said, still gently rocking Gabe. "I've been reading up. It's a bit of cross-body movement—encourages midline awareness. I think it might make a difference."

"Seems like you're the one making the difference." Dok reached for her coat out of the hall closet. "Where's Annie? I thought she'd be with you tonight."

"I dropped her off at home," he said, not quite meeting her eyes. "I just haven't been good company lately. Too bothered about . . . all the hoopla."

Dok raised an eyebrow as she slipped her arms through her

coat. "Finding out you have a different father than the one you thought isn't just hoopla, Gus. It's a big deal."

He nodded slowly, his expression sobering. Gabe's fingers curled around the fabric of his shirt. "Gabe and I—we both have a lot of unknowns."

Dok buttoned up her coat and turned toward him. "Not really," she said. "You've got a family who loves you and always wanted you. You have Annie. And you have a birth father who showed a lot of courage."

Gus let out a short scoff. "He abandoned my mother."

Dok tilted her head. "Can you remember what it was like to be fifteen? Sixteen? Because I can. I felt like I couldn't breathe. Like I was getting smothered in expectations. The only choice I could see was to get out. I ran away too."

Gus looked over at her, surprised.

"And I have to tell you—coming back is much harder than running away."

Gus's mouth tugged slightly, uncertain. His arms tightened around Gabe, the gentle rocking slowing.

"I'm not saying Sam Mustang did the right thing. He didn't. But he's trying to make things right now."

"We're alike, Gabe and me. We're the same. We both have fathers who bailed on us."

Dok took a moment to respond. "Yes, in a way, you are alike. You both had teenaged fathers who knew they couldn't give their child the life they deserved."

Gus didn't answer.

"If there's one piece of advice I could give you, Gus, it's that being angry might feel good for a while. But don't let it keep you from seeing what's right in front of you."

He shifted his stance, weight settling back on one heel, gaze dropping to adjust the blanket at Gabe's shoulder.

Dok sensed Gus was offended by her unasked-for advice. If her words landed harder than he liked, she didn't mind. It's the advice she wished she'd been given at a time in her life when she felt lost, untethered to the Amish world she had known.

She picked up her medical bag from the hall bench and grabbed an umbrella from the coat-tree. Quietly, she opened the door and left.

David heard the voice before he saw the face—familiar, bright, unmistakably Jimmy Fisher. He bolted from his chair in the back office and stepped into the store. "Jimmy Fisher, is that you?"

There the young man was, standing by the soda shelf, grinning like he always did. One of David's favorites. They shook hands, both smiling wide.

"What brings you back to Stoney Ridge?" David asked. "Are you here to stay?" He hoped so.

"No. Just for the weekend. Big birthday for my mother."

David didn't ask which big birthday. He knew better. Edith Fisher Lapp was not a woman who welcomed commentary on her age. She was sharp, proud, and not easily amused. Her son, on the other hand, was all warmth and charm—easy to talk to, quick to laugh. They couldn't be more different.

"Well, it's good to see you," David said. "How's everything going?"

Jimmy leaned against the shelf, casual as ever. "You mean at the hillbilly church?"

David fought back a smile. Jimmy had followed Sylvie King to her church in Big Valley, a far more conservative Amish community than Stoney Ridge. "I meant everything."

Jimmy laughed. "Not so bad at all. I miss indoor plumbing, but the people make up for it. Good folks. Strong community."

David nodded. He'd noticed that too, over the years. The more conservative churches tended to be tighter knit. More isolated, yes—but that seemed to deepen the way they leaned on one another. There was something admirable in that.

The store was empty, so David persuaded Jimmy to sit in the rockers for a catch-up visit. He heard about Sylvie, and her little boy, and all the horses Jimmy trained. Horses were Jimmy's lifelong love.

When the clock struck four o'clock, Jimmy bolted out of the rocker. "I'd better get going. Lots to do for Mamm's birthday party." He strode to the soda aisle, plucked four bottles from the shelf, and set them on the counter. "You and Birdy will be there, right?"

David kept his gaze on the register keys. "No, actually, we won't."

Jimmy's head tipped, his voice dropping to a murmur. "Oh. That's right. The pie plate."

That pie plate! Sally Fisher had brought it back to Edith with a chip in the rim, and Edith had been in here not long after, recounting the whole sorry tale to Sarah Blank in a voice pitched just loud enough for half the store to hear. No apology from Sally, Edith had said. In fact, she insisted that the chip was already there when she had borrowed it.

At this point, David had come from his office to cut in. "Edith, a friendship is worth more than any dish." He'd meant it too. But Edith had bristled, gathered her purchases in a muslin bag, and left in a huff—a scene they'd played out more than once.

As if Jimmy was listening to the replay going on in David's mind, he said, "It *was* Mamm's grandmother's pie plate."

David looked up. *Oh*. That shed a different light on the topic. He felt a prick in his stomach, where his ulcer lay dormant. It had a way of reminding him of his shortsightedness.

Time to change the subject. As David put the soda bottles into a box for easy handling, he said, "Jimmy, if you knew you were dying, what would you do differently?"

Jimmy froze. His mouth opened, then shut. Then opened.

"Boy oh boy." He blew out a puff of air. "You sure know how to hit a man where it counts."

"I just wondered—"

"I get it." He raised his hands in mock surrender. "You don't have to say another word."

David tipped his head. What had he said?

"I know exactly what you're thinking."

What? Because David didn't know.

"Stop waiting for the right moment. Or maybe it's not so much waiting for the right moment as stop waiting for my mother to approve, because she never will." Jimmy shook his head, half amused, half resigned. "It's high time I asked Sylvie to marry me." He blew out a puff of air. "I came in for soda pop and I'm walking out with a heavy burden that the bishop laid on me."

David smiled, but Jimmy didn't quite return it. "I think I'll wait to tell Mamm *after* her birthday party." He grabbed the box of soda bottles and headed for the door, noticeably less lighthearted than when he'd walked in.

Should David have left well enough alone? He hadn't meant to push Jimmy toward the altar or send Sally Fisher off in a panic to Dok's.

But he had to admit—Jimmy was particularly skilled at sidestepping matrimony. A great waffler. So perhaps the question was worth asking after all.

An hour or so later, David looked up from the ledger when Dok stepped into his cramped office at the Bent N' Dent. She didn't bother with a greeting, just dropped into the chair across from him.

"Brother or bishop?" he asked, half wary, half amused.

"Bishop, I think." Her eyes narrowed. "Why did you tell Sally Fisher she was dying?"

He cringed. "I didn't! I asked Sally the same thing I've been asking a lot of folks lately—what would you change if you knew you were dying?"

Dok leaned back, studying him as if she might try the question on herself. The silence stretched before she said, "Funny you should ask. Lately, I've been thinking about how quickly my life is passing. When you've lived more years than you've got left, you start thinking differently about life. There's just something about turning sixty. Some days I feel like I'm watching sand pour through an hourglass—running out of time for the things I thought I'd do . . . the things I still want to do." She rose, smoothing her white coat. "It's a good question for everyone to ponder, David. A very good question."

At the door, she stopped and turned. "And may I remind you, dear brother, we're not so far apart in age. Sixty is staring you in the face."

David swallowed hard, the truth of it landing heavier than he cared to admit.

Eighteen

Annie had never seen or heard anything like it in church. The bishop's sermon had been thoughtful, wise, like always. But then, at the very end, he paused. His voice lowered, and he turned in a slow circle to face both sides of the benches as he said, "What would you do differently if you knew you were dying? Perhaps it's an attitude we should all consider—to live like you're dying." That was all. No explanation. No elaboration.

And yet, the words seemed to echo through the barn like a bell. Annie glanced around. No one moved. No one coughed or shifted in their seat. The entire church had stilled. Men on one side, women on the other. Even the children, who usually fidgeted and whispered after more than three hours on a backless bench, sat frozen.

Normally, after the sermons, the ministers would add some affirmations or corrections or expand on a topic. Not this time. They seemed just as struck by the bishop's words as the church members. Even the swallows in the rafters above had gone quiet, as if the words had reached them somehow. It was as if something sacred had been spoken—something too large to grasp, but impossible to ignore.

After the service, the benches were quickly converted into tables for the fellowship meal. But the usual buzz of chatter was missing. Quiet side conversations here and there, but little laughter, little lightness.

After the women served the men, they took their turn to eat. Annie sat beside Sarah Blank, who usually had plenty to say about everything, from who she saw going into Dok's office and why, to who might be courting whom. But today, even Sarah Blank was quiet. She stirred her bean soup slowly, eyes distant.

Across the barn, Annie saw the bishop sitting with his ministers. He wasn't speaking either. Just watching. Not solemn, exactly—but thoughtful. Like a man who had dropped a stone into a deep well and was waiting to hear the echo.

"Live like you're dying."

The words kept circling in Annie's mind. She knew the bishop had Sam Mustang in mind—how could he not? Poor Gus was still reeling from finding out the news that Sam was his father. Annie could almost hear what he'd say if David asked him straight out—what would you do differently if you knew you were dying? Gus would say something clipped, maybe a shrug, just enough to shut the door on the whole thing. That was what made her heart ache. Sam was dying, and Gus acted like it didn't matter. Maybe it was shock. Maybe it was easier for him not to care. On Friday, during their ride to work in the morning, Annie had tried to remind Gus that a man's last days were worth something, no matter the wrongs behind him. The Lord's mercy could reach even into the darkest corners, right up to the final breath. But Gus had no interest in hearing her defend Sam Mustang.

With the back of a spoon, she smoothed peanut butter marshmallow spread over a slice of bread—a familiar motion she'd repeated hundreds of times at the Sunday fellowship meal.

It was the same as always, yet today the simple act felt different, as if the air itself had shifted. Only a month or so ago, she'd been quietly hoping Gus might ask her to marry him. Now everything was turned upside down, and she couldn't see how—or if—they'd ever set it right again.

Darcy dipped her brush into cobalt blue, the bristles whispering against the paint, and eased the curve along Neptune's orbit. For the past week, she'd been here most evenings in the garden-level waiting room of Dok's office—sleeves pushed up, music off, letting the quiet keep her company.

It had started as a simple idea: the solar system, bright and bold for the kids who came in for checkups, stitches, or a lollipop from Dok or Charlie. The garden level, to Darcy, was a sterile, cold-looking basement, and Darcy thought a mural would warm things up. Dok gave her the go-ahead so she started right in on it. Somewhere between Mercury and Saturn, it had shifted. It wasn't just a mural anymore. It was . . . something of herself she could leave behind. Because she knew her time in Stoney Ridge was almost up.

She stepped down from the stool, brush still in hand, and took it in. Planets floated in a deep indigo sky, their orbits curling like ribbons. Stars were scattered everywhere—tiny pinpricks of white. "The stronger the telescope," Sam had once said, "the more stars there are to count."

Off to the left, she had painted a "loner star." Sam's star. Small. Almost swallowed by the dark.

Her chest tightened. She could still hear his voice from that night in the hospital—low, tired—telling her he had ALS. She hadn't seen him since. No calls. No texts. Just silence.

Her mind drifted to something Evie had said: A fork in the road isn't really about circumstances. It's about God—what you believe to be true about him.

Those words had been circling her ever since, like a song she couldn't quite place.

Darcy pressed the brush against the rim of the jar, watching the bristles bend. The mural was good—better than she'd hoped—but it still felt like something was missing.

She looked at the night sky she'd painted. Vast. Bigger than her fears, her questions, her not-knowing. The scale of it pressed in, but instead of crushing her, it loosened something. If God could make all of that—every spinning planet, every burning star, every galaxy flung into the dark, billions of them—if he could hold the universe in place, maybe he could hold her together too. Whatever came.

It wasn't an answer. It wasn't a plan. But it was a shift. A quiet peace.

Without thinking, she dipped her brush again, climbed back onto the stool, and added another star beside the lone one—close enough that their light seemed to touch.

A binary star.

She glanced at the clock. Half past eight. If she hurried, she might still make it. She sealed the paint can, wrapped the brush, grabbed her keys, switched off the lights, and slipped out into the night.

Forty minutes later, Darcy heard Sam's truck before she saw it—the now familiar rumble of the engine. She'd been leaning against her car at the Wonder Pond trailhead, waiting, watching the road like some lovesick teenager. Which, apparently, she was. At thirty-two.

The headlights swept across the gravel pull-off as he parked beside her car, and she watched him through the windshield for a moment before he cut the engine. He climbed out slowly, then went around to the passenger side to unbuckle the case of his telescope. Even in the darkness, she could see the careful way he moved, like someone who sensed his body wasn't entirely trustworthy anymore.

"Darcy, what are you doing here?" he said as he walked toward her.

"Waiting for you." She pushed off from the hood of her car. "So Mustang is the name you chose for yourself?"

"When I was sixteen, all I could think about was buying a Ford Mustang."

A laugh burst out of Darcy. "Not the horse? You chose a car name for yourself?"

"I told you. I was a stupid kid."

Just a boy, really. "Did you ever get one? A Ford Mustang?"

"I did. Used. Over three hundred thousand miles on it. Got me through grad school and then it gave up the ghost."

Darcy's smile faded. "We haven't talked or texted since that night at the hospital."

Sam set the telescope case down carefully, like he was buying time. When he looked at her, his expression was gentle but tired. "Darcy . . . I want you to forget about me."

"Forget about you," she repeated in a flat voice. *Like that's possible.*

"You know what's ahead for me. You know it because of your brother." He shoved his hands in his pockets. "You have a life to live. Go live it, Darcy. For your brother . . . and for me."

The words hit like a slap, but she didn't flinch. "You think I'm going to run."

He scoffed. "I hope you're smart enough to run."

She stared at him for a long moment, this stubborn, infuriating man who thought he could make her decisions for her. "The problem is . . . those binary stars."

"Darcy—"

"That first night, you showed them to me. Do you remember?" She took a step closer. "Albireo. The golden one and the blue one. You said they were meant for each other."

Sam's jaw tightened. "Stars don't have feelings."

"Don't they?" She could see him wavering, the careful distance he'd built starting to crack. "You said they were born together. That they'll die together. That they can't exist without each other."

"That's called gravity."

"Exactly."

He ran a hand through his hair, a gesture she'd seen him make a hundred times when he was thinking too hard. "Remember Finland? Take that traveling nurse contract. See those northern lights. It's the happiest country on earth."

"It won't be . . . not without you."

The words hung between them like a bridge she'd just burned. Sam's face went through about six different expressions before settling on something that looked like pain.

"I'm not going to get better," he said quietly. "This isn't a movie where love conquers all. It's going to be ugly and hard and . . . a ventilator . . . and well, you know."

"I know." She reached for his hand, and after a moment's hesitation, he let her take it. He had such beautiful hands. Long, tapered fingers. "I think I would rather have whatever time we get than spend the rest of my life wondering what if." She squeezed his fingers.

"Why?"

"Something my friend Evie told me. She said that faith isn't about knowing what's going to happen. It's about stepping into the unknown anyway."

Sam searched her face like he was looking for cracks, for some sign that she didn't mean it. "I don't want to be the one who breaks your heart."

"Those binary stars," she said in a whisper. "They're not just bound by gravity. They're bound by choice. Every day, they choose each other. Sam Mustang, every day, for as long as we have left, I choose you."

He made a sound that might have been a laugh or a cry or

might have been something else entirely. His hands cupped her face like she was something precious, something he'd been afraid to want. Then he was kissing her, and she could taste the salt of tears—his or hers, she couldn't tell. Both, she decided.

Nineteen

The barn was silent. The kind of silence that settled deep, like snow falling. David could sense it was a quiet full of reverence. The men sat with hands folded on their laps or resting on their knees, most of them still. The women on the other side were the same—some with heads bowed, some with eyes fixed on the barn rafters. Children had been sent out to play after the lengthy church service—longer than usual, as the ministers had presented their views on the Attnung. Now was the time when faults must be confessed, and differences settled, before each member would be asked if he or she was ready for communion. David sat in the stillness, savoring this time of honesty and vulnerability, a time for repentance.

Sam Mustang had just spoken his piece. Stiff and stoic, Sam had named his sin plainly, acknowledging the pain he'd caused to others, to Mary, to Marcus, but especially to his son.

Then it was Mary's turn. She rose from the sinner's bench and walked in the silence to kneel between the benches that separated the women from the men. Tears streaming down her face, her voice had carried clear and steady as she echoed Sam's regret. "I am truly sorry," she said, "and I humbly ask for God's forgiveness."

As soon as Mary sat down again, David noticed that Gus Troyer, who'd been sitting in the far back corner of the men's side, rose quietly and left the barn. From where David sat, he could see Annie Fisher's eyes follow him out, a concerned look on her face.

When the barn door closed, David stood. He hadn't planned to say anything, but something inside him told him this wasn't a moment to let pass. For the sake of the church, for the sake of himself. He knelt between the benches. "Like Sam," he began, his voice steady but low, "I've wanted to run away at times. Many times. And I can't blame the longing to escape on being a frightened, overwhelmed sixteen-year-old boy. Because I'm nearing sixty and I still have moments when I want to run away from my responsibilities." Chin tucked, he paused a moment before landing on the heart of his confession. "Mostly, because of the burden I carry of being a bishop," David said. "Just last week . . . I was told I was the poorest excuse for a bishop they'd ever known. Said the church hadn't been the same since the last one."

David knew full well the previous bishop to Stoney Ridge had made some terrible decisions that damaged more than just church order. But even so, the criticism leveled at him had struck hard and stayed put. "I felt hurt. Offended. And once again I felt the temptation to run."

He kept his eyes fixed on a knot in the worn barn floor in front of him. It would have been easy for his gaze to slide to the right, to where Edith Lapp sat in the front row of the women's benches. But he resisted the temptation.

"So I confess my pride," he said quietly. "And my offense toward this individual. I am truly sorry and I humbly ask for God's forgiveness." Then he rose and went to the bench to sit down next to the other ministers.

The silence returned—but now it had a different feel. Expectant. Unfinished.

David let it sit.

From the women's side, his wife Birdy rose and came to the center. Her round face had a sheepish look. She knelt. "At our last comfort quilt, I brought a pie made by Fern Lapp. She wasn't able to come and had asked me to bring it for her. Everyone loved it so much that, instead of telling them that it was Fern's, I let them think I had made it. I don't know why I did it, other than pride. Fern's baking is legendary. And mine . . . always seems to be lacking. I am . . . truly sorry and I humbly ask God's forgiveness." She got up and returned to her seat on the bench quickly, cheeks bright pink.

Fern stood not half a minute later and walked to the center. David helped her kneel. "I knew Birdy claimed my lemon meringue pie as hers," she said. "And I have to admit that I've been nursing a little grudge toward her for it. So I confess that grudge. And I humbly ask the Lord's forgiveness." She put a hand out for David to help her up, then changed her mind. "And maybe I can get a bit prideful about my good cooking. I confess that, too, and humbly ask the Lord's forgiveness."

A few chuckles bubbled up on the women's side. Then silence again, until one by one, others rose from their seats to make their way to the center. One who'd agreed to split costs with a neighbor to build a fence but never paid up. Another who sold a horse to a friend and lied about its age. A married farmer who admitted he had gone to the library and used the computer to search out something that was not . . . defendable.

David wondered what that meant.

A young mother stood and walked forward to kneel. She had visited a non-Amish cousin recently and spent the entire night watching television. "One show right after the other," she said. "All night long. I couldn't stop myself." She choked up. "And they were not entirely . . . edifying programs."

Hank Lapp got to his feet and made his way to the center to

kneel. "I MIGHT take a NIP of my Englisch neighbor's homebrewed beer now and then."

"Now and then?" Edith Lapp whispered loud enough for Hank to hear. "More like now and again."

Hank scowled at his wife before tucking his head to ask the Lord's forgiveness, and then he sat down.

One of the sisters from the Sisters' House rose slowly to her feet, steadying herself with a cane. At her age, no one expected her to come all the way to the center, let alone kneel. But she did. Her voice was soft, almost fragile. "Once," she said, "I stole a dollar from my mother's purse to buy candy at the store."

David guessed that little transgression had happened half a century ago—maybe more. Still, it weighed on her. The guilt hadn't faded with time. And as he watched her, he reminded himself: God isn't bound by years or calendars. He's outside of time. What's old to us might still be fresh to him.

Bill Lapp came forward to kneel. "I suppose," he said, cutting his eyes toward Johnny King, "we could split the difference between where the creek used to be and where it is now."

From his seat, Johnny King nodded. "I suppose we could."

David felt tears prick his eyes. When he had proposed such a solution to the men, they had flatly rejected it. Only God could've softened those hearts.

Then Sarah Blank stood, near the back, came forward, and knelt. "A few weeks ago," she said, her voice a little shaky, "I went to the Bent N' Dent early when my dentist appointment was canceled. I noticed that the door to David's office was ajar—the lock on that door is just useless—so I came in that way to close it behind me. I heard voices coming from the store. The bishop and Mary and Sam were talking." She twisted her hands together. "I should've just gone back out again . . . The bishop's always telling me to turn away from temptation. I shouldn't have listened to their conversation, but I did. And then I left through the back door. A few minutes later I saw Sally

Fisher heading to the post office, and—well, I knew she'd want to know all about Gus Troyer because of her Annie . . . and the rest happened from there." She fiddled with the strings from her prayer cap. "So I need to humbly ask God's forgiveness for passing along news that might have been private"—she waved her hand in Mary's direction—"even though it was entirely true." She rose and returned to her seat.

So. Sarah Blank had been the one who had spread that tale. David should've known. If he'd been a little more wary, he would've called the dentist office to confirm that Sarah had been there when she said she'd been. He'd even noticed that she continued to rub her jaw, like the tooth was still bothering her. He wasn't sure whom he felt more disappointed in—Sarah or himself. He *should've* known.

All heads turned as Sally Fisher rose and came forward to kneel. "After I saw Sarah out in front of the post office, I went to the Sweet Tooth Bakery to get their day-old cinnamon rolls before they were gone, and it seemed like the whole church was waiting in line. I tried to keep the news to myself but it just spilled out. So I ended up telling, let's see, Molly, Lydia, Elizabeth, Kate . . . " She ticked off names on her fingers. "Let me see . . . who else?" She named more. A few more hands lifted in resignation.

David waited to see if there might be any others who felt the need to bring something to light. After a long pause, Hank Lapp leaned forward on the men's bench, stage-whispering, "Eddy, don't YOU have SOMETHING you want to say?"

From over on the women's side, Edith scowled at him. Slowly, reluctantly, she rose and slowly knelt, folding her hands neatly in front of her. "I suppose the bishop might be right about something. A friendship is worth more than a dish. Sally Fisher, I forgive you for putting a chip in my grandmother's pie plate."

Sally's head snapped up, eyes narrowing like she wanted to defend herself. *That chip was already there!* was practically written across her face. But then David saw the fight drain just a notch, her expression softening. He had a hunch what thoughts were running through Sally's head: Maybe she wasn't entirely sure about that chip after all. And maybe it would be wise to accept the forgiveness that Edith offered to her.

As Edith started to rise, Hank called out, "ANYTHING ELSE, Eddy?"

She frowned at him and settled back on her knees. "I didn't say David was 'the *poorest* excuse for a bishop,'" she said, chin up. "I said 'a *poor* excuse.' There's a difference."

David lifted his eyes and met hers. Really? he thought. Not much of one.

"But I confess that I said it. I shouldn't have said it out loud. I let frustration for his liberal and progressive ways get the better of me, and I humbly ask God's forgiveness for that."

Somehow, David felt Edith had gotten another swipe at him, but he refused to let it get to him. Birdy caught his eye from across the barn and raised her eyebrows slightly, a little smile on her lips. He knew exactly what was running through her mind: "If it be possible, as much as lieth in you, live peaceably with all men." This was as much peace, Birdy would say, as he could expect in a relationship with Edith Lapp.

Edith sat down, and a gentle hush returned. David waited in the silence to be sure there were no more confessions. There weren't, and there didn't need to be. Something in the air had changed. It felt as if someone had thrown open the windows and cleared out all the old stale air, letting in a rush of spring. As if something new had come in its place.

Later, as the benches were turned into tables for the fellowship meal, David's gaze moved through the barn slowly, noting the easy laughter, the smiles exchanged over ladles of hot soup and plates of bread and pickled beets and peanut butter spread. There was a lightness and joy accompanying this humble meal that he hadn't seen in the church for a while.

Yes, he thought. This is what preparing for communion should bring to a church, to each soul. No longer hiding behind sins, not trying to keep things tidy and acceptable. But confession. Repentance. Forgiveness.

Today, God's renewing spirit had lavishly filled their little church.

It was quiet along the creek that Sunday afternoon, the kind of hush that made every bird call seem louder than it was, every branch snap like a firecracker. Annie walked beside Gus, her boots soft in the leaf litter, her hands folded in front of her apron. He'd shown up at the house late in the afternoon with that hollow look in his eyes again, asking if she would take a walk with him, that he wanted to talk to her. She'd said yes, of course she had. But now that they were out here, far away from her mother's listening ears, he still hadn't said a word.

They passed the bend where the sycamores leaned toward the water, their roots gnarled like old fingers. The wind shifted, lifting Annie's cap strings slightly. Still, Gus said nothing.

Finally, she cleared her throat. "I saw you at church. I saw that you left after your mother's confession."

"I heard what I needed to hear," he said, barely above the creek's murmur. He kept walking. "Did they stay?"

His parents, he meant. All of them. "Your mother and father stayed, but Sam left. Darcy was waiting for him outside." Annie stopped walking. "I wish you would've stayed. You didn't get to hear the rest, how others started to admit their flaws and faults. One after the other. On and on and on. It was rather remarkable. I've never seen anything like it. You should've stayed."

Stopping, Gus turned, brow furrowed. "Why? What difference would it make?"

She met his eyes, steady. "Because it would remind you that everyone fails. That no one is beyond temptation. We're all so close"—she nearly pinched two fingers—"to doing something stupid or selfish . . . or something that causes harm to another."

His jaw tightened, and he looked away. "Annie, you make it sound easy, like I should just move on. But you can't possibly understand what it feels like to know you've lived your entire life with a lie."

"No," she said softly. "I can't. I'm not in your shoes. But from where I'm standing . . ." Her voice caught, and she made herself go on. "From where I'm standing, you have far more to be thankful for than you have reason to wallow."

"Wallow." He turned sharply toward her, shoulders stiffening. "You think I'm wallowing?"

"I do. I think you're angry. And hurt. And I don't blame you. But, Gus—why can't you see any of this as a blessing?"

He scoffed. "A blessing?"

"Yes," she said. "Can't you see that God might be doing something important in your life? That maybe bringing Sam into it now—at this time—isn't a curse, but part of something bigger? If not for you, for him. For heaven's sake, Gus, the man is *dying*."

Gus didn't answer. He just stared at the creek like it held the answers, his face tight with a kind of sorrow that had no words.

The breeze blew between them, and for a moment all Annie could hear was the rush of water and the caw of a distant crow. "No one was ever trying to hurt you," she said. "They were trying to protect you. Your mother, your father, and Sam Mustang too. Deep down, you must know that."

"Protect me?" Gus let out a dry, bitter laugh. "Everything I've ever known about myself . . . it's built on a lie. I became an EMT because it was the only way I could keep studying and still stay in the church. It was the only path the man I *thought* was my father would approve of. I shaped my whole future around that—around what I thought was the straight and narrow."

He shook his head, scoffing. "And now I find out my real

father isn't even Amish. He works at NASA, Annie. *NASA*. He studies stars for a living. Do you know how much I would've loved that? College. Grad school. A career like Sam Mustang's. That life was *in me* all along, and I never even knew."

And just like that, it was out. Raw and unfiltered. Annie felt like someone had thrown a bucket of cold water over her. If she'd been holding onto any hope, it slipped through her fingers in that moment. Gus—who had always been so grounded, so certain—was unraveling. And she knew what it meant. If he left the church as a baptized member, he'd be placed under the Bann. She would lose him.

Her voice trembled as she spoke. "I care about you so much. You know I do. But this . . . this is something you need to work through on your own."

His eyes snapped to hers, startled, but she didn't let him speak.

"I think it's best if we stop seeing each other."

She turned before her resolve could falter. She didn't run. Her steps were steady, her head held high. But the tears came anyway, slipping down her cheeks in silence.

Behind her, she heard nothing. No footsteps. No call of her name. Just the wind through the trees and the faint sound of water running in a nearby creek. By the time she reached the house, the sun was dipping low behind the barn, casting long shadows across the porch. She didn't look back. Didn't need to.

She already knew he hadn't followed.

On Monday morning, David had shown up early at the Bent N' Dent, the sky still smudged with sleep, ready for the week's first shipment. He greeted the truck driver with a steaming cup of coffee and a warm "Glad you made it," and just like that, the week was off and running.

As David watched the truck drive off, his thoughts drifted

to the Council Meeting service the day before. The image of so many taking a turn to kneel before the church, before the Lord—shoulders bowed, hearts cracked open—still stirred something deep in him. He was grateful, overwhelmed even, by the movement of God's Spirit in that room. It had felt sacred, like heaven had leaned in close.

And yet, beneath the gratitude, a quiet unease lingered in him. Something about the day felt incomplete, like a thread had been left dangling. He couldn't name it, couldn't put words to it, but it tugged at him all the same.

Setting that uncomfortable feeling aside, he focused his attention on the task of unpacking the boxes that the driver had dropped off. He'd emptied the contents of two boxes and was stocking a shelf with cans, trying to make dented cream of mushroom soup look appealing, when the bell over the door jingled. Sarah stepped into the store, cheeks pink from the cold.

"Morning," he said. "I made some coffee. I didn't expect you to be here so early. The sun's barely lighting the sky."

"I knew the shipment was coming," Sarah said, hanging her bonnet and coat on a wall peg near the cash register. "Figured you'd need the help." She grabbed a box cutter from the counter and started slicing open a case of cereal. For a while, the only sound was cardboard ripping and one box after the other, placed on a shelf.

David liked this rhythm. Quiet but useful.

Then, just as he was stacking the last six-pack of cans, Sarah came up his aisle. "I am truly sorry."

David picked up the empty box. "I know you are. And I appreciate you saying it."

She nodded quickly, like she wanted to move on, but David wasn't about to leave it hanging like that. "But I do hope you're feeling more than just remorse."

She blinked, caught off guard. "What do you mean?"

"It's one thing to feel bad. It's another to recognize the pattern." He started arranging jars of applesauce. "You've got a nice way with people, Sarah. You're friendly, warm. Folks like talking to you. But you tend to use your connections from the store to spread gossip."

"*Not* gossip." Her mouth pulled tight. "I like to pray for people. And I know other people like to pray. That's why I share information. It's not gossip if it's true and meant for prayer."

David stopped. "I don't accept that."

She stiffened, clearly surprised.

"You don't ask anyone's permission to share those stories," he said. "Most of the time, you're eavesdropping while people shop. Then you pass it along like it's your news to tell. That's not the same thing as sharing a prayer request."

"But people do pray," she said defensively. "Doesn't that count for something?"

"When you share news you overhear, you don't know the whole story. You're only eavesdropping on one side of it."

Sarah busied herself with straightening a row of cereal boxes that were already straight. David let the silence settle for a bit. *Let it do some of the work.* He went to the back room with the empty boxes and brought back a box of spaghetti sauce.

As he set it down, she picked up the conversation. "I didn't expect to blurt it out like that yesterday in church. But after hearing you and Birdy and Fern and Bill Lapp and the others . . . admitting how you felt or what you did . . . something just came over me."

"Conviction," he said, going back to his jars of spaghetti sauce. "It doesn't always knock politely."

They worked side by side for a few minutes more. The shelves slowly filled, the store warming up a bit from the morning sun slanting through the front windows.

After a while, Sarah spoke again, this time softer. "I don't mean harm."

"I know that," David said, without looking over. "But good intentions don't mean you're not causing harm."

"I guess I've always felt useful when I had news to share."

David turned to face her. "The best way to be useful is to keep a confidence. Carry burdens in silence. Pray for those people whose stories you might hear. That's how a person can be most used by God."

Sarah blinked, then gave a slow nod. "I'll try."

"Good. That's all anyone can do." He put a hand on her shoulder. "Sarah, you made a public confession. The sin's been named and forgiven. We don't have to keep talking about it."

"Really?" She gave a small laugh, mostly at herself.

David smiled faintly. "Really. You said what needed saying. And now you get to walk forward."

They didn't say much else for the next little while, just the two of them tending the aisles. The store smelled faintly of spices and cardboard, and outside, the world went on as usual—horses clopping down the road, cars arriving at Dok's nearby office.

Inside, the quiet felt like grace.

Twenty

The morning sun was just beginning to filter through the slatted blinds in Dok's office when she walked in with a steaming mug of coffee and sat down in her chair. Monday mornings were her favorites. The week felt full of promise.

"Got a minute?" Charlie said, poking his head around the threshold.

"No patients here yet?" Dok asked, setting her mug down.

"Not for another ten minutes," Charlie said. "I wanted to run something by you before the day gets away from us." He sat down in the chair across from her. "A new patient came in last Thursday afternoon—middle-aged, normally healthy, but she's been having headaches, fatigue, joint pain."

"Fever?"

"Low grade, off and on. She said she thought it was just the flu, but it's lasted three weeks." Charlie sat back and crossed his arms. "She's complaining of this weird combo of symptoms—some muscle weakness, fatigue, brain fog."

"What kind of brain fog?"

"She said her handwriting's been sloppy. Her husband noticed she's mispronouncing words now and then. And then she couldn't remember her neighbor's name at the post office, which really freaked her out. That's why she came in."

"You ran labs?"

"Yep. Just got them back. Everything came back within normal ranges. Slightly elevated CRP, nothing alarming."

Dok took a sip of coffee. Brain fog might mean neurological symptoms. Her mind began flipping through diagnostic possibilities. "Did she mention if she's had a recent fall? Head injury?"

"No recent injuries. I asked."

"Any history of arthritis?"

"Nope," Charlie said. "None of the usual suspects. I thought maybe early-onset Parkinson's. MS. ALS. But it doesn't really fit."

"Has she been traveling?"

"Um . . . let's see. She did mention something about hiking." He looked up at the ceiling, trying to remember. "I think she said she'd spent a few weeks in the fall hiking along the Pacific Crest Trail in California. She went on and on about it."

Dok leaned back in her chair. "Interesting."

"What?"

"Did you notice any rash?"

Charlie scratched his chin. "I didn't see any and she didn't mention it. But her knees are swollen, and she's not sleeping well. Doesn't it seem autoimmune related?"

"Could be," Dok said. "But this kind of cluster . . . it's odd." She tapped her coffee mug with her fingertips. "Sometimes Lyme disease can bring odd symptoms. It can look like other things."

Charlie tilted his head. "Seriously? I thought Lyme disease showed up with a rash."

"Classic symptom, sure," Dok said. "But not always—especially in the later stages. Chronic Lyme can look neurological. Brain fog, memory issues, speech slowness, even limb weakness. That's why it's called the Great Imitator." She turned to her computer. "It's worth checking. Ask her to come in for more tests. I'll get the information for you."

"I'll do that right now," Charlie said.

Dok sat up straighter as a thought began to tug at the back of her mind. "Sometimes people don't even remember being bitten, especially if the tick was in the nymph stage—they're basically the size of a poppy seed."

Charlie made a face. "That just killed my love of the great outdoors." He rose and went to the door. "Thanks, Dok."

"Actually, Charlie, you showed good instincts. Something felt off and you kept looking for an answer."

He froze, then an ear-to-ear grin of pure delight came over his face. He looked so genuinely pleased—and so surprised—to be complimented that Dok felt a pang of regret. She really needed to be more affirming of Charlie. He was trying hard . . . and she was too hard on him.

Then she turned her attention to her computer screen. Her fingers flew across the keyboard. On the CDC website, she typed in: *Lyme disease symptoms*. Up popped:

- Fever
- Chills
- Headache
- Fatigue
- Muscle and joint aches
- Swollen lymph nodes
- Erythema migrans rash (bull's-eye rash)
- Sleep disturbances
- Sensitivity to light
- Difficulty concentrating

Then she typed: *Late-stage Lyme disease neurological symptoms*. Soon came a list:

- Neurological symptoms: facial palsy, memory problems, dizziness, nerve pain, shooting pains in hands and feet
- Irregular heartbeat
- Shortness of breath

She leaned her head back against the chair, the words swimming in front of her. Her mind wasn't on Charlie's middle-aged female patient anymore. She leaned back in her chair, crossing her arms.

Sam Mustang.

He was convinced nothing could be done for him. She just hadn't been so sure he was right. There had been something that struck her odd in the way he moved—stiffness, yes, but also . . . discomfort. Each time she saw him, he seemed to be favoring a different joint—rubbing a knee one time. Next time, a wrist. ALS didn't cause migratory joint pain. Sam had mentioned his headaches to her. ALS didn't cause headaches.

Darcy had told her that she'd taken Sam to the hospital after a hike to Wonder Pond, convinced he was having a heart attack. ALS didn't cause shortness of breath. Or an irregular heartbeat.

What if Sam didn't have ALS at all?

What if he had Lyme disease?

She sat up straighter, heart picking up pace. Could it really be that simple? No. Not simple, she corrected herself. But an answer. But how could it have been overlooked?

She clicked a few more articles, cross-referencing case studies, scanning treatment protocols. Early detection, antibiotics, anti-inflammatory treatment for neuro involvement. *Recommend ELISA and Western Blot testing. If positive, consider IV antibiotics and referral to infectious disease*. She read further: *But if it isn't caught early . . .*

She jumped up and ran to the door that led to the waiting room, where Darcy sat at the little reception desk. "Darcy, can you get in touch with Sam Mustang?"

Surprised, Darcy nodded.

"Ask him to get in here. As soon as possible."

Twenty-One

A few hours later, Sam Mustang sat in the chair across from Dok's desk, his arms folded tight over his chest. "So tell me again. Why am I here?"

Darcy leaned against the filing cabinet, arms crossed, trying to look calm though her stomach was twisting and turning. "Dok wants to explain. She's just finishing with a patient and then she'll be in."

"Darcy, can't you just tell me what you know?"

She frowned. "Only that she's asked me to get some tests ready for you."

"More tests?" His face scrunched up. "I've told her no more tests. Which ones? I've probably had them."

Darcy knew better than to say more. "Sam, she'll go over everything with you."

"If she thinks I've been misdiagnosed, she's wrong. I'm sure Dr. Stoltzfus is a good doctor, but I was put through all kinds of tests at Houston's medical center. I saw specialists. The best in the country. There's no way they would mess up a diagnosis."

Darcy stayed quiet for a second, then pushed away from the

cabinet and came to sit on the edge of the desk. "Maybe so, but Dok doesn't just look at test results and check boxes. She *sees* things. She pays attention to what doesn't quite fit."

He gave her a skeptical glance.

"Working with her these last few weeks . . . I can't tell you how many times I've witnessed the way she notices things that I'm convinced other doctors would miss. They're looking at symptoms. Dok looks at the individual."

The door opened and Dok walked in. "Thanks for coming in, Sam." She took her seat at the desk. "Did Darcy tell you why you're here?"

Sam looked at Darcy. "No. She was very unhelpful."

"Good." Dok grinned. "She was following my directions."

"I'll leave you two to talk," Darcy said.

"Hold up," Sam said. "I'd like her to stay, if it's all the same with you, Dr. Stoltzfus."

That surprised Darcy, and pleased her too.

"I don't mind at all. Have a seat, Darcy." Dok leaned forward and rested her forearms on her desk. "Sam, when we first met, you said that you had first noticed some symptoms after a hiking trip. As I recall, you said you'd overdone it."

He looked surprised. "Yes. Good memory."

"Is there any chance you might have hiked in an area known to have ticks that might transmit Lyme disease?"

"Lyme disease? You think that's what I have?" His face looked unconvinced.

"At this point, I just want to rule it out."

"Dr. Stoltzfus, I mean no disrespect, but if you told me you thought I had cancer or a brain tumor, I'd have an easier time believing you. I've had every test imaginable."

"So you've had the ELISA and the Western Blot test?"

Sam frowned. "They don't sound familiar, but that doesn't mean I didn't have them." He clapped his knees with his hands. "It just doesn't make sense to me." He shifted in his chair, and

Darcy could see the way his hands trembled slightly against his thighs. "If I had Lyme disease . . . I would've had a rash."

"Not necessarily," Dok said gently. "Late-stage Lyme disease can display neurological symptoms that mimic ALS. But some of your symptoms don't fit the typical ALS pattern." She leaned forward slightly, her tone becoming more clinical but still warm. "Darcy said your reflexes are still strong, even with the tremors. Your speech doesn't slur—Darcy says it just slows when you're tired. And your symptoms come in waves instead of showing steady decline. That's not typical for ALS."

Darcy watched Sam's face as Dok spoke, saw the way his jaw tightened with each word. He shot her a side-glance that spoke volumes: He was annoyed that she was feeding Dok information about his symptoms. She responded with a shrug. Dok *had* asked.

"Two tests. That's all, Sam. No promises. I just want to rule it out." Dok folded her hands together. "Would you be willing?"

The silence stretched between them like a held breath. Sam stared at his hands, at the tremor he couldn't control, and Darcy could practically see the war happening behind his eyes. The part of him that had already started grieving his own future battling against the part that couldn't help but wonder. Hope was a dangerous thing when you'd already been handed a death sentence.

"I just don't want to get disappointed," he said finally, his voice so rough it was almost a whisper. The words came out like a confession, like admitting to some terrible weakness.

"I understand," Dok said, and her voice was soft enough that it felt like a benediction.

"How long until the results come back?"

"The ELISA takes about three days. The Western Blot can take longer—up to a week—and should confirm whatever the ELISA indicates."

Sam looked down, his frown deepening. Darcy knew he was

doing the math, counting days, imagining the wait. His head lifted. "But if you're wrong . . ."

He didn't finish the sentence, but Darcy heard it anyway. *If you're wrong, I'll have to do this all over again. All that work to accept it, to make peace with it—I'll have to go back to the beginning and face it all again.*

"Then you'll know," Darcy said, leaning forward to cover his hand with hers. His skin was warm, but the tremor continued beneath her palm, a reminder of everything hanging in the balance. "But what if she's not wrong?"

Sam's eyes lifted to meet hers, and for a moment she saw past the careful resignation he'd built around himself. Underneath was something raw and desperate—a man who'd been trying so hard to accept his fate that he'd forgotten how to hope for anything else.

"What if Dok's not wrong?" Darcy repeated, softer this time. "What if this is something that can be treated? What if you get to stick around and show me more binary stars?"

The corner of his mouth twitched. He was quiet for a long moment, his gaze moving between Darcy and Dok, weighing the cost of hope against the price of certainty. Finally, he straightened in his chair and gave a single, decisive nod.

Dok reached for her prescription pad, and the soft scratch of pen on paper filled the silence—a sound, to Darcy, of possibility. Of hope.

Spring was coming—David could feel it in the soft churn of the wind and the way the light lingered longer on the fields. But the season's promise didn't reach him this morning.

He sat alone at the table, his coffee untouched, cooling in the mug Birdy had set down before she left to walk the boys to the schoolhouse. The house was quiet now, save for the ticking of the clock and the occasional creak of the floorboards settling.

Preparation Sunday had gone better than anyone dared hope. The confessions had been honest, the spirit gentle. There had been tears, yes—but also laughter. Healing.

And yet.

David stared at the mug, watching the faint swirl of cream settle into stillness. Just a few days after that remarkable service, that wonderful sense of peace had faded. He felt hollow. Not because the service had failed—but because it had worked. The Lord had done the work that David had left undone. That service had revealed just how much had been left unattended by him in the last year. How many offenses had gone unchallenged. How many misunderstandings between neighbors had gone unaddressed. How long he'd waited, hoping time would smooth things over. Hoping silence would be enough.

It wasn't. And he felt painfully aware of his shortcomings as a bishop, a leader, a shepherd of a flock.

Yesterday afternoon, Billy's mother had come to the store to tell him they were leaving Stoney Ridge. It was the briefest time they'd ever lived somewhere, she said, because she knew this was not the right place for them.

She didn't actually say they were leaving because of David's failure to solve her son Billy's problem of getting bullied at school, but he felt the accusation, all the same. And she was right about that.

David had meant to speak to the teacher weeks ago—about the teasing, the bruised feelings. But he hadn't. As a rule, he didn't like to interfere with the schoolhouse, because he had a lot of confidence in Trudy, the teacher. And he'd reassured himself that the bullying would pass as Billy settled into school and made friends. That's what he told himself, anyway. But he was noticing a recurring theme in himself—passivity had seeped its way into his ministry. Waiting. Hoping. Avoiding.

The door opened, and Birdy stepped in, her round cheeks flushed from the walk, her eyes bright. She paused when she saw him still sitting there. “You didn’t finish your coffee,” she said gently.

David looked up, tried to smile. “Got cold.”

Birdy crossed the room and sat beside him, her gaze steady. “You’ve been awfully quiet since Council Meeting.”

He hesitated. “It was a good service.”

“It was,” she said. “So why the long face?”

He ran a hand over his beard. “I just keep thinking about everything I’ve neglected,” he said. “All the things that were simmering. All the people who were hurting. I didn’t see them. Or maybe I just didn’t want to.”

“Many of those confessions . . . they were hidden from view.”

“True, many, but not all. I’m the one who’s supposed to lead and I didn’t. I let things fester.”

Birdy reached for his hand, her fingers warm and firm. “David, it’s time.”

“For a deacon.”

She nodded. “You’ve carried too much alone. The ministers are fine men, but . . .”

She didn’t need to say another word. They were fine men, hardworking farmers with large families, who helped with Sunday services but avoided anything during the week that took them away from their farmwork. And, like David, they preferred to sidestep conflict. Or maybe that’s just the way of most men. Avoiders.

Birdy stood and moved to the sink, rinsing his coffee mug. “You should let Fern know. She’ll need to hear it from you. I think she’ll have a hard time accepting it. She’s always been so sure that Luke and Izzy would return.”

He gave a quiet smile. “I’ll stop by on my way to the shop.”

Birdy turned, drying her hands on a dish towel. She leaned down and kissed him on the top of his head. “Spring’s coming, David. Let it come.”

Fifteen minutes later, David turned his mare’s reins into the long drive that led to Windmill Farm. Overhead the red windmill creaked as it turned, one blade missing, as always.

Now that he was here, he was glad he'd come, glad Birdy had encouraged him to stop by Windmill Farm. It had been too long since he'd sat with Fern Lapp. He missed her—missed the way she listened to him, the way she could see straight through a problem and lay out the solution like it had been there all the time.

He tied off the reins to the hitching post, gave his mare a pat, and hurried up the porch steps to knock on the kitchen door. Only then did he smell it—warm peanut butter mingled with chocolate, the kind of scent that made you forget whatever burden you'd brought with you.

Fern Lapp opened the door with a brisk nod, her gray hair pinned back under a gossamer prayer cap, her apron dusted with flour. She was small and quick, like a sparrow in motion.

"Come on in," she said, stepping aside. "Coffee's brewing. Cookies will be done soon."

Pleased, as if she had sensed he might be coming, David stepped into the kitchen. It was a simple room—green-painted walls, chipped in places, with a calendar hanging beside the table of mismatched chairs. A lantern hung from the ceiling, casting soft light over the worn linoleum floor. And yet, the room felt full. Full of warmth, of memory, of Fern's quiet and efficient care. It was one of David's favorite places to be.

She handed him a cup of coffee and gestured to the table. "Sit while I get the cookies out of the oven."

David lowered himself into his favorite chair, the one with the cushion slipping sideways. Not a minute later, Fern set a plate in front of him—peanut butter chocolate chip cookies, still warm. He picked one up, took a bite, and let the sweetness settle him.

"It's always good to see you at my table," she said, settling into her own chair with her needlepoint hoop. "But I don't think you came for cookies."

"They're definitely worth a visit." He took a sip of coffee, savoring the bitter and the sweet. "But you're right about that." He set the coffee mug down. "I wanted to let you know that I'm going to speak to the other ministers about planning to draw the lot later this spring. For a new deacon."

Fern's needle paused mid-stitch. "Why?"

He looked down at the cookie in his hand. Was it his second or his third? "To be honest, I miss having a deacon. I miss Luke. He is an exceptional deacon. He has a way of addressing problems, of speaking hard truths, and he can do it without offending people. I seem to lack that gift. I saw it clearly after Attnungsgemee. I've been overlooking so many important issues in the lives of church members. I have let little problems grow into large ones."

"Seemed like there was a good clearing of the air at the Council Meeting." Fern resumed stitching, her fingers moving with quiet rhythm.

"Thanks be to God for all that. It certainly had nothing to do with my leadership." He put his hands around the coffee mug. "Fern, I need to find a new deacon."

"There's no need for that."

"But there is. And I know that there's no guarantee the new deacon will be anything like Luke. I have to trust God will provide the right person for our church. I just know that I'm not much good at deaconing. Disciplining church members, asking for alms . . . it's like working a weak muscle. I dread it. I delay it. And if I finally do address a problem, I often end up making it worse."

"What makes it so hard for you?"

"I've given this a lot of thought lately." He lifted the coffee mug and took a sip, buying himself a moment. "I've been in churches with harsh leadership. I know what it does to people, how it beats them down. Take Sam Mustang, that fellow who made the confession at Council Meeting. Not sure you know the whole story, but he was raised Amish, with a harsh bishop. Look what it did to him. He was barely out of boyhood, not anywhere close to being a man, and he couldn't see a way out of the problems he'd created. He felt his only option was to run. I think my sister lived with that same oppressive fear. If you couldn't stay within the straight and narrow way, you were better off running away. The problem is, we all have trouble staying within the straight and narrow way. 'For all have sinned, and come short of the glory of God.' If everyone felt like they had to leave because they sinned, the church would soon be empty."

Fern didn't interrupt him, just let him spill everything out. Which was good, because he was now on a roll and couldn't stop.

"I've never wanted to be that kind of a bishop. I wanted to show people the kindness of God, the overwhelming love of God, the Good Shepherd who's always seeking the lost lamb, to bring it back into the fold." He sighed. "But these last few months, I wonder if I've lost sight of what it means to fear the Lord. I think I've overlooked sinful behavior and let it become acceptable. Gossip, for example. I hear all kinds of gossip at the store—and I just let it go."

"Why's that?"

Good question. Why didn't he call Alma and Julia out for their gossip? "They're my customers, I suppose. It's hard to know when to be a bishop and when to be a storekeeper."

"Hard to be both."

"Yes." Exactly. "But I know I'm not doing anyone a favor by letting them sit in sin. I need someone like Luke. Someone who doesn't flinch." He paused, the silence stretching between them.

"Zu scharf schneid net—zu schtump as net." *Too sharp is as bad as too dull.*

"Yes. That's right. And I've been far too dull. That's why I need a deacon."

"David, you've got one."

Birdy was right. She had said Fern would have trouble accepting David's decision. Luke was like a son to Fern. "I've waited as long as I could for Luke to return. Birdy thinks they're not ever coming back, nor should they, she thinks. Land is less costly in Kentucky, and there's more opportunity for a young family." He reached for another cookie. "Fern, sometimes I wonder . . . is this what it's like to get older? There are days that feel like it's the day after Christmas or Easter—when you're just worn out, even from good things. Like you've had too much cake." He shrugged. "Or maybe I'm just using my age as an excuse. Maybe my weaknesses just seem more apparent than ever."

Fern tied off her thread and reached for another. "You're not weak, David," she said. "You're tired. Weary. There's a difference." She held up the sampler she'd been working on. The stitches were neat and tidy, the colors soft and gentle. It read: "Wo die Kraft fehlt, trägt uns Gottes Gnade." *Where strength fails, God's grace carries us.*

David stared at it. How had he neglected to remember that truth? He'd been leaning on his own finite strength instead of resting on God's infinite power. And hadn't the Lord proven himself to their church this last Attnungsgemee? The Lord had taken the humility of Sam Mustang and Mary Zook and used it to stir the hearts of the church in a powerful way. David had nothing to do with it.

The church didn't need a perfect leader. All that the church needed was the Lord. David read the sampler again, letting the wisdom settle over him like a balm.

"You don't need to draw the lot for a deacon because you have one." Fern rose and reached for a folded letter on the windowsill, then handed it to David. "This just came. Luke and Izzy are heading back. Should be here within a month or so. In time to help me with the orchards, he said."

David sat back, stunned. "Luke's really coming back?"

Fern nodded. "He called a few weeks back, right after you gave that blistering sermon."

"Blistering sermon?" David wasn't really a blistering-sermon kind of bishop.

"When you told everyone to live like they're dying."

Oh, that.

"I told Luke about it. He said it shook him to his very core. He and Izzy want to be back here to raise their little ones. He said they realized they were missing too much and it was time to get back home. Back to Windmill Farm."

Fern had a very, very pleased look in her eyes. David had a feeling that his eyes might reflect that same feeling.

"So it seems God knew what you needed before you did." She picked up her sampler to start sewing again. "He does that."

David looked around the kitchen—the mismatched chairs, the faded calendar, the green walls chipped with time. There was so much love in this room. So much grace. "Yes, he does do that." He took another cookie, eating slower this time.

Fern smiled. "Take two for the road. You need to keep up your strength."

He took two for the road, but he didn't really need them. He'd found his strength.

Twenty-Two

Tonight, skies clear, there was supposed to be a spectacular meteor shower. Everyone in town had been talking about it. All day, Annie went back and forth about whether she would join Darcy and Sam up at Wonder Pond. She wanted to see the meteor shower. She might be on the low end of amateur astronomy, but she had learned quite a bit this last month by listening to Gus and Darcy as they peppered Sam with questions. Knowing about constellations and planets made stargazing so much more interesting than when she had just stared at the moon.

On the other hand, Annie felt odd going without Gus. Almost like she was betraying him. She hadn't seen him for a few days, not even at work. She wasn't sure if he was the one avoiding her, or she him. Either way, it was working.

In the end, she decided she was overthinking and that was ridiculous. It was a perfect night for viewing. A new moon, cloudless skies. She was fond of stargazing and she wanted to see the meteor shower. Period.

Still, she lingered at the bottom of the hill, hoping Gus might surprise her. Might come face Sam Mustang at last.

The stars had already begun to salt the sky. The evening was still, the air cool with the promise of spring, but her shawl didn't do much to chase away the cold. She'd told Sam and Darcy to go ahead, that she'd join them soon.

"Annie, I don't think he's coming," Sam said, and he sounded as sad about it as she felt.

She waited as long as she could. She could just make out Sam and Darcy ahead, their outlines slowly making their way up the trail. Sam had the telescope case, awkward in his arms, shifting it from hand to hand every few steps. Annie let out a sigh and told herself it was time to give up. Gus wasn't coming. She flipped the switch on her flashlight and hurried up the hill, shining the light ahead of her, trying to catch up with Sam and Darcy.

She was halfway up the trail when she heard footsteps behind her. Then a voice, low and just a little winded. "Annie. Wait."

She turned and shone the light on a figure. There Gus was, coming toward her, his hat pushed back slightly.

"Can you drop the flashlight? You're blinding me."

"I didn't think you'd come," she said, flipping the flashlight off. "But I also couldn't imagine that you'd miss the meteor shower."

His eyes met hers and held. "You were right," Gus said. "About everything." He took in a deep breath and let it out. "I've been acting like my parents had intentionally tried to hurt me. They were only trying to protect me from getting hurt."

She couldn't stop the slow smile that spread across her face. "So you're ready to face Sam?" She turned her head toward Sam and Darcy, who had paused on the hill. They were only ten or twenty yards ahead of them, unaware of Annie and Gus, and their conversation carried easily downhill.

"I told you I could carry it," Darcy said.

Sam set the telescope case on the ground and was rubbing one shoulder. "It's too heavy for you. I've got it."

But before he could reach down to pick it up, Gus strode to meet them, saying, "Let me carry that."

Sam spun around. Even in the dim light, Annie could see emotions flash over his face—surprise, hope, happiness. He hesitated, but only for a second, then nodded and handed it over. The two men exchanged a glance—brief but not without weight. Nothing was said but something had passed between them. Respect, maybe. Curiosity. The beginning of something new.

It was a start. Annie couldn't hold back her smile. She was beaming.

Then, still without a word, the two men crested the hill together. Darcy waited for Annie, gently squeezing her arm as she whispered, "Can you *believe* this?"

Yes and no, but more no than yes. Annie had hoped Gus would sort things through, to right himself, like one of Gabe's bath toys that would turn upside down, only to pop up again. She'd prayed for it. She'd longed for it. But, she realized now, she hadn't truly *believed* that God would answer her prayer. And she certainly hadn't expected the answer to come sooner rather than later.

Maybe that had something to do with Sam's illness. God, in his wisdom, had used something so unlikely as disease to bring about healing.

Darcy was waiting for a response from her. All Annie could think to say was, "Joy often comes when it's least expected." She wasn't sure why that phrase popped out of her mouth. Had she heard it somewhere? Or maybe the Lord dropped it into her mind.

"Yes!" Darcy threw her arms around Annie and held her tight. "Yes, that is so very, very, very true!" She said it with such conviction that a laugh burst out of Annie, which made Darcy laugh. The two men were far enough up the trail that they didn't hear them.

Noise traveled downward. Annie could hear the low rumble of conversation going on between Sam and Gus. She was struck again by how much they shared in common—the tenor of their deep voices, their height and body shape, even their gait as they climbed the trail. She thought of Marcus Troyer, short and stout. She thought of Mary. Short and stout. Same with all of Gus's siblings. Short and stout. Watching Gus and Sam crest the hill, Annie could so clearly see the obvious: father and son.

Up on the ridge, waiting while Gus set up the telescope and Sam fiddled with the dials to adjust the focus, Annie tilted her face upward. The night felt larger than she remembered, large enough to swallow up old regrets and make room for new mercies.

Far away, she heard the sound of murmuring voices. Of footsteps plodding up the trail. Darcy heard, too, and they exchanged a questioning look. Then two figures, one in a black hat and one in a large bonnet, appeared at the top of the trail.

Sam looked up in mild surprise as more and more began appearing along the ridge, their figures taking shape in the dim moonlight—families, couples, even a few elderly people. "They've come for the meteor shower," Darcy said. "Didn't I tell you to expect a crowd? People were talking about it all day at Dok's office."

"You told me," Sam said, "but I didn't think they'd come."

"Amish love stars too," Gus said, a faint smile tugging at his mouth.

"You don't have to tell me that," Sam said. "My grandfather was the one who taught me all about the night sky. Your great-grandfather."

Gus tilted his head, and Annie saw the shift in his expression—subtle but sure. He'd probably never considered Sam's parents or grandparents. Never thought of them as part of him too.

Sam cleared his throat. "I just didn't think the Amish would want to be around me."

"They have respect for you, Sam." The words flowed from Annie, surprising even herself. Normally, she would think twice before speaking aloud in a group. Maybe three times. And then the moment would've passed before she said a word.

More and more started to arrive, in pairs and small clusters, nodding greetings as they made their way toward the telescope, standing patiently in line for a turn. No one spoke loudly. Sam helped each one, adjusting the height of the telescope to accommodate their height, answer their questions, explain what they were seeing. Darcy answered questions, too, as she walked along the long line of patient stargazers all craning their necks to catch the streaks of falling light.

Satisfied after a turn at the telescope, each one would thank Sam, then head to the trail to return to their buggies. Morning came early for farmers.

And then Annie touched Gus's arm. "Look."

Gus turned—and his face froze in surprise. His mother, Mary, was making her way to them, her husband Marcus beside her.

"We've been hearing a lot about that fancy telescope," Mary said, her eyes crinkling with a smile. "I'd like a look through it myself."

"Here's your chance, Mamm," Gus said. He adjusted the scope down so she wouldn't have to stand on her tiptoes as she gazed into the lens. Marcus stood beside her, waiting a turn. Gus stood a few feet away, watching his parents—Mary, Marcus, Sam—standing together near the telescope. His brow was relaxed, the tension Annie had seen in him had finally eased.

Then he left them to come over to stand close to Annie, so close their hands were nearly touching. Their eyes were on the night sky. Even without the telescope, the meteor shower was now visible to the naked eye. Against the black was another streak of light, fast and sudden, like a firefly on its last flight. It was glorious.

After a moment, Gus said, "You think God puts these shows on to remind us how small we are?"

"Maybe how small," Annie said. "Or maybe how loved."

He glanced sideways at her, his fingers finding hers. "Thank you. For being you."

Annie leaned into the moment, into the warmth of Gus beside her, and let the silence stretch again. She thought they might just find their way through this. Together.

Yes, joy often came when it was least expected.

Days passed, then a week, and still no word from Dok about Sam's test results. Finally, late in the day on Monday, Dok told Darcy to ask Sam to come to the office after the last patient was scheduled for the day. And then Dok was called out on a house call.

Darcy and Sam sat in Dok's office, nervously waiting for her to return to the office. Sam was visibly tense, his foot tapping the floor. He kept glancing at his watch. "Tell me again what she said to you."

"Dok said she'd like you to come to the office at the end of the day."

"That's it? Nothing else?"

"Nothing else."

"Darcy, that first test—the one with the girl's name—"

"ELISA."

"Dok said that one would only take a few days to get a result." His eyes glanced at the computer on Dok's desk. "You can access it. I'm sure you know how to find it."

She did, and she'd been tempted to look to see if the ELISA results had come in, but she couldn't do it. It wouldn't be right, not without Dok's permission.

Or maybe Darcy just didn't want to know the test result. Hope was a very pleasant companion.

Before she could respond, the door opened and Dok stepped in. She closed the door behind her, set down her bag, took off her coat, and hung it over the back of her chair. Darcy's anxiety ratcheted a few notches as Dok seemed to be avoiding Sam's eyes.

"Well," Dok said, easing down into her chair. "I'll get right to it."

Sam sat up straighter.

Dok turned to look directly at him. "You, sir," she said, with a small smile, "do not have ALS. What you do have is Lyme disease."

Darcy's hand flew to her mouth as tears welled up. Sam blinked. Once. Twice. He looked stunned, like he couldn't quite hear the words.

"You're sure?" Darcy said.

"Absolutely, positively sure. I saw the ELISA result last week but wanted to have the confirmation of the Western Blot test before I said anything." Again, she looked right at Sam. "You do *not* have ALS."

He made a raw, gasping sound, as if he'd been swimming underwater for too long and broke through the water's surface for air. Perhaps, in a way, he had.

Darcy let out a breath that turned into a sob. She didn't mean to cry, but the tears came anyway.

"Is there . . ." Sam cleared his throat. "Is there a cure for Lyme disease?"

"Yes," Dok said, nodding. "And we're starting treatment right away. We'll begin with doxycycline—oral antibiotics—and then assess whether we need to move to IV depending on your response. You'll need to be thoroughly consistent, no missing doses, and will need regular follow-up labs. But yes, there is a cure."

Sam swallowed hard. "And I'm really going to be okay?"

Dok gave a slow, measured nod. "Assuming we caught it before it caused permanent neurological damage. There is something called chronic Lyme disease, but I'm hopeful that won't be your outcome." She smiled. "Bottom line . . . you're not out of the woods yet, but you're certainly not lost in them either."

"Dr. Stoltzfus," Sam said, his voice trembling. "I saw the best of the best in Houston. No one ever mentioned Lyme disease as a possibility."

"I told you, Sam," Darcy said. "Dok sees things others don't see."

Dok smiled. "Just lucky."

No, Darcy thought. Luck had nothing to do with it. Call it instinct, experience, education. Whatever it was, this woman had a gift.

Dok stood. "I'll go grab samples of antibiotics. We'll start tonight." She left the room, and the door clicked softly behind her.

For a long moment, Sam just sat there. Then he looked at Darcy and held out his hand. "Come here."

She was still wiping her eyes, smiling through the tears. She took his hand, rising, and he pulled her gently to him to sit on his lap. She didn't hesitate—she fell into his arms and let him hold her tight. Neither of them said anything. The moment didn't need words. They just sat there, wrapped in relief.

There weren't many stories that had a happy ending like Sam Mustang's. Dok sat at her desk, in the quiet after Sam and Darcy had left, feeling so thankful to God for calling her to a life in medicine. Whenever she had a really bad day, she needed to remember this day. Remember how it felt to tell Sam that he did not have ALS. Remember the look on his face as she told him he was not going to die from that terrible disease. That he was going to get well, God willing, and get his life back. Return to his important work at NASA. A bright future which, Dok had a pretty good hunch, might include Darcy Delaney.

A ping came from her phone and she saw that Matt had texted, wondering when she was coming home. Soon, she texted back:

Just finishing up for the day.

Take your time. Gus and Annie are with Gabe.
I'm off to work.

Any change in Gabe today?

None

Dok rubbed her temples. No change. Her mind flipped through last evening. Matt had tried to get Gabe to play with his toy tractor. No response. Matt tried singing to him—he liked the sound, but he didn't react like most babies would, no swaying, no clapping, just silent watching.

Gus, bless him, was convinced Gabe was coming alive before their eyes, but Dok had seen no sign of that. In fact, she thought he was growing weaker.

It was just so baffling. Gabe's medical records offered no real answers. Just the usual well-baby checkups, vaccinations, growth charts. Nothing alarming, nothing that pointed to why he was so different from other toddlers his age.

She'd ruled out lead exposure. She'd done every panel she could find. She'd consulted neurologists. Gabe had low muscle tone. Developmental delays. Lack of eye contact. Matt was pressing her to accept the obvious. Everything pointed to autism.

"Let's get on with it," Matt told her last night after he'd put Gabe to bed. "Just because *you* don't want to acknowledge that Gabe is autistic doesn't mean he's not."

There was just something in Dok's gut that rejected that

diagnosis. She trusted her gut instincts. God had given her those instincts, and she'd had enough experience in life to trust them.

Sam Mustang popped into her head, the shock in his voice as he said, "But no one had ever mentioned Lyme as a possibility."

That's because Lyme was known as the Great Imitator. Its symptoms could mimic a wide range of conditions, making it a challenge to diagnose. That could result in misdiagnoses and delayed treatment, which only meant symptoms grew more severe.

She thought of Gabe.

Then, before she could stop herself, she typed: *Can Lyme disease mimic autism?*

Her finger hovered over the Enter key. This felt like a wild-goose chase. She thought again of Matt. If he were here right now, he would scold her for trying to collect more and more data about Gabe. He would tell her to stop avoiding the reality of his condition.

Lyme disease in an eighteen-month-old? Highly unlikely. Besides, what were the odds of having two undiagnosed cases of Lyme disease in her practice? It seemed completely improbable. Lightning didn't strike twice.

But still, she pressed it.

The first article that popped up made her sit up straight. *Neuroborreliosis in young children can present with developmental delays, hypotonia, and social withdrawal.*

Dok's heartbeat picked up the more she read. *Neuroborreliosis.* Also known as Lyme neuroborreliosis. Late-stage Lyme that affected the brain.

The symptoms listed weren't a perfect match, but they were close enough to give her pause. She clicked on Gabe's file and skimmed the intake notes from the social worker. He had lived with his father in a rural area, outside State College. A woodsy area.

Pennsylvania was a hot spot for Lyme disease.

Her mind raced. If Gabe had been bitten by a tick, the symptoms could've taken time to appear.

She reached for her pen and tapped it against her desk.

It was a long shot.

But what if she was right?

She needed to get Gabe tested immediately. She reached for her cell phone to call Matt at work to tell him her plan, then paused. Matt would object, tell her that she had promised the last test was the end of testing.

Again, she thought of Sam. *No one mentioned Lyme as a possibility.*

Gus and Annie were at the house, watching Gabe until Dok got home from work. She could go home right now and bring Gabe to the office to get tested. No need to even mention this to Matt until the results were in. Why give him false hope? If her hunch was wrong, she might not tell him at all. After all, it was a long, long, long shot. Probably no chance at all.

As she backed up the car, one thing went through her mind. *Please let it be Lyme*, she prayed. *Please let it be something that can be fixed.*

Twenty-Three

Spring had arrived. Temperatures climbed to the low sixties in the afternoon, and the evening didn't have its typical winter chill. Darcy and Sam were on a blanket side by side, on the ridge overlooking Wonder Pond, the telescope set up beside them. The night was hushed, the stars sharp and clear in the dark sky overhead—the first clear night all week. Crickets filled the air with a soft rhythm, and somewhere across the pond, a bullfrog gave a throaty call.

Sam leaned back on his elbows, relaxed in a way Darcy had never seen in him. His laugh had come easily tonight, his steps stronger. No stumbles on the trail. The tremor in his hands seemed to have lessened, though that was probably just her imagination. He'd been on the antibiotics only a few days. Still, Darcy was noticing everything. The way he stood taller. The way his eyes shone, not with fear or fatigue, but with happiness.

She crossed one ankle over the other. "As much as I appreciate your dazzling telescope, it's nice to sit here and just take it all in." She craned her neck. "'Can you bind the chains of the Pleiades? Can you loosen Orion's belt? Can you bring forth the constellations in their seasons or lead out the Bear with its cubs?'" She grinned. "I've been studying."

"The book of Job?"

"You know it?" She was impressed. "Actually, I've been trying to memorize verses that talk about the stars. Annie gave me a list." She turned to him. "Do you know any? Bible verses about the stars, I mean."

"'Lift up your eyes on high, and behold who hath created these things, that bringeth out their host by number: He calleth them all by names by the greatness of his might, for that he is strong in power, not one faileth.'" He was quiet for a long moment. "That's me, Darcy. I was missing."

She turned to him. "But no longer."

He cleared his throat. "No longer."

The quiet spun out between them. "You know," she said, nudging his shoulder lightly, "Evie's cast is off."

He turned his head. "Really?"

Darcy nodded. "Dok thinks she'll be back at the office within a few weeks."

He pushed himself up and leaned back on his hands. "So," he said, eyes on the sky. "You'll be out of a job soon."

"Yep." Darcy drew her knees up and rested her chin on them. "I need to start looking for my next traveling contract."

"Finland?"

She smiled. "Maybe. Though I hear the northern lights are better in the winter. I might hold off and look for something else for summer and fall."

There was a beat of quiet between them. Then Sam said, softly, "Houston is nice."

"Nice?" She laughed. "You're kidding, right? Houston in the summer is supposed to be a greenhouse. I've heard it's the only US city with tropical diseases."

He cleared his throat. "It can get a touch warm. But what I mean to say is . . . Houston would be nice. If you were there too."

Her breath caught. Was he joking? She turned her head and

looked at him. He wasn't joking. "You want me to come to Houston?"

He nodded, his expression earnest in the moonlight. "Lots of hospitals down there. And my friend has an ADU in his backyard. Really nice. Air-conditioned. It's available. I, uh, checked."

Sam had a *friend*? Darcy had assumed he was a loner star. She smiled, her chest tight and full at the same time. "Maybe Houston could be nice for the summer."

"And maybe . . . next winter, we could go see those northern lights in Finland. Though Lapland is better."

"Listen to you, Sam Mustang. Making plans for the future."

"Our future." He turned and looked at her for a long moment, his eyes searching hers. There was a quiet understanding between them, something that didn't require words—which was quite a change for Darcy. Sam leaned over slowly, his lips meeting hers in a kiss that felt tender yet strong, filled with a promise.

When they pulled back, Darcy's heart was beating a little faster. She wasn't sure when it had happened—this shift in her—but she'd gone from anxiously moving from place to place to wanting to stay right here, right beside Sam Mustang, wherever he happened to be. She didn't need to chase the world anymore to find what she was looking for. She'd found him.

Spring was fickle, Dok thought, as she pulled her medical bag from the back seat of her car. A few days ago, she had opened the windows to the house to let the fresh air in. Tonight, Matt would need to turn the furnace back on. To keep Gabe warm. Her fingers tightened around the handle of her medical bag.

She'd barely reached the path that led to the house when Matt opened the front door. In his arms was Gabe. She caught the flash in his eyes before he even said a word. He was upset.

"What's wrong? I know I'm not late." She was early, in fact. She'd let Charlie finish up the rest of the patients so she could get home as quickly as she could.

"Ruth, we agreed there'd be no more tests." His voice was low, but the anger was there, steady. "I ran into Gus at a scene today. Police had been dispatched to assist with a medical call. He asked me if I'd heard what the test results were. He said that just a few days ago, you'd rushed home to take Gabe back to the office for another test."

Argh. She hadn't expected Gus and Matt to see each other. "I was going to tell you—"

"When?" He wasn't just upset. He was angry.

She blinked. "Matt, calm down a minute—"

"I'm not going to calm down. We're supposed to be a team, Ruth. I don't like you sneaking around behind my back."

"Let's go inside," she said, quieter now. "Please. I have something important to tell you."

He hesitated, then stepped aside and followed her in.

Inside, as Matt set Gabe gently into the high chair, Dok handed him a box of Cheerios from the pantry. "Feed him a few while I get this ready." Her medical bag thumped softly onto the kitchen table. She unzipped it and pulled out a cooler pouch, then began unpacking vials.

"What are you doing?"

"I'll explain in a minute."

Matt stood stiffly, shaking some cereal onto the high chair tray. Gabe reached out for them clumsily, knocking most of them off the high chair's tray.

Dok took a bottle from the cooler pouch and began shaking it gently. "You know about Sam Mustang, right?"

Matt nodded, arms crossed. "He's the guy who showed up in town and claimed to be Gus's birth father."

"Well, yes. But there's more to Sam Mustang's story. Much, much more. I told you parts of his story a couple of months back. Do you remember? He had been diagnosed with ALS and wanted to make amends before it was too late. He asked if I could help him find the woman he had wronged . . . who turned out to be Gus Troyer's mother."

Matt had crouched down to pick up Cheerios on the floor. "You're avoiding my question. Why did you take Gabe for another test when we'd agreed not to?"

"I'm *trying* to tell you. So last week, Charlie told me about a patient with odd symptoms . . . and it dawned on me that this patient might have Lyme disease. Something clicked. Sam Mustang has odd symptoms too. Ones that fit ALS, but some that don't. So I ran some tests and it turns out that Sam Mustang has Lyme disease. *Not* ALS."

Matt frowned. "Okay. So that's good news for Sam."

"Very good news," Dok said, setting the bottle down.

He narrowed his eyes. "But what does that have to do with Gabe?"

She drew in a breath. "Some of Gabe's symptoms . . . the blank stares, how he flinches from sound one day but not the next—"

"Ruth, those symptoms point to autism. I've been reading."

"Those symptoms overlap with autism, yes. But other symptoms don't. And when I read up on untreated Lyme disease in babies and toddlers, Gabe fit the profile. He has nearly every symptom."

Matt had a skeptical look on his face. "So you think Gabe has Lyme? Come on, Ruth. That's pretty far-fetched."

"Not if he was living in a high-risk area. And when I read his file, I found that his father had been living in a wooded area near State College. So a few days ago, I came home, picked Gabe up, and took him to the office for tests. I didn't tell you because—" Because she knew he'd say no, get upset with her, accuse her of avoiding reality, blah blah blah. "Because I just didn't want to get your hopes up." She turned to face him fully.

"But the first test result came in this afternoon, and as soon as I read it, I came straight home to tell you. Matt, Gabe has Lyme disease."

Matt stared at her, stunned. "Are you sure? Absolutely, positively sure?"

"There's one more test result to come in that will confirm it. But I feel confident that the first test result was accurate. That's why I brought these antibiotics home. I want to start treating him right away."

Matt had a look on his face like she might be speaking a foreign language. "You mean—Gabe doesn't have autism? He's not going to be like this for the rest of his life? He's going to get better? Be . . . normal?"

"I . . . don't know. I hope so, but I can't promise anything. If the disease has been caught in time, we should see him start to recover, gain strength in his muscles, maybe even meet some of the milestones he's been missing. It'll take time, but there's a chance that he will have a normal life." She hoped so, with all her heart.

Matt let out a long breath. He looked at Gabe, then back at her, and she noticed that his eyes were glassy. Then he stepped forward and pulled her into a hug. "I'm sorry," he said softly. "For doubting you."

She held still for a moment, then nodded against his shoulder. He meant it. And she knew it hadn't just been about the test.

He had doubts about her too. About her desire to become a mother at age sixty.

And the worst part was—he wasn't wrong.

Not in the least.

Twenty-Four

Darcy pulled her jacket tighter against the cool April night, the zipper catching a strand of hair before she freed it. She stood by her car on the road where she and Sam always met before hiking up the trail to Wonder Pond. Above the dark tree line, the stars pricked through the deep blue sky.

She tilted her head back, scanning the cloudless sky. Venus was already bright in the west, and just above it, Jupiter glimmered faintly. The pale new moon was just a sliver tonight. Ideal for stargazing.

Her thoughts drifted to Sam. Since Dok had started his treatment for Lyme disease, he'd changed in ways that still caught her off guard. The hollowness in his cheeks had filled in; his shoulders looked broader under his shirts. There was a lightness in his step now, a bounce that made him seem younger, more himself. It was like she was getting to know a new and improved Sam Mustang. And she liked what she saw in him. Loved him, if she was honest.

She thought about Houston. A traveling nurse contract in an internal medicine clinic had been easy to line up, starting in a few weeks. Three months—that was the deal she'd made with herself. Three months to see if what she and Sam had was real, if it could last beyond the quiet magic of Stoney Ridge.

When she'd told him about the contract, he'd grinned and said she'd better ask for a longer contract because he wasn't letting her go. Not ever. The memory warmed her now, and she felt the corners of her mouth lift. It was nice—more than nice—to be someone's forever.

The rhythmic clop of hooves pulled her from her thoughts. She turned to see Gus approaching in his horse and buggy, the lantern swinging gently at the side. He pulled up beside her, reins in hand.

"Evening," he said.

"Evening," she said, stepping closer. "Where's Annie tonight?"

"Helping her mother with something," Gus said, glancing toward the trail.

Darcy nodded, a thought forming. If Gus had come without Annie, maybe he was feeling more at ease with Sam. And if he was, maybe it was time for the two of them to have an opportunity to talk, really talk. Sam had a lot he needed to say to Gus before leaving town.

"Gus," she said, touching her temple lightly, "I think I feel a headache coming on. Would you mind if I left the two of you to stargaze without me tonight?"

He hesitated, his brow furrowing. "Just me and Sam?"

"Just you and Sam."

Uncertainty flickered in his eyes. He dipped his chin, paused, then lifted his head. "You go on home and take care of your headache."

She gave him a small, knowing smile. "Thanks. I'll do just that."

She slipped into her car, the seat still warm from driving here, and started the engine. As she pulled away, she glanced once in the rearview mirror. Gus was still there, the buggy lantern casting a soft glow around him. Sam, always late, would be along any minute.

Darcy smiled to herself, pleased. Tonight belonged to the two of them. And that felt exactly right.

Late in the day, David swept up the empty peanut shells left scattered on the ground by the graybeards who missed the open door of the woodstove. The bell over the store's door jingled, and he glanced up to see his sister step inside, still wearing her white doctor coat. A smile tugged at the corners of his mouth. "Sister or doctor?"

"Sister," she said.

It didn't matter. Either way, they would head back to his office to talk privately. Sarah was busy helping a customer at the register, and while she seemed to be genuinely working on her habit of eavesdropping, he didn't want to chance it. Even a saint is tempted by an open door.

"Please. Sit down," David said, gesturing to the chair in front of his desk. "What's on your mind?"

Ruth took a seat and leaned forward, as though the weight of the conversation had already settled on her shoulders. "Gabe. He's on my mind. He's all I think about lately."

"How's he doing?" David knew that he'd been finally diagnosed with Lyme disease. What were the odds—two patients showing up with the same misdiagnosed illness? Both ending up in the care of his sister, whom God seemed to have bestowed with remarkable intuition. Who but the Lord could have herded both Sam Mustang and little Gabe to Stoney Ridge, just in the nick of time? Only God could have orchestrated such a plan. Into his head popped a phrase Birdy liked to say whenever something unusual occurred: Schreib's in her Schannschtee, daett waert's net ausgewischt. *Write in the chimney, where nobody will erase it.* "Improving, I hope?"

A smile filled Ruth's face. "Lots of improvement. He's making steady progress. The meds are working. His strength is improving. He's eating better. He's less tired. He's even standing for longer and longer periods. No steps yet, but I think that'll come soon."

Then her smile faded, just enough to make David realize there was a cloud over her that he hadn't noticed at first. "But something's bothering you."

"Matt wants to start the process to adopt Gabe."

David stayed silent. He'd known this was coming. Matt had led the charge to adopt Gabe when he and Ruth had first fostered him.

"David, I just can't do it. I've prayed and prayed, but I can't find any peace about adopting Gabe." Her voice grew shaky, as if this was hard to say out loud. "Matt asked if I'm incapable of being a mother to Gabe. Or maybe incapable of being a mother at all." She blew out a puff of air. "I do love that little boy, David. He's very dear to me. It's just . . ." She trailed off, as if unsure how to continue.

David leaned back in his chair, folding his arms across his chest, and gave her the time to collect her thoughts. A year or so ago, Ruth had joined Matt in being fully committed to adopt this little boy. Matt had talked about taking early retirement to be available for Gabe. Ruth had tried to find a partner so she could work less. They'd finally completed the half-finished remodeling projects in their house. After a long pause, David gently said, "What's different from a year ago?"

Ruth stared at the desk for a moment, her voice softer when she spoke again. "I think it has to do with turning sixty. Staring at the decade ahead. There are days when I feel every one of my sixty years. I don't have the energy I did. I don't know if I can handle raising a child, not the way I should." She swallowed before she continued. "I can't stop thinking that the best family for Gabe would be one with much younger parents—with more energy, maybe even siblings. I just don't think Matt and I can give him the childhood a little boy deserves."

David sat quietly, taking in her words. He could well understand what she meant. He knew the difference of being a young father, with his first wife Anna and their six children, and now being an older father, with his second wife Birdy and their two young boys. He knew that the energy and patience required to raise them weren't always easy to muster, even while he loved them dearly. "Sometimes, the best thing you can do is recognize your limits."

Ruth met his gaze, looking uncertain. "I love Gabe, David. I want him to have the best life possible, but . . ."

David nodded slowly. "Maybe you're not meant to be his mother. Maybe you're meant to be a part of his life in a different way. You've already had a special role."

"And I don't want that role to be over. I really don't. But I just can't get on board with adopting Gabe." She let out a breath, the weight of her decision pressing on her. "How do I tell Matt that I can't do it?"

David leaned forward slightly, his voice lowering. "You've been able to be honest with me, Ruth. Now you need to be honest with Matt. Go home and tell him exactly what you told me."

Her phone pinged and she pulled it out of her coat pocket. "I have to get back to the office." She lifted a hand in thanks.

David watched her walk out of the office's back door, the one with the bad lock. *Lord*, he prayed, *give Matt ears to hear Ruth's heart without any resentment. Give him an understanding heart. And mostly, Lord, provide a loving home for this precious little boy.*

On the heels of that prayer came a fleeting worry: Ruth might share her misgivings with Birdy. As sisters-in-law, they were close, and it wouldn't take much for Birdy to decide that she and David ought to adopt Gabe. She'd always wanted more children.

Lord, he added silently, *as you search to find Gabe a good, loving home . . . please don't let that home be ours.*

Dok sat on the edge of the bed, her hands loosely clasped in her lap. The house was quiet, dinner dishes stacked in the sink, the porch light catching a flutter of moths outside the window. Matt was across the room, checking the lock on the back door like he always did before bed. She waited until he turned around and looked at her. "We need to talk," she said. "About Gabe."

Matt stilled for a second, then nodded and walked over, sitting beside her. "Okay. You go first." He just folded his hands and looked at her, waiting.

Ruth took a deep breath.

"I love him, Matt. I hope you know I do. But I can't come to peace with the idea of adopting him."

Matt exhaled through his nose, slow and steady. "Why not?"

She searched for the words. "I've tried to imagine what our lives would look like with him here permanently, but it just doesn't feel right."

Matt's voice was quiet. "You don't think you can love him like a mother?"

"I can. I already do, in a way. But that doesn't mean I should be his mother. Not legally." She looked at him now, really looked. "I'm sixty, Matt. I feel it every morning in my knees and every evening in my feet. I don't bounce back the way I used to. And parenting isn't just love. It's stamina. It's saying yes to baseball practices and science fairs and sleepovers and teen angst. It's going the distance, and I'm not sure I have that in me anymore."

Silent, Matt's eyes remained on the worn rug that covered the room.

After a long pause, she added softly, "Matt, I'm just tired."

He rubbed a hand across his jaw, then let out a quiet laugh that wasn't really a laugh. "I understand, Ruth. I do."

She blinked, surprised.

"I mean . . . I'm disappointed. In both of us."

"What do you mean?"

"Well, I had this plan for us in mind. Our next chapter. I hoped that if you made Charlie a partner, you could start easing out of the practice."

Charlie? Dok stayed silent, though inwardly she felt a flicker of doubt. Charlie still had a way to go before she could trust him as a partner.

"I thought that we would have more time, more flexibility."

And that wasn't happening. Not yet. "I get why you're disappointed in me . . . but why would you be disappointed in yourself?"

Matt crossed an ankle over his bent knee. "Because . . . there's a lot of things on my list. I want to travel. Do some volunteering with Habitat for Humanity, maybe even spend a winter or two somewhere warm. And when I start thinking about what a kid needs, it's not me. Gabe needs a dad who can coach soccer or lead Boy Scouts. Not one who's pushing sixty and needs a nap after mowing the lawn."

Dok gave him a sidelong glance, and he offered a wry smile in return.

"When Gabe graduates college," he said, "we'll be close to eighty. That's a hard thing to think about."

They sat in the quiet for a while, the hum of the old heater the only sound that filled the house.

"I get it, Ruth," Matt said. "I get that we're getting older. And I get that Gabe deserves a family—maybe even brothers and sisters."

Dok felt her throat tighten. She reached over and placed her hand on his. "Maybe we're not supposed to be his parents,

Matt. Maybe we're supposed to be something else. A bridge. A blessing in the middle."

Matt nodded slowly. "Yeah," he said, his voice low. "Yeah, I know. What I have a hard time with is . . ." His voice cracked, and he cleared his throat. "If we don't adopt him—if someone else does—we might not see him again. Not really. And that's what I can't quite come to terms with. I love that little guy. He's in our life for a reason."

David's advice to be honest with Matt was right, Dok thought. This conversation had gone better than she had imagined. They weren't on opposite ends of adopting Gabe, like she'd worried they would be. But once again, just like she'd feared, letting go of this little boy was breaking their hearts.

Annie sat quietly beside Gus as he drove the buggy down the winding road to Dok and Matt's house, her hand tucked into his, both of them comfortable in the silence. The last few days had been full—talks that stretched late into the night, long walks, longer prayers.

Gus had spent time with Sam. Real time, just the two of them, getting to know each other. Annie had seen something in Gus's attitude for Sam that she hadn't expected—mercy. Compassion. Acceptance.

And then, tonight, as they'd sat on a blanket on the banks of Blue Lake Pond to watch the sunset, Gus had turned to her and blurted out, "Annie, I'm ready. I want to marry you now. Not wait until November, not wait any longer. I want us to get on with our life. That is"—he suddenly looked shy—"if you'll have me as your husband."

Her heart wanted to shout a yes, but her mind had the final say-so. She had a few things she needed to know. "What about the longing you've felt for a life like Sam's? I don't want you to have any regrets about living a Plain life." This would be harder to say, but she needed to say it. "I'm not leaving this life, Gus. Not even for you."

"No doubts, not anymore. I've worked them through with Sam. He told me that anything I might gain by leaving doesn't compare to all that I would lose." He reached for her hand, pulled it to his heart. "And I can't lose you, Annie Fisher. I love you. I want to spend the rest of my life proving that to you."

That was the moment when her heart and mind came together, and she said yes. Yes, she would marry him. And they didn't need to wait for the traditional wedding month of November.

They had spent the next few hours talking about their future. All their hopes and dreams and what-if ideas. And then they decided to go see Dok and Matt. And Gabe.

As they pulled into Dok and Matt's driveway, Annie glanced at Gus and felt a quiet certainty settle into her bones. They were doing the right thing. All of it.

The front door to Dok's house was unlocked, as it usually was. Gus didn't hesitate. He knocked, walked straight into the house, and found them in the living room. He knelt in front of Gabe, who was playing with a set of mismatched blocks on the rug. "Hey, buddy," Gus said softly, and Gabe beamed, lifting his arms to be picked up.

Watching them, Annie felt something tighten in her chest. She wanted to hold that picture in her mind forever, to remember this moment. She felt a happiness that she didn't know was possible. Yes, this decision that she and Gus had made, their first one as a couple, was the right one.

Gus looked straight at Dok and Matt, no wavering in his voice. "We wanted to share some news. Annie and I are getting married. As soon as possible."

Dok let out a delighted gasp, jumped up, and pulled Annie

into a hug so tight it left her breathless. "Oh, honey. That is happy news!"

Matt smiled, shook Gus's hand, then clapped him on the back. "Good choice," he said, his voice gruff with approval.

Gus, holding Gabe, standing next to Annie, cleared his throat and asked Dok and Matt to sit down. "There's . . . something else," he said. "Annie and I—we'd like to adopt Gabe."

Annie held her breath. She was watching Dok closely, not sure what to expect. Surprise, certainly. Hesitation, probably. But instead, she saw something she'd never seen before—Dok's face crumpling as tears filled her eyes and spilled over. Annie froze, then glanced at Matt—only to see him lean forward, elbows on his knees, hands covering his face, his shoulders shaking.

Annie and Gus exchanged a puzzled look. Had they offended them? She crossed the room quickly, crouching next to Dok and put a hand gently on her back. "If you're planning to adopt Gabe, of course we'd never want to interfere. We just—we knew you'd agreed to being foster parents, but you'd never said anything about adopting Gabe. We just love him so . . . and we thought we'd ask you, that's all."

Gus seemed as flustered as Annie. "I should've asked first. Not just walked in and told you what we wanted to do. I'm sorry. This is all my mistake. We just want to be part of his life. Even if all we ever get is to see Gabe from a distance, we'll take that."

Dok shook her head, tears splattering. "Annie, Gus. You don't realize. This . . . this is such an answer to our prayers. For us. For all of us."

Annie glanced at Gus, unsure she'd heard right. "You mean . . . ?"

"Ruth and I love Gabe," Matt said, "but we don't feel as if we can adopt him and give him everything he needs. Yet we want to be a part of his life, and giving him up means we would lose that. We've gone round and round . . . asking God what to do . . . and now here you are."

"But hold on," Dok said, wiping tears from her cheeks with both hands. "Yes, this is an answer to prayer for us. But we need to make sure this is the right decision for you too. Gabe might have some developmental delays from Lyme. It's too soon to know—"

Gus lifted a hand to stop her. "Dok, we've talked that possibility through. We want Gabe, no matter what his recovery looks like. We accept him just the way he is."

Dok and Matt exchanged a look, one that Annie thought she might never forget. Full of relief, of gratitude, and something like awe. Annie felt it too. Such a clear answer to so many prayers for Gabe, coming from so many different directions. She smiled. Joy often came in the most unexpected ways.

"Do you think," Gus said, "that we'd have any problems with the court allowing us to adopt him?"

Matt lifted a shoulder in a shrug. "We'd need to talk to the social worker, of course." He glanced at his wife. "But hopefully Dok can work some magic."

Annie's heart thudded with something fierce and bright. She looked at Gus, holding Gabe, his chin tucked protectively on top of his head. He held out his other arm for her to join them. She rose and crossed the room, leaning into his solid warmth. They felt . . . like a family.

But then she caught sight of Dok's face. Her skin had blanched, her expression caught between worry and hesitation. Annie felt a spike of alarm. "What's wrong?"

Dok waved a hand as if shooing a fly. "I shouldn't even say it out loud."

"Go ahead, Ruth," Matt said gently. "If you have any concerns, now's the time to air them."

"I'm hopeful that Gabe will have a full recovery. I pray that he was diagnosed before there was any permanent neurological damage. We all want that. I just wondered . . ." She drew in a breath. "I just wondered that if he does make a full recovery, if his father would try to reclaim his rights to him."

For one dizzying moment the world tilted—Annie's bright hope threatened by a shadow she hadn't even thought to fear.

Twenty-Five

It had been a long week. A good week, but long. Dok was finishing up for the day when she heard a knock at the front door of the office. She squeezed her eyes shut and frowned. *Not now. Not another patient, or emergency, or house call.* She wanted to get home and see how Gabe was faring. To see if there was some improvement. To have dinner with Matt. To pick up the book she'd been reading and finish it off tonight. To savor the fact that Charlie was handling night calls with more skill than she'd given him credit for.

The knock persisted.

She rose and went to the door, opening it. A boy stood there, ball cap in his hands, his curly brown hair mussed from where he'd shoved it off and on. "Ma'am?" His voice cracked slightly. "I saw a car in the parking lot. I—I hoped it belonged to you."

Dok's pulse caught. She remembered who he was before he said another word. It was his features that struck her first—fine-boned, almost delicate. A dimple cut his left cheek, his ears were finely shaped, his eyes had a familiar almond tilt. A beautiful face. For one dizzying instant, it was like looking at a future version of Gabe—more than a boy but not yet a man. "Of course I remember you. You're Gabe's father."

He nodded, shoulders hunching. "Yeah. I didn't know if you'd talk to me. The social worker . . . she wouldn't tell me anything. Said I signed away my rights, so I don't get to know nothin'. File closed, she said."

File closed. That sounded like Sandra. She had used the same words with Dok and Matt, over a year ago, when they had been asked to relinquish baby Gabe to this man. This boy. This boy-man.

"But I need to know." His voice cracked again. "Ma'am, he's still my son. He's part of me, y'know?"

Yes, she knew. Dok probably shouldn't be talking to him. She should let Sandra deal with him. But she couldn't bring herself to send him away. She stepped back, gesturing toward a chair in the waiting room. "Come in. Come and sit."

He sat stiffly, twisting the cap between his hands, his knees bouncing.

She lowered herself into the chair opposite him, folding her hands. "What is it you want to know?"

"How is he doing?" He lifted his eyes. "Please. I need the truth. Did you figure out what's wrong with him? Is it autism?"

She drew in a steadying breath. "No. Gabe has Lyme disease."

The boy's mouth dropped open. His face blanched. "Lyme disease?"

"Yes. He must have been bitten by a tick in the last year."

He looked stricken, like she had just slapped him. "So it's my fault."

Dok wasn't sure how to answer that. Yes, in a way, it was his fault—for not taking better care of his child. For not getting treatment sooner. For not being aware of the chance of getting a tick bite. And no, in a way, it wasn't his fault. A tick bite could happen to anyone, especially in Pennsylvania, a hot spot for ticks.

"But that's . . . Lyme . . . it's treatable, right?" His voice came fast, like he was afraid of the answer. "He'll get better?"

"We hope so," Dok said carefully. "Lyme can cause neurological damage if it goes untreated long enough. We don't know yet how advanced it was before we caught it. Some children recover completely. Some don't."

He blinked hard, his lips trembling. "But he might be okay?"

"It's too soon to tell." Dok leaned forward. "But I'm hopeful."

The boy dropped his head, staring at the floor. "Everyone kept saying autism. Everybody. They told me he'd need all kinds of special help—therapy, doctors, specialists, all that. And I . . . I just—" He shook his head and rubbed the brim of his cap. "I'd just gotten laid off. Couldn't even pay my own rent. I'm trying to find a job, but nobody hires you steady when you don't even have a high school diploma. I know I gotta finish school if I want something better. But Gabe—he needed more than I could give him. That's why I signed the papers." His breath came uneven, jagged. "Not because I didn't want him. Because I thought it was best for him."

Dok's throat tightened. She gave him a moment before asking quietly, "Are you trying to reclaim your rights?"

He looked away.

"When you signed the papers to relinquish your parental rights, did you understand it was permanent? Did Sandra explain it to you?" This was a critical question.

"Yeah." He scrubbed his palm against his knee. "Yeah, I knew. She was clear about that. But it didn't mean it was easy. I didn't want to let him go."

Silence stretched, the wall clock ticking loudly between them. After being with Annie and Gus, Dok had made it a point to find out the law in Pennsylvania—once parental rights were relinquished and the court finalized it, it was permanent. "The law is designed for the child, to make sure they have stability. It isn't meant to punish parents, but it does mean you can't change your mind later."

He nodded miserably, eyes fixed on his shoes.

"You know this back-and-forth is no way to raise a child, don't you?"

His shoulders hunched. He didn't look at her.

Dok hesitated, unsure if she should say more, but then decided to lay it all out there. "There's an Amish couple who wants to adopt Gabe. They're good people."

His head snapped up, alarm sparking in his eyes. "I thought you were going to adopt him."

"My husband and I thought about it. We prayed about it. But we didn't feel a peace about it. We're both getting older, and it didn't seem fair to Gabe to be raised by people who could be his grandparents. So in the end, we decided Gabe should be part of a family, with brothers and sisters. It seemed like the best option for him. I think you know that too."

His throat worked, but no words came.

"And if it eases your heart," Dok said, "if Gabe does have any developmental delays, an Amish family is a good place for him. The Amish see every life as valuable. They call those with special needs 'special children.' Not as a burden. As a gift."

He sagged against the chair back and rubbed both hands over his face, dragging them down until they trembled in his lap. "Do you think . . ." His voice was hoarse. "Do you think I could still be part of his life? Would they let me?"

Dok tilted her head. "Why?"

"Because I don't want him to grow up thinking I didn't love him. That I just threw him away." His voice cracked, and this time tears spilled over, quick and hot. "I couldn't take care of him, but I wanted the best for him. I just want him to know that."

"I'll talk to this couple," she said. "I'll see what they think about letting you maintain some kind of connection."

His shoulders shook once, relief and grief tangled together. He pressed his cap against his eyes, muffling a sob. "Thank you, ma'am."

"I can't make any promises." But Dok already knew Annie and Gus would say yes. Gus, especially. After meeting Sam Mustang the way he did, he would want Gabe to know his own birth father's story.

There was always more to a person's story.

In the quiet of his back office, David gently set the receiver down. The rain tapped a steady rhythm on the roof above, a soft percussion to the hum of voices drifting in from the store's front room. Around him, cardboard boxes stacked waist high waited patiently—cereal from this morning's delivery, still unopened. His desk was a scatter of invoices, some half checked, others still untouched. There was work to be done, but for now, he let himself pause.

He closed his eyes briefly and breathed in the moment. The scent of rain, the muffled laughter of shoppers, the warmth of the woodstove in the corner. Gratitude welled up in him. He thanked God—not just for the tasks that filled his days, but for the joy stitched into each one. For the steady rhythm of family life. For the quiet honor of being a bishop. And today, especially, for the news that Luke was coming home. His deacon. His friend. His balance. The call had just ended, and David felt the world tilt gently back into place.

A knock broke the reverie.

Sarah leaned in, her apron dusted with flour. "That Englischer's back. The one who looks like a cowboy. Says he wants a minute of your time."

"Send him in." David moved quickly to clear a box from the spare chair, making space for Sam Mustang.

Sam stepped in, rain still glistening on his shoulders. "Looks like I've caught you at a busy time," he said, nodding toward the clutter.

David smiled. "It looks worse than it is. Cereal boxes unpack quickly. It's the invoices that test a shopkeeper's patience." He extended his hand. "Come. Sit."

Sam took the seat, and David noticed it immediately—the shift. The man who had arrived in Stoney Ridge weeks ago had worn his pain like a coat too heavy for spring. But now, his posture was lighter, his eyes clearer. He looked younger. Renewed. "I've heard good things."

Sam gave a quiet nod. "Thanks to your sister. I'm still wrapping my head around it."

"The medication's working?"

"Better than I hoped."

David could see it. The way Sam moved, the way he sat—there was ease now, where once there'd been strain.

"We started a conversation," Sam said, "but never finished it."

David tilted his head. "Remind me."

"I was going to ask you if God could forgive me."

The room fell still. David chose his words with care. He knew the weight they carried. Sam had been raised Amish, but he'd walked a different path. He wasn't coming back—not to the Ordnung, not to the life David knew. And yet, here he was, seeking something deeper. Something eternal. While David would never presume to tell anyone if the Lord had forgiven them—only God could answer that question—he knew that Sam was looking for a sign from the Almighty. He leaned his elbows on his desk. "Tell me how it felt when Mary forgave you."

Sam exhaled slowly. "Unexpected. Overwhelmed. I didn't think I deserved it. I still don't." He paused. "And she gave it so readily."

David nodded, his voice low. "I believe that kind of forgiveness doesn't come from us alone. It's a reflection of something greater. If Mary could forgive you, don't you think the Lord was at work in that moment? And if he was, isn't it possible that he's offering forgiveness to you?"

Sam looked down, his hands clasped loosely. When he raised

his head again, his eyes were shiny. "Thank you," he said. "For everything."

"You're leaving?"

"Heading back to Houston. It's time."

"You won't stay for Easter?"

Sam stood, adjusting his coat. "I'm ready to get back to work. But I'll make you a promise." He met David's gaze and reached out a hand for a shake. "I'll be in church on Easter morning. You can count on it."

That was good enough for David. Easter was coming and the Lord would continue his work in this man's life. Shaking Sam's hand, David smiled. The kind that comes from deep within.

Darcy tucked the last supply into the cabinet, her fingers lingering on the pulls before closing it shut. With it came the finality she hadn't expected to feel. It was her last day working for Dok. The end of one chapter. Bittersweet.

And the beginning of one she was looking forward to. Quite a bit!

Evie had returned to the office, easing into her full schedule like a woman reclaiming her rhythm. On her first day back, Dok had made the point to add a plaque on the front of the building below her own: DR. CHARLIE KING, GP, AND PARTNER. Evie sobbed when she saw it. Literally sobbed.

The practice had found its heartbeat, and Darcy knew it was time for her to go. She was ready. Still, her feet felt heavy as she moved down the hall. She hadn't expected to have such strong feelings about this office. She had never felt an attachment to other medical practices. She'd always been ready to leave when her contract was up.

Working with Dok Stoltzfus had changed her. She was a better nurse from these last few months. She didn't know when it started—maybe with that first house call, or maybe the second or third, when she realized how much more there was to nursing. Listening to what wasn't being said. Noticing what wasn't being pointed out. Forevermore, she would take Dok's example of keen observation with her.

She'd grown fond of these Amish of Stoney Ridge—these quiet, surprising, often stubborn people. Hank Lapp, with his booming voice and that perpetual twinkle in his eye. Edith Lapp. That woman could give frostbite with a glance, but Darcy had come to admire her, in her own way. There was steel under that bonnet.

Fern Lapp had a different strength, like she knew more than she said. And David Stoltzfus—he had shattered every image Darcy ever had of what an Amish bishop would be. Wise, yes. But warm too. Approachable. Humble.

His kind wife, Birdy, who towered over her husband and probably outweighed him, yet they were a perfect match.

Quiet Annie Fisher, whose silence held so much more than words ever could. Darcy had come to appreciate her presence, like the calm of early morning.

Even Sally Fisher—Annie's mother, who'd self-diagnosed with everything from kidney stones to gout—had made Darcy laugh more times than she could count. Not in front of Sally, though.

And Sarah Blank from the Bent N' Dent store, who always treated her to a cup of her good coffee when she stopped in to pick up some supplies for Dok. Sarah was the one who said, "You'll miss us more than you think," with a wink.

Darcy knew she was right. She'd learned that these people—who looked alike at first glance, who dressed in a way that set them apart from the rest of the world—were each startlingly different. Unique. Complex. Capable of surprising tenderness and raw honesty. Yet they were so much the same too. They believed God was sovereign over all things—every person, every circumstance. To them, there were no accidents.

Darcy had always believed in God, but she was leaving Stoney Ridge making peace with God about her brother's death—and for that, she had the Amish to thank. Jonathan's life had been complete, full of purpose and meaning, albeit short.

One more thing she'd learned, too, what an apology could do. How one sentence—"I was wrong"—could set a whole new thing in motion. Heal. Mend. Build something better.

Sam had taught her that.

Darcy raised her hand and knocked gently on the door to Dok's office.

"Come in," Dok said.

Darcy stepped inside, a little unsure what to say now that it was time to say goodbye. But she didn't have to. Dok jumped up from her desk and wrapped Darcy in a hug that felt more like a benediction. "You were just the right person at just the right time," Dok said, her voice low. "There'll always be a job here for you, if you want it."

Darcy smiled, the sting behind her eyes sharper than expected. "I'll keep that in mind. Thank you."

Before either could say more, a knock came at the door and it opened. Sam popped his head in, his smile tentative. "Just wanted to add my own thank you," he said. "For everything you've done for me. I owe you my life." He stepped inside to offer Dok his hand.

Dok ignored the hand and pulled him into a hug instead. Sam looked embarrassed, but also . . . pleased. It was a look Darcy had come to recognize. One she'd seen slowly stretch across his face more and more lately. A look that said, *I like this. Having people care about me. Caring about people.*

When Dok released him, he turned to Darcy. "You ready to go?"

Darcy nodded. "I'm ready."

She took one last glance around Dok's office, then stepped

through the door, walking side by side with Sam into the light spilling from the front windows.

The day was waiting. So was the road.

Annie Fisher was so right. Joy came often when it was least expected.

Discussion Questions

1. There's a theme of observation in this novel. Dok observes the behaviors of both Sam and little Gabe, Darcy observes the Amish and how they differ from the non-Amish, David observes festering problems among the church members. And, of course, there's a lot of stargazing going on. How does the theme of observation—whether through telescopes, medical symptoms, or emotional cues—shape this story?

2. Sam Mustang left at sixteen, walked away from a pregnant girlfriend and a whole life he didn't feel ready for. Now, years later and facing an ALS diagnosis, he's come back to apologize. Honestly, humbly, and without excuses. And somehow, that simple act stirred something in the Amish church. People started opening up, owning things they'd buried for years. Why do you think one person's apology can have that kind of impact? What makes a heartfelt apology so powerful—and why does it sometimes take just one to help others find the courage to follow?

3. What does Sam's return say about the power of repentance—not just for the person owning their mistakes, but for the people left behind? Can healing begin even when the damage was done long ago?

4. Sarah Blank has a habit of sharing everything she overhears at the Bent N' Dent—as prayer requests, of course. "I like to pray for people," she told David. "And I know other people like to pray. That's why I share information. It's not gossip if it's true and meant for prayer." David warned her that it's not true if it's only one side of a story. What do you think—where's the line between caring and oversharing? And is it still gossip if a person's heart is in the right place?

5. Mary Zook Troyer may not take up much space in the story, but her choices ripple through it in powerful ways. Her quiet strength, her grace in forgiving Sam Mustang, and her decision to make a public confession—for her sake and her son's—spark a wave of honesty and vulnerability in Stoney Ridge. Her husband Marcus said that Mary always seemed to know the best way forward. What does Mary's example show us about the kind of wisdom that doesn't need a spotlight to make a difference?

6. Annie stands firm in her faith, even as she loves Gus through his doubts. How does her quiet strength shape their relationship, and what does it say about the role of conviction, even in love?

7. At first, Gus felt a pull toward Gabe and wanted to find a way to help him. Later, as Gus wrestled with his

own identity after learning that Marcus Troyer wasn't his biological father, his bond with Gabe grew even stronger. Like Gabe, he would be facing a future with adoptive parents. How might Gabe's experience—being relinquished by a father who wanted the best for him—bring understanding and healing to Gus?

8. Annie and Gus don't know whether Gabe will make a full recovery or only a partial one. He may grow into what the Amish call a "special child." In their community, differences in ability and intellect are accepted as part of God's will, and a person's worth is not measured by productivity or wages. What does this act of commitment and care reveal about Gus's and Annie's growth, and how does their willingness to adopt Gabe reflect the Amish belief in valuing every life?

9. "When you've lived more years than you've got left," Dok said, "you start thinking differently about life." As you age (regardless of how old you might be), have you started thinking differently?

10. Bishop David Stoltzfus can't shake the feeling that he's let too many things slide in the church—grudges, bitterness, quiet divisions. He wonders if he should've spoken up more, stepped in sooner, been willing to face conflict. But maybe those doubts aren't a flaw. Maybe they're what make him a good shepherd to his flock—more humble, more willing to lead by example. What do you think? Can self-doubt actually be a sign of wisdom? And how might it help someone lead with more grace and honesty?

11. "Live like you're dying." Those four simple words rippled through the little church of Stoney Ridge in a profound way. They prepared the community for Council Meeting—a significant season in the Old Order Amish Church. It's a time of solemn reflection before partaking in the sacrament of communion, a time to ready the heart for Easter Sunday, for forgiveness, wholeness, and new beginnings. Live like you're dying. It's a reminder to keep short accounts, make amends, release grudges, and mend fences. As Scripture says, "If it is possible, as far as it depends on you, live at peace with everyone" (Rom. 12:18 NIV). How might your life look different if you truly lived "like you were dying"?

Author Note

Writing this book introduced me to something completely new: astronomy. Honestly, learning about the night sky left me, to quote Darcy Delaney, just gobsmacked.

Over 250 million stars are born every single day.

The observable universe contains more than 200 billion galaxies (thank you, Hubble and Webb).

And in our own Milky Way, there are over 100 billion stars—many with exoplanets orbiting them. In just *one* galaxy.

It's staggering. The scale of it all makes you feel impossibly small. And yet, Scripture tells us that not one star is missing to God. That each one is called by name. That the fall of a sparrow is noticed. That even the hairs on our heads are counted.

"Lift up your eyes and look to the heavens: Who created all these? He who brings out the starry host one by one and calls forth each of them by name. Because of his great power and mighty strength, not one of them is missing" (Isa. 40:26 NIV).

Sam Mustang believed, because of his messy past, that he'd gone missing before God. But Scripture reminded him that he hadn't. Not one person is missing to God. Not Sam Mustang. And not you.

So lift up your eyes. There's beauty above—and assurance beneath it.

If you're curious about the stars, here are a few simple stargazing tips to get started:

Find true darkness: Get away from city lights for a clearer view. At the very least, choose a moonless or new moon night.

Get comfortable: Recline, bundle up, and bring snacks—your neck and stomach will thank you.

Let your eyes adjust: Give yourself twenty to thirty minutes without screens or bright lights.

Start with the bright ones: Look for planets like Venus or Mercury, or the Big Dipper.

Use binoculars: They're easier than telescopes and still reveal plenty of wonder.

And get ready to be gobsmacked!

Read on for a sneak peek at the final book in the

NATIONAL PARK SUMMERS series

Available May 2027

Eleven years earlier

Colt first saw her in the gift shop at the Ahwahnee Lodge—the girl who would change everything, though he didn't know it yet. A woman in line ahead of the girl had dropped a twenty-dollar bill from her wallet without realizing it and walked away from the register. The girl bent down, scooped it up, left her place in the long line to hurry after the woman, tapping her gently on the arm to return the money.

Colt watched from behind the postcard rack. She didn't make a show of it. Just smiled and walked to the back of the line, like returning lost money and losing her place in line was no big deal.

The next day, he saw her again outside the Yosemite Mountaineering School. A group of kids stood in a loose circle while a guide talked about harnesses and knots. One small boy fumbled with his gear, frustrated. The girl stepped closer, crouched beside him, and helped straighten the straps.

Colt lingered at the edge of the scene, pretending to read a notice board, watching the girl instead. He couldn't decide whether her hair was blond or red. Somewhere in between. She usually wore it in one long braid down her back, and it swayed when she walked.

He couldn't seem to look away. It wasn't just that she was pretty—though she was, the kind of pretty that made his teenaged brain go numb. Twice now, he'd seen her go out of her way to do things nice things. The kind most people might not do. And somehow, watching from a distance, it made an impact on him.

Finding out more about her turned out to be easier than he expected. Being the pastor's kid at the Yosemite Valley Chapel meant Colt had grown up in the valley. It also meant he knew people—like the older woman who ran the reservation desk center at Curry Village, who played piano at the chapel and had known him since he was little.

"Tent cabin 244?" she repeated when he asked. "The MacIntoshes. A nice couple from Fresno. Two girls—Jenny and Lexi. They've been coming for the same week each summer for the last three years now." She opened her mouth to ask why he was interested, but the phone rang sharply from the front desk. He was on the move, out the door.

Jenny. So her name was Jenny MacIntosh.

Colt found it hard not to think about Jenny. He wasn't alone. She didn't exactly go unnoticed. He saw how many guys stuck close to her, doing ridiculous things in hopes she'd look their direction. Colt couldn't blame them.

Not even TC. A kid too cool for a regular name. TC was never far from Jenny. Colt had his own name for him—The Coyote—borrowed from his grandmother, who had a gift for seeing people clearly. In the old stories, Coyote was never simply bad, he was appealing. Charming and dangerous, she said, in that order.

More than anything, Colt wanted to talk to Jenny. The problem was, on the best of days, he rarely spoke. Colt had what the audiologist called severe-to-profound sensorineural hearing loss. He could hear some low-frequency sounds (like deep voices, engines, doors closing), but speech was muddy and unclear. Hearing aids helped, but he hated them. They were bulky, uncomfortable, and amplified everything.

So he wasn't fully deaf and he wasn't fully hearing. Stuck between worlds, which was pretty much the story of his life.

Colt was one-fourth Ahwahneechee—the Native Americans who had lived in Yosemite for centuries until forced out in the 1850s. His full Ahwahneechee grandmother, Gram, spoke of their shared heritage like a wound and a treasure all at once. He had grown up with her stories—names of places that no longer belonged to them, ancestors who had walked the valley before uniforms—but he didn't carry those stories the way she wanted him to. He kept them folded up inside, unread. Ignored.

And if he could have hidden his resemblance to Gram, he would have. He had her dark eyes and dark hair, her olive skin. He even had her build—short, solid, impossible to overlook. Puberty was slow to find Colt, unlike The Coyote, who was already working on a mustache. Colt held out hope that one day he'd wake up taller, thinner, blonder, more like his dad. At school, his stocky size made him an easy target. Even more so, his silence.

Colt could talk, he just didn't like to. He'd rather use sign language, and while his parents and grandmother had learned to sign, his mother still wouldn't let him off the hook. She had forced him to endure twice-a-week speech therapy for as long as he could remember. She insisted that he keep working on his speech, that relying on ASL would keep him out of most conversations, and that he was just being lazy.

All true.

But as far as Colt was concerned, ASL was all he needed.

And then Jenny MacIntosh came to church on Sunday and sat in the pew right in front of him.

Colt knew he'd been handed a gift—a chance, finally—but what was he supposed to do with it? He couldn't just lean forward and start talking. He never knew what to say, especially to girls, especially to her. And then TC slid into the pew beside Jenny, close enough that his shoulder bumped hers. *Great, just great*. The Coyote, who'd made it his personal mission to make Colt's life miserable.

Colt had learned early that saying nothing hurt less than answering back. Silence gave him a kind of control. So he ignored the comments, the snickers, the way kids, all led by TC, leaned too close to his face. Mute boy, they called him. They flapped their hands crudely, mimicking sign language they didn't understand. They exaggerated their words when they spoke, or shouted as if volume could make them heard.

Most kids assumed Colt was completely deaf. He wasn't. And dumb, too—which he definitely wasn't. He could hear some things, especially if he was watching a person's mouth. He'd taught himself to read lips better than anyone ever realized. Words, to him, were often something you saw before you heard.

But explaining took effort. And it never changed anything anyway. So why bother?

And then he met Jenny. Actually met her.

Up front, his dad told everyone to turn around and say hello to someone. As Jenny turned around in the pew, TC saw him first and sneered. "Hey look, it's the mute kid."

Colt ignored him, and stared intently at Jenny. Up close, she was even prettier. Brown eyes. Freckles scattered across her nose. One strand of hair had slipped out of her braid, and he wanted in the worst way to reach out and tuck it behind her ear.

One of TC's posse leaned over the pew. "Hey, Injun boy." He spoke like his mouth was full of marbles.

"Stop it," Jenny said, whirling around and confronting the boys on either side of her.

"Don't bother with the dunce, Jenny," TC said.

"Don't call him that," Jenny said.

"He doesn't talk."

She turned to Colt, smiling at him. "Hi, I'm Jenny." She waited, expectant. Friendly. And Colt's throat locked up completely. He couldn't manage to get out a single word. He wanted to tell her she was pretty and that he'd noticed her before.

That he was touched by how kind she was to strangers. How much he liked the color of her hair, but he couldn't get that out, either. Her eyes flicked to his ears, and he could see that she had noticed his hearing aids. He looked away, hating those telltale signs.

"See?" TC said with a taunt. "Mute boy."

"Stop it," she snapped. "That's mean." And then the reservation desk center lady started banging away on the piano and Jenny turned back around.

The opportunity had come and gone, and Colt had missed it. At least he could watch her for the rest of the service. He memorized everything he could—the thick braid slipping over her shoulder, the gold necklace that caught the light, the way she kept twisting it.

When the final song ended, Jenny spun around to him immediately. She smiled, then lifted her hands and signed, *Hello*.

Colt froze for half a second before his own hands came up. *Hi*, he signed back. His eyebrows lifted. *You sign?*

She smiled again, that easy, knowing kind of smile. *My whole family knows ASL.*

Before Colt could ask why, a small girl appeared and tugged at Jenny's hand. Her sister, he could tell, though the little one seemed frail, almost breakable. Maybe it was the pink fluffy earmuffs she wore, despite the summer heat. Jenny, by contrast, seemed unbreakable. Solid.

"Come *on*, Jenny. I need to go. This is too much for me."

But Jenny didn't move. Her gaze stayed on Colt—steady, open, curious in a way that didn't make his chest tighten or his shoulders hunch. She lifted her hands and signed, *Are you deaf?*

Colt blinked, surprised. Not at the question—he was used to that—but at how naturally she asked it. How easily her hands moved. She knew more than the alphabet. He answered without thinking, rocking his hand side to side. *Not totally.*

She nodded, then signed again, pointing briefly toward TC. *Some things people say aren't worth hearing.* Then she smiled.

And something in Colt's chest shifted, like a door he hadn't known was shut eased open. For a second, it felt as if the world sharpened—edges clearer, colors brighter—like he'd been squinting his whole life and had finally adjusted the focus. Before he could stop himself, he smiled back.

Her sister tugged harder, her voice anxious. "Let's *go*!"

Jenny took a few steps backward, still signing as her sister tugged her toward the door. *We'll be back next summer. Watch for me.* She added an exaggerated wink—part emphasis, part play, the way ASL invited expression—then lifted her hand in a lingering wave before she was pulled away.

Colt watched until she disappeared into the sunlight. Next summer. One year. Three hundred and sixty-five days.

Maybe this would be the year he'd finally agree to the cochlear implants—something his mom wanted him to do, to increase speech clarity. Maybe he'd actually try at speech therapy instead of just showing up. Maybe next summer, when she came back, every word he said would ring clear as a bell.

That was exactly what happened. Colt kept watch for Jenny that next summer, but she didn't return to Yosemite.

He looked for her the summer after that too. And the one after that. He never really stopped.

And then, eleven years later, she walked back into his life.

One

Yosemite is a place where one's past and future meet.
Ansel Adams, photographer

Mid January

Jenny MacIntosh had spent the past two years studying silence—or rather, listening for what broke it.

Not library hush or nighttime quiet. The real kind: old-growth forest silence, where wind moves through high branches and owls call across dark timber and woodpeckers peck their way up dead snags. The kind of deep, layered quiet that meant an ecosystem was slowly pulling itself back from the edge. That's what she was listening for now, hunched over her laptop in her cramped Austin apartment, headphones on, coffee going cold.

She'd just finished her master's at UT Austin, a place she loved for its chaos. Cities meant energy, life, movement—she couldn't get enough. But her thesis had taken her somewhere else entirely: boreal forests in northern Alberta, thousands of miles from the nearest traffic light, where a massive wildfire had swept through and left behind nothing but ash and standing black timber.

Her research was built on a simple idea. As a burned forest healed—as understory plants crept back, as insects returned, as the soil knit itself together again—the birds would follow. And when the birds came back, they'd sing. So she'd spent two years poring over audio recordings, tracking the slow reappearance of birdsong against a backdrop of wind and silence, building a picture of forest recovery. One bird call at a time.

And now, she had a shot at something that could lead to a coveted spot in UT's PhD program in environmental acoustics.

Dr. Elise Marchand—*the* Dr. Marchand, whose lab was pioneering AI-based soundscape mapping—had invited Jenny to interview for a summer position as a research assistant. Marchand's work was reshaping the field: decoding biodiversity from audio alone. No cameras. No boots on the ground. Just sound.

Jenny closed her eyes and listened harder.

In her pocket, her phone vibrated. *Mom.*

Jenny sighed and pulled off her headphones. She loved hearing from her mom, but her timing was always terrible. "Hey, Mom. What's up?"

"Hi, sweetie," her mom said, cheerful and familiar. "Just checking in to see if you'll reconsider Yosemite. Your dad said he might even splurge for Sunday brunch at the Ahwahnee." She paused. "You know what a big deal that is for him."

Yep, Jenny got it. Her dad was a true Scot, a tight penny pincher. Brunch at the Ahwahnee sounded lovely, though she knew her sister Lexi wouldn't go. Still, Jenny had already explained to Mom why she couldn't join them. She leaned back against the sofa. "Mom, I told you—I'm heading to Canada for a big interview next week. I'm prepping for it now."

"I know, I know," her mom said. "But I hoped you might change your mind. Maybe you could ask to postpone the interview. We haven't been to Yosemite as a family in years. And we've never seen it in winter. Your sister's so excited. She's even bought snowshoes."

Jenny smiled faintly. "Snowshoes?"

"A big snowstorm is hitting in a few days. Perfect time for our trip the following week. Lexi is determined to hike to Mariposa Grove. She wants to see the giant sequoias in the snow. It'll be utterly quiet, she says."

"That's . . . ambitious."

Her mom laughed, then softened. "Come on, Jenny. You need fresh air. Real trees. Real birds."

"I'm studying real birds," Jenny said. "Just . . . remotely."

Her mom paused. "I still don't get how you can study forests without actually being in a forest."

Jenny bristled. Sometimes Mom could make her work sound like a hobby. Like playing with tape recorders in her bedroom. "I'm analyzing soundscapes. I don't need to be physically there to understand what's happening. And I've told you before—this interview—it's huge. Dr. Marchand's work is groundbreaking."

"Surely you can spare a few days for us. Yosemite in winter is supposed to be magical. And Lexi is really hoping you'll come."

"I'll go next time," Jenny said, already reaching for her headphones. She needed to end this call, get back to her studying. "I do have a life to live, you know." It came out a little sharper than she had intended.

Her mother's sigh crackled through the phone. "Don't be like that."

"Like what?" Jenny pulled at a loose thread on her comforter, watching it unravel.

"Like being with us is an imposition." Her mother's voice held an edge. "Family's important too, you know."

Jenny squeezed her eyes shut. She'd already missed Christmas at home—she'd gone to Cancun with friends from her program instead. Mom was still holding that over her head.

The truth was, Jenny couldn't face going home. Not after

breaking off her engagement to Tanner. Her parents had loved him, called him the son they never had. If she'd gone home, Mom would've spent the entire visit trying to get them back together. *You're so perfect for each other. You both listen to the world—you above ground, him below.*

Tanner was working on his PhD in Seismic Engineering at UT. And yes, ending their relationship had been hard. But it had been the right thing to do.

She glanced at the clock. "Mom, I'm sorry, but I need to get back to work."

"Yes, yes, I know. But honey, Lexi needs you. She's had a tough time lately."

"What do you mean? I thought she liked junior college."

"She had to take a leave this semester. A little too much for her to cope with."

When had that happened? Jenny had been so absorbed with her own life these last few months that she'd hardly given much thought to Lexi. She sent her memes and always gave a thumbs-up on ones Lexi sent to her, but that was about it.

She'd almost forgotten what it was like to feel worried about Lexi. Constantly worried. The kind that made her twelve-year-old self cover Lexi's ears during fireworks, that made her check on her sister three times before bed. She'd forgotten how it felt to wonder if Lexi could ever have a life of her own. Or much of a life at all.

"This trip . . ." Her mother's voice brightened with forced optimism. "Lexi's been looking forward to it, Jenny. And don't forget she's the reason you're doing what you're doing."

Jenny winced, feeling the familiar tug. Mom knew exactly which buttons to push.

Lexi had always been different. Misophonia, the doctors called it—a sensory processing disorder that made certain sounds unbearable. She just couldn't seem to manage on her own. Everything had to be arranged to suit her needs. Not her *wants*, her mother would quickly add. Her *needs*. Misophonia wasn't a choice Lexi made. Crowds, sudden noises, the scrape of a fork on a plate—those could send Lexi spiraling. Nature was safer. Trees didn't honk or shout. Birds sang, but gently. Mostly.

So yes, Lexi *was* the reason Jenny had first noticed how sound shaped an environment. But did that mean she owed her something in return?

The thing was, as difficult as it was to grow up with a sister who had a serious issue, and with parents who did everything they could to accommodate her, Jenny did love her sister dearly.

Her mother seemed to sense she'd gone a little too far with the guilt. "Lexi just admires you so much, sweetie. So much more than you realize. You make such a difference in her life."

Jenny's throat tightened. She could picture Lexi, probably already packing, imagining the two of them hiking through snow-quiet sequoias together.

She felt herself weakening. Maybe she could ask Dr. Marchand if she could interview the following week. Or maybe it could be done over Zoom.

But then Jenny looked at her headphones lying on the desk, at her open laptop with its seventeen browser tabs of research articles. "Mom, I'm truly sorry to miss the trip, but I really, really want this summer internship. It would be huge for me, especially to help me get into the PhD program. I'll try to come home soon, though."

The silence on the other end lasted three seconds. Four. Long enough for Jenny to hear how hollow her own words sounded, echoing back at her through the phone.

"Promise?"

Jenny glanced at the time. "Promise. Gotta go, Mom. I'll call soon. Love you."

"Love you too. Bye, honey."

And they hung up.

A week later, Jenny was packing. Her passport lay beside her field recorder. She'd printed her CV, triple-checked everything. Her flight left in a few hours, and she wanted to get to the airport early.

Her phone rang.

Lexi.

Jenny answered, distracted. "Hey there."

There was silence. Then a shaky breath.

"Jenny . . . something's happened." Lexi could barely get the words out.

Accustomed to these kinds of phone calls from Lexi, Jenny kept packing. She made her voice sound calm and soothing. "Lex, take a deep breath, in and out. You'll be fine."

"No, no. Not me. This isn't about me." She started sobbing. "I don't . . . I don't even know how . . . I don't know . . . how to tell you."

Jenny glanced at the clock. She needed to keep moving. "Take all the time you need." *But please hurry!*

"It's . . ." Lexi sucked in a breath. "Mom and Dad."

Jenny stilled. "What about them?"

"They . . . were . . . driving." She was having trouble even getting the words out between sobs. "Driving early this morning . . ." Her voice trailed off.

"Lexi, please just tell me what's happened."

"I'm trying!" Big sob.

A chill went down Jenny's spine. "Okay, take a deep breath. So they were driving . . ." She heard her sister inhale big gulps of air, then exhale them.

One more deep breath. "Dad wanted to fill up the car at that cheap gas station, you know, before we left for Yosemite. Mom went with him to get some coffee. We were out of coffee."

"Okay. So what then?"

"And they hit black ice."

Jenny's hands felt cold. "Are they hurt?"

Lexi didn't answer her question. She only sobbed.

"Lexi, where are they now?"

Deep breath. "The police said . . ."

"Police?" Jenny echoed. "What do you mean? Lexi, where are they?"

No response.

Jenny let out a breath. "So where are Mom and Dad? Are they in the hospital? Which one?" She grabbed a pen and paper to write down the name of the hospital. She could call and get more information. She glanced at the clock. She could be there in a few hours.

"Jenny." Lexi was sobbing hysterically, while sucking in deep breaths between her words. "You . . . you . . . don't understand. Mom and Dad . . . they didn't make it."

Jenny stood slowly. The room tilted. She pressed one hand to her forehead, the other keeping the phone pressed to her ear. Lexi's voice sounded distant, underwater, like she was calling from the bottom of a well. Lexi wasn't making any sense to her. This must be a mistake. "They're fine, Lexi. Mom texted me last evening. She said the car was all packed for Yosemite."

"The policeman said . . . it happened so fast . . . they probably didn't even know what happened."

Her chest locked. She couldn't pull in air. Her mother. Her father. The words didn't connect to anything real.

Jenny's mind couldn't absorb what she was hearing. Her sister's sobs echoed in her ears and seemed to be reverberating against the walls of her head.

"Jenny?" her sister sobbed. "Are . . . are you there? Say . . . something."

"I'm here," Jenny managed to whisper. She inhaled and followed her own advice, breathing slowly, hoping the technique would calm the rising sense of panic that threatened to overcome her.

Lexi.

Jenny needed to be strong for her sister. "Are you at home?"

"Yes."

"Okay, good. Stay there. I'll head out the door right away. I'll be there as soon as I can. If I can catch a flight, I'll be there by this afternoon."

How calm she sounded, she thought to herself, like she was talking about people she hardly knew. She felt completely numb.

Jenny sat on the edge of the bed, phone in her hand. She wanted to crawl back into bed and pretend this was just a dream. Just a terrible dream. She couldn't breathe. Everything got louder. The fridge humming. A siren wailing blocks away. Her own heartbeat hammering in her ears. Too much. All of it too much.

She let the cell phone slip out to the floor and pressed her hands to her ears.

Lexi.

There was always Lexi to worry about.

Jenny zipped her suitcase, her hands moving faster than her thoughts. Purse. Keys. Door.

She pulled it open—and froze.

Tanner stood there, his hand lifted mid-knock.

For a second, neither of them moved. She hadn't seen him in months. Not since she'd told him it was over, that she couldn't do this anymore.

"Jenny." His eyes scanned her face—the tears, the suitcase behind her. "What's wrong? What's happened?"

She should tell him to leave. She should close the door. But her mouth wouldn't form the words, and her parents were dead, and she couldn't think, couldn't breathe—

"I need to get to the airport," she heard herself say. "Right now."

He didn't ask why. Didn't ask questions. Just stepped forward, steady and sure. "I'll take you."

She knew this was a mistake. She knew she might regret it later. But later felt impossible to imagine. Right now, her legs were shaking and the floor felt unsteady and Tanner was here, solid and real and offering help she desperately needed.

He stepped closer—close enough that she could smell his soap, the same one he'd always used—and then his arms were around her. Steady. Familiar. "I've got you," he whispered against her hair. "You can always count on me."

Jenny let herself lean into him, just for now, just until she could breathe again. She'd figure out the rest later. Right now, she needed to get to Lexi, and Tanner had a car, and nothing else mattered.

Suzanne Woods Fisher is the award-winning, bestselling author of more than forty books, including *A Hidden Hope*, *Capture the Moment*, and many other beloved contemporary romance and Amish romance series. She is also the author of several nonfiction books about the Amish, including *Amish Peace* and *Amish Proverbs*. She lives in California. Learn more at SuzanneWoodsFisher.com and follow Suzanne on Facebook @SuzanneWoodsFisherAuthor and X @SuzanneWFisher.

Connect with SUZANNE

SuzanneWoodsFisher.com

Be the first to hear about new books from Revell!

Stay up to date with our authors and books by signing up for our newsletters at

RevellBooks.com

FOLLOW US ON SOCIAL MEDIA

@RevellFiction